THE DELIVERANCE OF MARIA

George Houston

Blue Moon Adventures

ISBN-13: 9798649571067
ISBN-10: 1477123456

Cover design by: Mandi Knight
Edited by: Martin Karlow, Barbara Houston,Sandy Houston

Library of Congress Control Number: 2018675309
Printed in the United States of America

For Ellen
and Mary my always

"The best protection any woman can have ... is courage."

– ELIZABETH CADY STANTON

CONTENTS

CHAPTER ONE: AN END AND A BEGINNING

Just outside a small Mexican village stood a young girl who held a pearl. She did not know exactly what it was. She had no idea of its value. Or what she should do with it.

In this same small village there was a doctor. He did not know the girl and she did not know him. They met, as is so often the case, by accident. Or fate. In the end, who is to know?

Inside the village the doctor, an American, walked, slightly bent, taking his time, on his way to the local cantina, where he would drown many of his sorrows in mescal and beer. He knew his barking and his tears would be a reason for laughter among the others. And so, in this way, he did not have to be alone. And in this way he was content, for he was aware of no way forward for himself.

There was unrest in the land and many men with guns who sought to find for themselves a good future. The guns, they felt, more than the land, were a sure way to provide it, if they could but align themselves with the winners. Sadly, it was difficult to know who the winners were and there was much bloodshed. Entire towns had been set in flames for a victory no one could see coming anytime soon. The innocents tried very hard to stay out of the men's way but this was not always possible. So the town became a very dangerous place to be.

The young girl's name, a name as countless as the all the waves in the sea, was Maria. She was going home that day, but no home awaited her. Only ashes and corpses and the bitter wind that carried the scent of hopelessness, along with the betrayal of future hope.

Into her village, at sunset, Maria made her way, along the pebbled trail. Oh, she thought, I have the best pebble of all. Dressed in her brother's overalls with the pearl tucked inside, she felt grown up, strong, as a man must feel. But the first man she saw coming into the village didn't look strong. He was running toward her, a frightened look on his face. Many times he looked back over his shoulder as if something was chasing him. Now she became frightened by still more men running. Strong men, running all around her. She saw flames. She saw a man sitting on the ground, leaning against a plaster wall dressed in a red shirt that was not all red. He was staring at her, but he saw nothing. He said nothing. When she moved away, he continued to stare at where she had just stood. He would never see anything again. His story was over. She, knowing nothing else, suddenly did not want to go home. Something inside her knew something she did not want to know. She made no sound but her eyes were large with fear. There was noise too. The horses that used to amuse her with their gentle nickering were now screaming in high voices. In the distance she heard crying. The dust was everywhere. It was beginning to be hard for her to see.

The beach that afternoon had been so beautiful. The sand, warm and comforting, the sea, playful, and in it, the color of Maria's eyes. The dolphins had spoken to her, as usual, in nicks and nacks, and of this and that. The gossip of the sea. And they were so insistent! Maria laughed to hear their chatter. She thought they laughed as she did. At such a time what should there be but laughter? What, in such delight, could not produce laughter? Such is the life of innocents. Searching, searching, opening every door, every shell, every curiosity, with the wonder given only to a child. She made her marks all along in the sand, and she was happy. Usually, it is said God will favor such innocence. And offer protection.

And then ... the pearl. She had knelt in the sand, as if praying, pried the shell open as she had done so many times before. To find a new and incredible thing. An unfathomable thing. The openings of a door, after so much repetition, open to see such as this!

For even children begin to suspect all things revealed begin to be the same. But not this. Not this one time.

She had heard the word *sacred.* Her papa and mama both knew of this word. They said it was not of this world. And she felt that this thing she had found fitted the word. She felt sure this word she had learned was not to be spoken lightly. She felt this thing she had found was no small matter. She did not know why, but it didn't matter. She had found a treasure and she knew the word. It became one and the same and it was enough. She shared her find with the dolphins, holding it up for them to see as they leaped from the water and played.

In the town, the doctor knew the men were coming. The men with guns searching for victory. The doctor was a man not given to deep thinking, but he knew that victory was elusive. (The doctor was an educated man and knew of words as large as *elusive.*) But that was nothing. What good was education in the face of this? He continued to bark and cry, hiding within the laughter of others. Still, he held one eye firmly fixed to the door.

For the doctor, in spite his drunkenness and the tortured soul within him, knew of his surroundings, of the danger, and of things that had gone past his understanding. Simply, he knew of what he did not understand. He knew, he thought, he was soon going to meet his end. A dead gringo would be a prize. So his eye never left the door. Men are always this way. For them the end is always possible. Always final. Always waiting.

But through the door came his beginning. Through the door, her small body reflected in the flickering orange of flames, came Maria.

The cantina in such a village is always a busy place. Always there were many men there in the evening. Some women too, but not nearly as many as the men. The women painted themselves in bright colors and sometimes wore feathers. The men talked and laughed with big voices. Always they talked at the same time, so much so that Maria often wondered how they heard each other or if they could hear at all. Maria was never allowed to enter such a place as this, but she had peeked in sometimes when no one was watching. Her mama and papa had told her it was no place for children.

In fact she was not allowed inside anywhere but her home, the stables, and the church with the big bell. She would go often to the church with her family, when the bell told them to, all dressed in their stiff clothing, the clothing that made her feel too tight and was worn only to church.

In the church with the big bell, men and women were silent. No one talked but the priest. Everyone had to listen and be quiet and, worst of all, be still. The priest talked so much it made Maria's ears tired. For the priest's story was not a happy one. At least it seemed that way to Maria. His sad eyes never twinkled; his voice never laughed, and out of his mouth came words Maria did not understand. She was told by Mama and Papa that here, in this place, she would give herself to God and that God would keep her safe and protect her.

But God was nowhere to be seen this night, for the church was in flames, flames that grew high in the sky, and the big bell, once so close to the sky, had come crashing to the ground. And so it was that Maria went to the only place left with people who were not running. The cantina.

A story can be such a delicate thing to tell. Everyone has one. But so many are lost. Some people tell a story with words, some with song, and some by action. Some stories are easier to tell than others because they are happy ones. Many are not. Some stories are short, some long. And so it is with Maria's story. It is all these things. In some ways, to tell a story like Maria's is to tell of the best companions a person can have. Courage and spirit. As Maria entered the cantina she could find neither.

The doctor rose to look at the vision that appeared at the door. The mescal and beer burned completely away in the bright light of this child. This was no vision. This had nothing to do with all that he had been and had witnessed. This was his new beginning and it took the form of a small young boy ... No! A girl! She who regarded him squarely with huge eyes the color of the sea. So out of place, yet not at all. Yet, there it was, amid all the hell that surrounded them both. He was not a man of God. Yet he could think of nothing but the word *holy*. So this was it, then. This was the answer. Not the end, but a beginning. She was here for him. He wanted to wonder at this. To give it the silence and stillness such a miracle deserved. But the doctor knew there was no time. He saw it was so in an instant. He rose from his stool, feeling unbroken for the first time in so long. He crossed the room quickly and swept the girl up. She did not cry out or try to run. She simply looked up at his ragged face as he ran with her out the door. For Maria knew, now, the something she did not want to know. All things end. For Maria, the haze of what would happen would find its way through her because it was to be. It was that simple for her. For the doctor it was so much more. It was rebirth.

CHAPTER TWO: THE ESCAPE

The setting sun had finally abandoned the village. Even the memory of it was going fast. The gathering dusk and looming shadows brought more angry pops and cracks that were getting closer with each passing second. The doctor ran with all that this newness gave him, but he could not run forever. He heard his breathing in between the bursts of gunfire and knew their only chance was the sea. It was a mercy that their way took them downhill and he could hear the breaking waves so close. Still, the mesquite and sage tore at his clothing and threatened with each step to bring him down. The slopes became steep, dangerously so. The girl, once as light as a feather, was becoming unbearably heavy and she clung to him with such force that he could only breathe in heaves and grunts. There came flashes of gunfire to the left. The girl was shaking in his arms. The doctor felt his eyes burn bright with fever and fought with a vision of the girl and him lying face down and broken, encased in blood, the two of them only steps from the sea.

The moon had not yet risen but the sea offered up its own queer ghostly light outlining the shadows of fishing vessels at the pier. Something was wrong with the shadows. The outlines were not right. Perhaps a trick of the mind. A cry arose from deep within him. It was an animal sound and filled with despair. "The boats!"

The doctor stopped in his tracks, his chest heaving in and out.

Tears that had blinded him now cascaded freely down the deep lines of his face, tracing the old familiar tracks of sorrow. He rocked Maria like a mother would rock an infant and whispered to her softly, "They have smashed the boats."

It was true. The boats lay like drunken men, bent this way and that, half-submerged in the waves that lapped at their sides as if trying to comfort them, the way that old friends did. The pier the boats were tied to seemed to be trying to hold them up.

Urgency pushed away the sickness, and the doctor staggered on. He and the girl could hide in one of the broken boats. The one turned upside down. There would be air to breathe inside and a hiding place. He had made it knee-deep in the salt water and was only steps from their hiding place when he heard a voice behind him.

"Doctor." The voice didn't so much call his name as state it as a rather unfortunate fact. It was a voice he had not heard in a long time, older perhaps and filled with weariness now, yet he recognized it.

Holding Maria more tightly than ever, he turned to face what was to come and squinted at the figure at the shore's edge. "Martin."

Martin stood on the shore regarding them. "It is said that rats swim away from ships that are sinking; they do not go toward them."

The doctor shifted the weight of the girl in his arms and said nothing but merely inclined his head to indicate the girl, all the while looking ahead at what was once an old friend, hoping for another miracle.

Miracles are mere impossibilities, and if one happens, who can say there will not be another? Yet in such a place as this, a place God has tried his best to forget, a man who believes in no God at all would be wise to not have expectations.

Martin cocked his head toward the left of them and bade them follow. Torches appeared at the top of the hill and there was much yelling. Rifle shots cracked the air. Martin led them to a small inlet away from the pier. There, hidden away from the rest, tied to a rickety dock, was a small sailboat. Martin's fishing vessel, the *Pelican*. "Quickly, doctor, get in." The doctor lost no time in complying, for the torches were descending the hill and coming toward them. Excited voices growing near and directing others to follow.

"Lie down on the bottom of the boat," Martin whispered urgently. He began to push the boat out to sea. When he was at chest level in the water, he heaved himself upward and was halfway over the gunwale. Bullets sang and caused the water near them to splash. The doctor reached for Martin's hand. At this moment the expression on Martin's face vanished. He coughed blood. "Stay invisible, it is the only . . ." His eyes glazed over in surprise, his grip loosened, and he slipped down into the water. The men gathered on the shore laughed and congratulated each other on their marksmanship while their torches danced in celebration. The doctor turned to Maria in the bottom of the boat and put a finger to his lips. He needn't have bothered. Maria would not speak a word for a long, long time.

Every second that passed was an eternity. They lay on the bottom of the boat and the doctor's breath came in quick hisses. All they could see were stars as they lay, quiet as heartbeats, in the stinking water that filled the bottom of the boat. The voices and laughter rose and fell but there was no sound of water splashing. The doctor knew from the voices onshore that liquor was being passed around and it was possible that he and Maria would be safe after all. And they were laughing. Laughter speaks of satisfaction. Although the doctor wondered if men like these could ever be satisfied. The voices spoke of a mission accomplished. Of traitors and justice. As the men drank more liquor they began to sing. They sang of the glory of no one telling them what to do. Of their exploits and of loose women. Of tequila and its magical properties.

The doctor knew all about tequila and its magical properties. One can wipe memory out for hours, even days. But it will inevitably return. Magic that is useless. The doctor looked over at the girl. Her eyes were closed and she seemed to be breathing very evenly. Perhaps she had exhausted herself and was sleeping. But who knows? The only thing the doctor was certain of now was that he had been a good man once and this girl was his chance to be one again.

The doctor's fall from grace had been a simple one. The desire for more life made him willing to trade his soul for it. For years he had been a good doctor to the village, bartering care mostly for food, sometimes furniture, and, once, a donkey. He had moved to Mexico from Texas with his wife many years ago. They had come to love the simple way of life and the happiness of the people. But in time, despite all he could do to save her, his wife had passed away from the fever. With no way forward, the doctor stayed in the village. Yet sorrow cannot live forever. After a time the buried life must rise to the surface once again. And so it was with the doctor. One morning he saw children jumping rope and the look of concentration on the face of one of the girls as she tried to manipulate two ropes at once made him smile. He found the courage to go on with life. But for everything given, something is taken. The doctor developed diabetes mellitus. He diagnosed it himself. He was very certain of this for he had kept up with his practice through trips to a dusty post office in Cancún to retrieve his monthly journal. It could have killed him very quickly. It should have, he thought to himself.

There were Americans who had come to the village and sought him out to translate for them. They said they would be coming regularly on business. He had drinks with them and asked of news of America. They asked in turn why he drank so slowly when this was an occasion to celebrate. Although he was a private man, the drinks had loosened the doctor's tongue and he told them of his illness. He had a favor to ask of them. There was a new medication, insulin, that could help him and he wondered if they might bring some back with them on their next trip. I would pay handsomely, he had said to them. Handsomely indeed!

The Americans were gunrunners, selling arms to the Mexican rebels who seemed to think that war was an endless sport. The Americans needed names ... the names of those who they could sell these arms of theirs to. And the good doctor supplied them. The killing started soon after. And poor Martin, a man whose son his medicine had once saved from death, was killed in the fighting the doctor had made possible.

All this went through the doctor's mind while the *Pelican* rocked like a baby on the small waves and the tide was carrying him and Maria very slowly and quietly out to sea. After a long time the voices began to fade. But neither the doctor nor Maria made a sound or a movement until the first light of dawn.

CHAPTER THREE: UNTIL THE SEA SHALL FREE THEM

Day 1

Maria's eyes opened. It was true, then. Many times before she had opened her eyes and closed them because such a thing could not be true. It was all in dreams. But the man was still there. Not looking at her now. He slept and snored, his breath stopping for a while and then, with a *kah-kah* sound in his throat, started again. She was cold and shivering in the morning air. She was wet through; her overalls sopping. She felt for the pearl and found it was still there. She brought it out to look at it. Its beauty remained, untouched by all that had happened. As quietly as she could, she rose to look around. She was at sea. Sea all around. No land anywhere. She had been fishing with her papa before, but always she had been able to see land. She looked down into the water for her friends the dolphins, but they were nowhere to be seen. Perhaps they could not swim this far out from the land. She was very thirsty, but she knew she could not drink of the sea. She was hungry too but that was nothing. She had known hunger before and it was not much of an enemy. It could only bite from the inside and could not get out. She looked back at the man. He was not her enemy. He had saved her from fire and from becoming one of those people on the ground who looked but did not see.

He had saved her from the bad men. Papa had told her about bad men. Men who cared nothing for the land but lived only to take all they could, using guns and showing uncaring eyes. Now she had seen how bad they could be. The tears came.

Because there is mercy, so there is sleep.

The doctor awoke suddenly and not without pain. He looked up at the sky for a long time. He was no philosopher, no ancient one. But he knew inside he was dying. One did not need wisdom for that. His insulin was gone. His opiate. His thirty pieces of silver. He looked over at the girl. Still sleeping. He moved to her carefully, touched her forehead. No fever. Good. She had been awake before and moved herself out of the stinking water. Good. He looked out from their nest at the sea and it was obvious that they were hopelessly lost. He rummaged through the boat with more noise than necessary hoping the girl might wake. If she did, she didn't let on. He breathed easier at finding fishing gear. He smiled when he discovered a small canteen of water. There was a St. Christopher's medal too, but one cannot eat or drink that.

Most of all there was mast and sail. He had watched Martin raise the sail when he had gone out with him. Now it was for him to do. It was their only chance. *Her* only chance, he corrected himself. His fate was already decided. The girl was meant for something. He had already ceased to be; except ... for this. He would deliver this girl unto all of what he did not know. Would never know. But she must survive. And without his help she would not. He began to roll out the nets and placed the canteen beside her.

Day 2

She rose when she was sure he was asleep. She had been awake, of course, before, but she chose not to let the man know. She had heard him moving about. She had heard splashes in the water. She had smelled him, the stink of him, close to her, and felt, with fear, his touch. His hands had been strangely gentle.

He was not a bad man. She was sure of that now. Next to her a canteen. She cautiously reached for it, looking at him all the while as he snored. She drank and drank more. She moved toward him. Looked at him closely. No, she decided finally. He was not a bad man. A creature of circumstance. Like herself. She was bold now. She moved to look out at the sea once again. No change. The sky, the water, this boat, and the man. Why had she been brought here? What was to be? Looking out at the endless sea, she felt charged with courage. No fire, no men, just this water. Then she noticed the nets. Already fish were in them. The man had done this. This was the splashing she had wondered about, not daring to open her eyes. The fire in her stomach, her hunger, was more than she could bear. Maria once again looked at the man. She would no longer hide from him. She lifted an oar from the oarlock and threw it to the bottom of the boat with such force that the sound shocked her. The man jerked his eyes open. His eyes were terrible. Not as she had imagined at all. They held no surprise or danger. His eyes were knowing. And somehow, even though they were open, his eyes were far away. He was not well. But mercifully, his eyes were also kind. "Girl, I will need help to raise the sail," was all he said. And there was, for the moment, the feeling in her that she was home.

They spoke no words, but eyed each other carefully, and when what they saw satisfied them, she followed his lead. He would gesture, she would obey. There was little else to do. Little else to want. They raised the sail. It caught the wind. This should have been victory, it should have been the hand of providence, but his only reaction to it was a brief smile. Why his smile should make her smile as well, she did not know. Still, they had fish for their supper. And the little water that remained in the canteen. He reached to touch her forehead. She shrank back. He mumbled that he meant her no harm. Strangely gentle, he asked about things that were of no use to her anymore. About what she knew and did not know. He promised that he would see her get well and he would see her safe. Man talk. That was all. But ... but the vile black water was gone from the bottom of the boat. He had found blankets, and she wondered where and how. While she was looking at the sea, trying her best to feel the senseless pride of being alone, he was in motion. How, she had wondered, would he bring the fish from the nets by himself? While she looked out at the sea, he had busied himself with work. He had bailed the vile dark water, had set out blankets, and her bed was nested in the bow, far from him. When she saw what he had done and saw him bend in pain, reaching for their food, Maria helped him with the nets, to bring in the fish that would feed them. Honesty seldom needs recognition. But so often it needs help.

Day 3

The doctor knew that the circumstances were not the ones he wanted, weren't what she wanted ... But what of that? He knew his mission was unique. Still, for some reason, he longed to tell this girl, not of his pain, but of the time when his muscles were like ropes and his eyes were clear. Of his medical knowledge that had saved so many, perhaps even those she knew. But his pride loomed before him like a silly curtain, preventing him from seeing. It would not serve him, he could not eat it, and he doubted very much whether it had ever done him any good. He dispensed with it as easily as a snake sheds its skin.

He stopped to consider. This child's pride, though, misplaced as it was, worried him. What if that was all that was left her? Take away pride in someone so young? Why did they learn pride so quickly and not their lessons? A nervous thought. He must not be nervous now. Although he was becoming sure that she trusted him, she would not speak. Not a word. Not so much as a syllable. It didn't matter. Her history, her before time. He needed her to know certain things. She had watched him, helped him, with the nets and the sail, but there was little time and so much more for her to learn.

So he talked to her in the boat and on the endless sea. While they were fully under sail, he told her of the ways to survive, how to fashion an arrow and bow, of poisonous creatures and how to recognize them. How to gather plants that could feed her ... make her better if she were ill. He found paper and pencil in the boat ... drew pictures as he talked.

Later he talked of the futility of men. Could she understand? It must be. He was her instrument. The doctor was sure of that. And so he went on as the waves went on ... about the importance of truth, the importance of temperance only a drunken man can attest to. His talking grew fainter and his voice grew dim and bleak. She listened, in the bow of the boat, the wind showing her hair the way she had come...She had listened and now knew the lesson was at an end. He was growing weaker and soon he would die. She had known the word "die" and now she would live it. She turned to the doctor, badly wanting to say she understood. But all she could manage was to touch his hair and smile at his face. Somehow, she was sure he understood.

Day 4

The doctor looked out upon the sea. And then at Maria. They were one and the same, he thought. Who am I to teach this child? he thought. She came to him, sat beside him in silence. He turned to look at her. In the short time they had been together they had shared so much. And now here she was, looking deep into his eyes. And touching his hair.

Day 5

They had not eaten. Who knows in how long? He had given her water ... when? They had had a little rain and he had showed her how to gather the precious drops. She learned quickly. Then sun ... the sun ... fortunately no storms, but ... now he was going. His thoughts formed and disappeared in his fever like birds in the mist. She knew he would soon be gone and she would be alone. But now she was not so frightened. In the end, he spoke words she did not understand. He called out names ... she understood names but that was all. In the end, when his eyes rolled back for the final time and his breath stopped, she could do nothing but watch. His last words were in a language she could not and would not try to fathom. But it was this foreign language that helped her not to cry. It is one thing to look at a man in the street, looking at nothing, she thought. It is another to have a sightless one in your arms, his final words tugging at your heart. Still, it amounts to the same. She would miss the doctor. He was one of the last true things she would know.

But now he was gone. She looked up at the sail. The doctor had showed her. She would remember him for that. And perhaps for many more things as well. She would remember the strange way he had smiled at her. She sat with the doctor for a long time after he had gone. No tears would come. A gull came and perched on the side of the boat, cocking his head this way and that, studying them both. After a time she rose to trim the sail, and to her great surprise and relief, land shimmered on the horizon! She adjusted the boat's course toward the shore. Toward still another new beginning.

CHAPTER FOUR: A NEW HOME

It was difficult. The breakwater. There was coral that cut into the underside of the boat and waves that pounded it. Maria silently asked the quiet one for help and found she was in luck. The timber in the boat struck against the coral but did not break. She managed to get close enough to jump out and it took all her strength to pull the boat to shore. Her lips were full of blisters and hurt very much. Her legs and feet were cut from stepping on coral and stung in the salt water. Her tears came then. She pulled and pulled until she fell and could pull no more.

The waves were in agreement however, as they sometimes are, and nudged the boat closer. She walked the last few feet onto the sand and fell. She rose again, made it to the dry sand, and fell again. When at last her eyes opened, the sun was setting. Maria looked all around her. Nothing she could see but herself on a beach and a boat with a dead man in it. She scavenged around the boat, looking for anything that might help. She took the scribblings the doctor had made. She took rope. She took nets. And she was very thankful when she found a machete.

But her strength was at an end, she bowed her head for several minutes on the bottom of the boat, and as she lay there, she made a decision. With her throat catching like she was sick, and taking care not to look at him, she searched the doctor's pockets. She found matches, some pesos, and a cigar. She retreated back to the shore and now felt the fear of the animal in the gathering dusk. She needed a hiding place. The sand led to trees, and beyond the trees to jungle, where perhaps more danger was hidden. Hunger was gnawing at her insides, but no enemy inside her could defeat her. Only from outside could the danger come. Water . . . she would need fresh water. But that would have to wait. She could not think anymore. She was tired and needed sleep. Perhaps the sail could be used to ... She scrabbled at the mast, hacked at the ropes with the machete. The sail came crashing down, the canvas smashing her to the bottom of the boat and shrouding her completely. Maria took the weight upon her and slept. In her dreams, she went back home. On her way to the dolphins, she said goodbye to her mother. Her mother told her to take care. That's all. Like the day was just like any other day.

Another day came sooner than Maria would have liked. The boat that cradled her, the sail that was her blanket—their use was now at an end. There was nothing they could serve to accomplish in the presence of this new day. She must find a place. A safe and special place. She rose with great difficulty, struggling to free herself from the canvas. An overwhelming smell threw her off-balance. It came from the doctor. She forced herself to look at him, and looked away at once. Maria must care for him on his final journey. It was not a thought so much as a knowing. She must do this above all things. Before she ate, drank, or slept again.

She thought on this a long while. She had not the strength to move the body far enough away to bury him. She could conceive of nothing to help her with the task. So, the sea, then. The sea would take him. Perhaps the dolphins ... no, they had deserted her. She would do this alone. She would take the boat once more, beyond the coral and the breakwater. For him. This she must do for him. The danger of it helped her, strengthened her somehow. This would be a fitting tribute. This, she would do. While onshore, she managed to wrap the doctor in fish netting and weighed down what was to be his seagoing shroud with stones and anything heavy that she found in the boat. She hacked at the mast with her machete until it was in pieces. She would keep the wood. She scavenged all she could, and although Maria struggled with her task, soon enough she had maneuvered the boat past the breakwater.

Taking a gaff, she lunged at the timbers of the boat until it was filling fast with water. She made her way back across the breakwater, taking special care to avoid the razor-sharp coral. Only when she reached the shore did she look back. The *Pelican*, the doctor's final resting place, had disappeared under the calm sea. He would never see the beautiful sunset this night, or feel the stirring of the warm breeze that now played at Maria's hair. The thought made her heart ache and flutter so that she turned away and got busy setting up her special place. As quickly as she could, she made good use of the machete and slashed away at a small space under a palm. She would come to know this special place well and it would be easy for her to find again as the palm she had chosen grew in three different directions. Soon she had cleared an area where she felt protected as the darkness deepened all around her. She searched the materials she had scavenged. The canvas of the sail would serve again as her blanket. Mangoes from a nearby tree would make a delicious breakfast. Although she had no idea where she was, she was home.

The next morning dawned clear and so very bright, with the sun beating down on the white sand making it hard to see on the beach. Maria kept to the trees just far enough away from the beach so she could still see for some distance in three directions. Nothing on the sea but gulls. No one to the left or right as far as she could see.

She set about gathering driftwood, and was able to find both mango and coconut. The coconut yielded up its milk to slake her thirst. How sweet and tasty it was. She felt the heaviness in her begin to lift. She gathered as much of the wood, mangoes, and coconuts as she could carry and stored them for future use. Over the course of the next couple of days she was able to fashion a crude shelter for herself and a storehouse as well. She felt pleased with her work. Satisfied, but not without worry.

In her shelter under the three palms she took out the pearl from her overalls and looked at it a long time. It looked so white and ... pure. But since she'd found it, nothing had come to her but bad luck. How could something so beautiful bring such misery? Still, Maria reasoned, perhaps it was not the pearl itself that brought bad luck. She thought this must be the case, but she could not be certain. She thought about it; and then had another thought. She placed the pearl in a tiny wooden box she had taken from the boat. Then she buried it, as deeply as she could, just outside her shelter. Now she would see. Perhaps her luck might change. Who can say?

On the third day Maria awoke to the sound of a voice. It was soft and low but still she could hear it. It was a woman's voice and she was singing! She crept from her shelter without making a sound and looked out toward the beach. She opened her mouth in wonder at the sight of a woman on a horse walking slowly along the beach. The woman had long red hair, and she sang softly to her horse as they made their way along. Maria had never seen hair that was of a red color. The woman was not young, not old, and she was certainly very beautiful. Her skin bore the paleness of angels. Her song was gentle and sounded wonderful to Maria's ears. This woman was dressed in fine clothing that looked newly made. The yellow of her shirt and the blue of her trousers were so bright! The horse chortled and tossed its head up and down. The horse, too, was magnificent, its coat glistening and gleaming in the sun, with a mane that was long and graceful.

Maria was filled with excitement and fear and hope all at the same time; and something else. Something she had not allowed herself to feel until this moment: yearning. Perhaps this woman was an angel. Perhaps she was Maria's own angel. Her hand flew to her mouth; afraid she might call out or utter a cry. She watched with such intensity that her body began to tremble. The woman went on some distance down the beach and then ... she was turning around! Had Maria been seen? She crouched low, her eyes never leaving the woman. Still the woman's song went on, so light and filled with such music. Maria began to cry. She held her hand tight over her mouth to muffle the sound, but her chest heaved and tears welled up in her eyes, brimmed and then flooded, running down her face. The woman was going back the way she had come and soon would be gone.

Sometimes a person will do what they never thought they would. It is at such times that the head loses all control and cannot intervene. No matter how determined or measured or stubborn the mind, it suddenly finds itself powerless to stop the heart.

Maria's mind was angry with her, was still in her hiding place, but her feet took her away, running down the soft white sand toward the woman. She ran like she imagined the wind might run. But such words are only for stories. The sand was pulling at her feet, slowing her, making her courage small again. Her heart, only seconds ago so big, had shrunk and left her.

But the woman had seen her! She turned her horse and was coming toward her. The sun was bright in Maria's eyes and there were so many tears that she couldn't see, and she lost her footing. Suddenly Maria did not know anything anymore. She sank to the sand. If this was the end, she thought, so be it. She wiped the tears the best she could from her eyes and looked for her angel once more. She saw only her tears. The horse approached and blocked the sun, casting a shadow on this small child. But Maria no longer looked up. This sudden darkness must mean the end.

Kate, which was the name of the woman on horseback, had stopped her singing quick enough when she spotted the child. What in the name o' God is this? she thought. She rode up to Maria, dismounted, and just stood, at a loss for a moment, looking at the poor collapsed child. But quick enough, she squatted down beside her, whispering, "Sure, you're lost, my darlin', but you're found now as 'twere."

She lifted Maria's face to hers, produced a handkerchief, and wiped at her tears.

Maria was lost in a glorious, mysterious scent and in a whisper of silk touching her cheek as her angel enveloped her so completely she could see nothing or care for nothing but to have this moment last forever. She did not understand the words of her angel; that was of no matter. So much was of no matter now. Having listened to the priest in the village, she knew she was not meant to understand. The language of God was given only to priests. Yet this angel's language was different from that of the priests. It was like the doctor's, but not. Well, perhaps the language of angels is different from God's language. The doctor had been an angel. She was sure of it. It mattered little to Maria now. She only felt more and more swirling in her head and the blackness came.

When she awoke, she was certain she had died. The angel had taken her to heaven. She opened her eyes to find herself floating in the air. It did not feel exactly that way, but when she looked at the ground, it seemed to be a long way down. The ground was made of white squares. She was lying upon something soft, something that was not the ground yet not just a blanket. There were, though, blankets over her, puffy and light like clouds. She closed her eyes once more. She remembered she had not wanted to die. But now ... who can say?

She opened her eyes to look at the ceiling. Many candles were burning and there were jewels beside them, jewels that reflected light like fire, and with ... no bad smell. It was so strange and yet true. There were no bad smells. All around her were smells of feathers and of firelight. Flowers had been placed on a window ledge. She could smell their sweetness too. She could look through the window, but could not pass her hand through it. The window was empty yet solid. Such are the ways of heaven, she thought. Out of her window she could see farmland and farmers toiling away. She suddenly wanted to go to them, her people. She wanted to be herself once again. But she was now in heaven. What was heaven, then, if it could not take a want such as this away?

A door opened, and her angel came near. She had beautiful long red hair if such a thing were possible; but with angels, who can say? Her face seemed clouded with care. She talked more of her angel language and her hand pressed Maria's forehead, and her angel's face brightened and turned into a smile. A smile from God, Maria thought, to welcome me into this place. Her eyes were green with tiny brown parts; the most beautiful green. But then her face clouded once more and she leaned close to whisper, holding her finger to her lips.

"Silencio. Muy importante." It was pitiful really. The Spanish Kate had learned could be contained in a thimble. Still, she would need the girl to understand, for if Vicente were to find her out, it would go badly for the girl. The fever was gone, that was something at least. She would see to the girl's breakfast herself. Then arrangements would have to be made, and quickly. Vicente would be home soon. She left the girl and busied herself in the kitchen preparing a tray. When it was ready, she called to her son. "Miguel, you'll be taking this upstairs to the girl, and remember now what I've said. You'll say nothing to anyone."

"Yes, Mama," the boy answered.

The boy was growing but not yet fully grown. He had the green eyes of his mother and the darker skin and hair of his father. He carried the tray carefully as though it held treasure. When he entered the bedroom, the girl was awake. She stared at him with huge eyes and leaned away warily at his approach. He set down the tray and looked up at her, smiling. It was a warm smile that made his eyes shine. “I am Miguel, and Mama has made you breakfast.”

And so it was that Maria found herself with a new home.

CHAPTER FIVE: FIRST STEPS

Maria had discovered that she was not in heaven after all. Yet it was like no place she had ever known. Miguel spoke to her in her own language, and although he was older than her, he had none of the mean, teasing ways of boys that were his age. He helped his mother care for her those first few days before she was moved to the small cottage by the stables. She learned many things quickly. She was to stay in the cottage. They were hiding her, Miguel explained, because his father would never give permission for her to be here. His mother's name was Kate. Kate would hold Maria's eyes with her own while she spoke to her. Although Maria could not understand what she was saying, Miguel would tell her what his mother had said. She would be kept safe. She would want for nothing. There were many workers and servants on their property. She must make sure they did not see her. If she wanted, she could take the path out of the back door and it would lead her to the beach, where she could have time outside.

Kate and Miguel wanted to know things about Maria too, and wanted to know most of all why she would not speak to them. Miguel tried again and again to get her to say her name ... anything. But after seeing the frightened look on her face many times, Kate shook her head at Miguel and they bothered her no more about it. She was given food to eat such as she'd never known. Golden pastries and juices served in glasses shaped like flowers. Eggs served with hot bread, cheeses, roasted meats. She could scarcely believe food could be so delicious. The first days passed in this way. Maria grew strong once again and her cuts healed well. In the evenings, when the workers had gone home and the servants were in the main house, Maria would take the path down to the beach and swim in the sea. She found that her special place was not too far from the hacienda and visited it sometimes. It was just as she had left it. She thought of the pearl in the little box buried deep but was afraid to dig it up lest her bad luck return. So she contented herself with poking through her belongings which she had taken from the boat. She found the old cigar she had taken from the doctor and thought about him awhile. Then she put the cigar in her mouth and lit the end. It smelled a little like the doctor used to smell. So she smoked the cigar and grabbed the machete, swinging it around and played at being a pirate. Pirates could have anything they wanted. They never had to ask for anything. They always had pieces of gold and jewels and all kinds of treasure. All they had to do was take it with their swords and pistols. Still, pirates did not have eyes like Kate, which were gentle and kind. She thought Miguel might not be so nice if he were a pirate. But she was only playing after all. Still, the thought made the game not so much fun. She put the machete carefully back into her storeroom and walked back to her cottage alongside the moonlit sea.

CHAPTER SIX: VICENTE ENRIQUE SANDOVAL

Vicente Enrique Sandoval held himself in high regard. He was a fortunate man, it was true, but there were many other reasons for this opinion. He was a righteous man who gave money to the church. Although he was a just man, a temperate and a wise man, Vicente Sandoval was a man who knew the meaning of hard work. He could be shrewd as well, and because of this, along with his hard work, he had become a man of property, someone who was held in the highest of standing. He knew himself to be very strong yet he was capable of great kindness, he thought. He had traveled to America; to England and Europe. He had brought back with him a beautiful bride, Katherine, who had given him a son. Life was good, it was true. But it was this way because he worked very hard and had an eye for opportunities. He was a man of rare quality. He could be impatient, but what of that? The way people spent their time meant a great deal to him, and when people didn't make use of it properly, it made him angry.

These were the thoughts of Vicente Enrique Sandoval as he returned to his hacienda in the early evening. He would have time for a ride on his prize horse, King, before eating his dinner. That was a magnificent specimen of horseflesh. He had been given to Vicente by the Americanos after their latest business dealings at the plantation. The horse was a token of their great respect for him. Vicente thought they showed much good sense in this, the Americanos. His own government was beginning to annoy him greatly. Foreign investment must be monitored closely, they said. Someone would have to pay the outrageous export fees they had set. He was determined not to bear this additional cost. Still, perhaps the right people could be persuaded to change their minds. For a price.

Vicente motored into the yard and applied the brake as he had learned to do. He had studied the automobile for some time before purchasing one. He had mastered the handling of it as he had mastered all other things; with determination and patience. He was harnessing the future to suit it to his needs. One must do so in order to prosper.

As Vicente got out of his horseless buggy he caught sight of his son, Miguel, making his way to the main house. Rather than call out a greeting, he swore under his breath.

The boy annoyed him. He didn't want this to be so, but so it was. His son spent too much time with his face hidden in books, too little time in the cane fields. Too much time dawdling with the workers and their children and too little time playing with his cousins when they came to visit. His cousins were proper young people of quality. They studied hard and had ideas about their future. It was of no importance to Vicente that they were somewhat older. Miguel should be learning from them when they came to visit. Still, he tried to put this out of his mind. There were more important matters to consider. He crossed the yard to the main house and went in for dinner.

Two weeks had passed since Kate had found the girl. She was sure now that the child was not from the village. Since her arrival, the tranquility of the people remained both as steady and as limp as a dishrag; among the workers, there had been not so much as a flutter of concern. Kate had often found them a frustrating people; their voices flat, nasal, every subject too simple in their minds, either this or that, as if they were thick She shouldn't think such things but it vexed her. In spite of the depth and the knowingness in their eyes, she somehow couldn't ... Well, never mind that now, she thought. We've a mystery here, still, the girl needs a home in the meantime. Kate found she had worked herself into a dread of this moment. Now her husband was standing in the doorway with his arms outstretched and she would have to be careful. The balance of power between spouses is a very delicate business.

"Darling!" She called, and laughed playfully, as her husband liked her to do, rushing to him in a flirtatious fashion. He embraced her closely, but quickly, with something else clearly playing on his mind. This evening was clearly going to be more difficult than she had imagined. "We've all been missing you so. Rosa has been so busy making a special homecoming dinner."

"Very well, my love: by all means, let us discover what surprises Rosa has to offer." And with that, Vicente left her and strode into the dining room, taking off his jacket and loosening his tie (a bad sign, that), and sitting down at the head of the table.

Kate followed, her head bowed, picking up all the signs she could on her journey to the other end of the table. His eyes did not follow her. This was another bad sign. There was to be a battle.

Well, the skirmish had begun, and rules be damned, she would fire the first shot. She placed a hand on Rosa's arm as the servant set a serving dish on the table. "Rosa, leave us, please." Rosa, eyes suddenly wide, nodded and scurried from the room. Kate did not make the entire twelve-foot journey to the end of the table, but chose a chair to Vicente's right, close beside him. She spoke softly but with no question in her voice. "So, then, things aren't going so well in Havana."

Vicente looked at her sharply, as if he were biting his tongue, then looked to his plate. “Zayas will run for the liberals. He is urging distrust of the Americanos yet again and spouting his usual drivel. This time he has the idea to suggest that women should have the vote! Who can say where this comes from? Radicals are like rats during a plague; there is no end to them.”

Kate had failed. The first shot in the battle should not let your enemies know what you yourself knew. The first diplomatic step with the enemy should not involve reaching out for understanding. Now Vicente was angry and would express this anger. She had lost the first battle. But in retreat, there was time to learn. She would use this great weight on her husband’s mind to her advantage. She must work quickly and directly.

She clasped her hands together purposefully and laid them on the table. “We found a young girl on the beach. She is staying in the cottage by the stables.”

Vicente turned to her, momentarily confused, as if not hearing properly. “You ... We?”

Victory! The first success. Vicente was off-balance. Now she must press on. “I ...” began Kate, “I found a girl on the beach and brought her here. Miguel and I have been caring for her. She is not from this part of the country. We have waited two weeks; the people are silent, so she cannot be one of them, the girl is a mystery, she ...”

Kate knew she must be strong, now more than ever. Her plan had worked! She had broken through the enemy’s defenses and now must advance as far as she could before the counter-attack. She swallowed and strength returned to her voice. “She was very ill, but now the girl’s well, and I want to keep her with us! I want so much to keep her with us! If you will meet her, you will see . . .”

Kate was disgusted to hear the pleading in her voice.

Vicente rose from his seat and glared at her with diamond-hard eyes.

Now the counterattack would come. But in spite of her fear, Kate held him with her gaze.

"Two weeks! You've lied to your husband for half a month!" Vicente glared at her, but the hatred and the thunder would not come. What is it, he thought, that enables women to cast such spells? She met his eyes all the while, blaze for blaze. Finally, he broke the silence. He tried to make his voice gentle, but anger remained. "Katherine, there is no place in this house for a girl like this. If she is not of the village, she must go to the church. They will know what to do."

Kate knew what must be done. His dreaded counterattack had had little effect. It was blunted by his love for her. She heard it in his voice and moved instantly to seize the advantage. "The church can be damned. You want to give her over to the likes of that drunken priest? If the girl does not stay with us, Vicente, hear this. I'll not share your bed. I'll not speak to you. I'll not appear with you at what you call your business dinners. Ever!" Well, there it t'was, all guns firing at once. Her Irish had risen. Now she would see.

Vicente's eyes lost their intensity and clouded over. Unknowable. Yet still he stared at his wife. Always this fury she barely held in check, he thought. For a long time he had laughed, calling her his thoroughbred. But to denigrate the church in such a fashion...

Finally, he rose and walked out of the room. Kate had lost. For the moment.

Until a few moments later, when Vicente walked back into the room, wagging a finger playfully at her. And light on his feet. He had done this many times before. His love dance, she called it. "We will talk further of this . . ." Quickly he turned and left the room again. Kate had won another battle for Maria and the girl didn't even know it. Yet.

The next morning Kate went to the village. She returned with a Sunday dress for Maria and shoes that were almost new. The seamstress was told they were for a visiting niece. Tongues would wag. But soon enough, there would be no need for these petty deceptions. She brought the dress and the shoes to the little cottage and dressed Maria herself, washing her hair and singing to her all the words she could remember of "A Kiss in the Morning, Early." The child certainly cleaned up very well, Kate thought. She tried out some of the Spanish Miguel had taught her.

"Buenos dias, Maria. Presentamente y dice a persona importante! El hombre a Grande. Mi gusto." She hesitated. Maria looked at her with wide eyes. Perhaps her Spanish was not up to snuff. "Mi Española no buena. Yo embarazada."

Maria did not know what to make of Kate's coming to her that morning singing. She trusted this woman very much, but now it seemed there might be something wrong with her. She washed Maria's hair with bubbles, and put a beautiful dress on her, which was also very stiff and itched at her skin. She had Maria put on shoes which felt tight and not comfortable at all. Then she spoke to Maria about an important man who was a big man and was to her taste. Then she said her Spanish was not good and she was with child. She was not at all sure Kate was not becoming a crazy person. She wished Miguel was there.

Miguel had visited her twice. Both times he had come alone. The first time, Maria was badly frightened when a knock came on the door. But it was a soft tapping and he entered whispering hello to find her hiding under the bed. He did not laugh but smiled and beckoned her to come out. When she did, he presented her with books. From the look on his face, Maria thought he must think of the books as a treasure and a wonderful gift. Maria did not know of books. But she tried to smile at him and accepted them. He seemed to understand her uncertainty.

"You do not know reading?" he asked. Maria shook her head. "It is all right, there are pictures too." He set all the books but one on a chair by her bed. He took this last book, the heaviest one, and opened it in front of her. He turned pages of the book until he found something. He showed her a picture. It was very beautiful, but Maria was a little frightened, as she had been frightened when she went into the sea and strayed too far from shore.

But no. She knew what it meant to be far from shore now and would not let it frighten her. She told Miguel she thought the picture was beautiful and nodded happily to thank him for his gift. "It is the great general Washington, crossing the Delaware," he said proudly. "He was a great revolutionary."

Maria did not know what any of these words meant. She smiled and nodded again to Miguel in thanks. It was then that she noticed that Miguel's eyes burned in a strange way. "The pictures are beautiful, yes. But the words are beautiful too, and you should know about them and what secrets they hold." Maria lifted her shoulders up and down to show she did not understand. Miguel suddenly became angry at her movement. "No, you must never do that, it is what too many of our people do. It shows not only that you don't understand but that you do not care!"

His sudden anger frightened Maria, for she thought perhaps she had just lost a friend. But as quickly as it came, his anger left him. He looked down, then up to her eyes, and asked her the question she would remember always: "Will you let me teach you how to read?" She would remember his question and the sound of his voice in that moment much longer than she would remember his face. She did not know the word "read." But she nodded her head. She would learn.

The second time Miguel came he brought with him a chalkboard and chalk. Maria remembered them from the school in her native village. She had been to school and knew the word "teacher." She had lined up to be assigned a desk, with a huge chalkboard, much bigger than Miguel's. Maria wasn't sure she remembered how that day in the school ended, but she remembered angry voices. The day had ended with angry voices.

Miguel said all she needed to know for the first lesson was twenty-six letters. This meant "alphabet." He wrote out each of them and had her do the same. He said the letter and she was to repeat it. He talked to her of mysteries and what a mystery was. He talked of puzzles and what a puzzle was. Each time she understood the word he used, she had to repeat the word and explain its meaning. It all seemed slow and made her head hurt, but she wanted to help him. He seemed like his mind was made up about the truth of these things and he was so serious, so she tried hard.

When he getting ready to leave her the second time, he said: "All the words in the books are mysteries, they are puzzles. You have learned three words this day. Mystery and puzzle. And also you have learned the name of the big book. You have seen the letters of the alphabet and the sounds they make when spoken. It is like a game. I hope you like this game. I do. I play the game mostly by myself. But it would be exciting to play it with you, Maria. Will you play this game with me?" He smiled and stood to leave. She wanted to touch him before he left. To let him know she understood. She did smile at him. It would have to be enough.

He had left her with this other thing. The big book. It had no pictures. It was not black, so it was not the Bible. It held no interest for her. Yet he said it was a key to the lock. He had said the name of the book. She played the game long after Miguel had left. She practiced the sound and saying the word as he taught her. "Dic-shun-ario." She said it to the air. Why would someone say a thing out loud without speaking to anyone? Somehow, it didn't matter, for Maria, for the first time in as long as she could remember, was happy.

CHAPTER SEVEN: KATE AND THE PRIEST

Kate was satisfied with her work. She took the girl by the hand and led her out of the cottage toward the main house. The girl hung back. She was plainly frightened, and it was all Kate could do to move her along. "It will be all right, you know. Este buen. Este muy buen." She gave the girl's hand a gentle squeeze as they entered the hacienda. Rosa greeted them at the door. The girl turned her face into the folds of Kate's dress. "Rosa, this is ... this is our special guest. My husband is in the library?" Rosa, looking oddly nervous, nodded quickly and moved past them to close the main door.

Well, it's time, Kate thought. With both arms guiding the girl beside her, coaxing her, they entered the library. Kate's excitement had been building all morning and had taken flight. Now, as they entered the library, it dropped from the sky as quickly as a stone, her smile frozen in the sudden chill of the room.

"Katherine," Vicente began, "Father Gregorio here, you know, but he has brought with him Sister Celia. Father Gregorio has most generously consented to help us with our present ... situation."

The room filled up with silence. Kate did not, would not, acknowledge the presence of the father and the sister, and her eyes remained locked upon her husband. The man who had just stabbed her. So, she thought, the tenderness in him was a bloody disguise. And the strength of him had taken refuge in his weakness. The coward would let the church speak for him. The girl, with her face hidden in the folds of Kate's dress, was trembling.

Father Gregorio cleared his throat and carefully set down his glass of wine. "The girl is not from the village." He allowed himself a small smile. "I would be the first to know. But with God's help perhaps ..."

Kate turned on him. "God has not helped the girl. I have."

The priest smiled his most patient smile. There were always those in his flock who questioned the wisdom of the Lord. It was in these times they came to him, and though at times he found them to be filled with anger or bitterness, he had given them comfort and guided them back to the path of righteousness. This woman of Sandoval's had never approached him, not a single time. She perhaps did not know how helpful he could be. She was filled with the sin of pride. He must show her the way of things but in a gentle way.

"The holy father has worked through you," the priest told Katherine. "You are fortunate to have been so chosen. In time you will see this. Such kindness and care as you have given will do much to atone for your sins."

Vicente could no longer meet his wife's eyes. Instead he gave a brief nod of thanks to Father Gregorio. The priest beckoned to Sister Celia, who moved toward Kate and the girl. Kate held tightly to the trembling child and turned her back on them. So, the decision had been made. There would be no discussion. Her voice would not be heard and did not matter at all. They were closing in on her. Her husband's voice came, gentle but firm behind her. "Please, Katherine, it is for the best. The girl belongs with the church. You must see that. She belongs with the church."

Kate saw the open bottle of wine on the sideboard. She snatched it up and turned to them, lifting the bottle high above her head. She saw them pause, saw the incredulous look on the priest's face. Saw the sister bow her head. "Forgive me, Father" she said, and let the bottle crash to the floor, exploding on the white ceramic tile beneath her, its contents creating what seemed a river of blood between Kate and the others.

"God sees the little sparrow fall, isn't that right, Father? Sister, perhaps you belong with the church; Father, you belong with your wine, and you, my husband, may very well belong with the devil, but the girl belongs with me!"

She took the girl by the hand, turned, and ran.

Vicente glanced at the priest, red-faced and at a loss. "I am truly sorry, Father, I beg your forgiveness. My wife is very headstrong. But I'm sure with time ..."

Father Gregorio reached for his hat and stepped carefully so as to avoid the spilled wine. Sister Celia followed him to the door. The priest turned to Vicente. "At least she keeps her silence in church."

His little joke having fallen on deaf ears, the priest brought out his stern voice. "God has patience, my son. But you should understand, this house has become a sinful place. You must do what is right and bring the child back to God. As for your good wife ... she will be much in need of our prayers. Good day to you, Señor Sandoval."

Vicente paced the room like a caged tiger. Rosa mopped up the wine, trying her best to be a ghost, to think of nothing. She finished as quickly as she could and silently left the room.

Vicente watched her slink out of the room. He slammed the door behind her to be alone with his thoughts. They began with Rosa. My people, he thought. They have the courage of sheep, the ambition of donkeys, and the intelligence of fleas! Still, at least they have loyalty. But what of that? Of what use has their loyalty been? I have done my duty to the church and now I am to be told that my house is a sinful place! Vicente's fury intensified at the thought. He goes too far! This priest has overstepped himself. He was quick as a rabbit to take money for the repairs he said were needed for the church. I was an angel then, thought Vicente. How blessed I was! And now, how quickly I seem to have fallen. He remained furious with his wife. He needed her now more than ever, but how could she have embarrassed him so with these dramatics of hers? Over some vagrant child? There were more pressing matters. Zayas was stealing away his conservative friends with his liberal posturing. It was so simple to go against the Americanos. Popular now too, it seemed. But the Americanos were the source of his livelihood, and if things did not change soon, Zayas would win power and make things impossible for a man like Vicente to make a living. If he were a drinking man, now would be the time to hit the bottle.

His thoughts were interrupted by his son, Miguel, coming into the room.

CHAPTER EIGHT: VICENTE AND MIGUEL

Miguel made sure to keep as much distance between himself and his father as he could. “Father, Mother wishes me to tell you she has gone riding.”

“And the girl?” asked Vicente? Miguel lifted his shoulders and put them down again. He turned to go. “Miguel, come. Sit here by me.” Miguel was frightened now but there was little choice. His father usually wore a sour look when he spoke to him. Miguel knew Vicente had not much use for him, no matter how hard he tried. But strangely, his father smiled as he motioned to the place beside him with a friendly gesture. Miguel did as his father commanded. He tried to sit as straight as he could and stared straight ahead at the books that lined the wall.

There were many of them in rich red leather bindings; the books filled every wall in the room and made this room a kind of holy place. Some of the books were about the production of sugar, and told of the many diseases the cane could come into contact with. Some were about accounting. These were not the ones that interested Miguel. There were many, many books about history, not just the history of his country but of countries around the world. His favorite was about the Americano revolution, the book that held the picture of Washington crossing the Delaware. There were map books too, showing every part of the world and the oceans and seas between them. Miguel used to love to come into this room and read. He was never allowed to sit at or near his father's great desk but there was a comfortable leather couch and comfortable armchairs. There were heavy carpets laid over parts of the porcelain tile, so the room was very quiet. Miguel had loved to sneak away and read here for hours with nothing but the heavy ticking of the grandfather clock to break the silence.

But his father had become impatient with his presence, saying he was always underfoot. From now on, his father said, he would be allowed to take only one book at time and read it in his bedroom. His father added he must always ask permission before borrowing any books.

His father's question, asked in a curious, gentle fashion broke into Miguel's thoughts. "Miguel, how many years have you now?"

"Fourteen years, Father," came his reply.

"You are quickly becoming a man, my son. It is time we took some time to talk together. This girl, how many years has she?"

"Twelve years, Father." His father looked at him closely, making Miguel's heart beat faster and his face go red.

"She has told you this?"

"No, Father, the girl does not speak. But she understands. I asked of her this question, and she held up both her hands and then put them down and raised two fingers."

"I see. So she can't speak and yet she understands."

"I do not know if she can speak, Father. But she has not spoken to Mother or to me."

"There is nothing to be afraid of, Miguel. You must tell me all you know of this girl."

So Miguel related everything he knew, how she had been very ill and full of cuts. How his mother had cared for her. He did not dare speak of his visits to the girl. Vicente rose, crossed to the window, and looked out. He thought for a moment then crossed back and sat down beside his son, placing his hand lightly on the boy's knee. "Do you remember the story of Washington, and the revolution, Miguel?"

Miguel could not help but be a little excited. "Oh yes, Father, it is one of the best stories."

Vicente frowned. "Miguel, look at me. It is not a story. It is history. It is the history of a great general."

"Yes, Father." The sudden light that had shone in Miguel's eyes quickly died and Vicente was hurt to see the boy's enthusiasm go with it. He felt a small electric shock inside himself to realize this. He had done this many times, stolen his son's joy. Stolen it in the name of constant corrections of his behavior, presenting himself as an exemplar of righteousness, shutting the boy out when the smallest detail was not perfect. He was overcome with an urge to take the boy into his arms ... yet even this, he must do this correctly.

"But, of course, you are right. It is history, yes, but a great story too." Miguel nodded and a very slight smile returned to his face.

Vicente studied his son for a moment, and then continued: "Now, Washington was a very great general, to be sure, and he became one because he knew many things instinctively. You know this word, 'instinctively'?" The boy gave a nod, seeming to listen more carefully.

"Well then, on one occasion, he learned from his scouts that his forces now outnumbered the forces of the enemy, and he thought about encircling them! He thought a long time before he acted. Do you know what he did when he did act?" The boy shook his head, now wanting very much to know the answer.

"He pulled back!"

The boy's mouth dropped open in astonishment. "He retreated? He ran?"

"No, my son, he did not run." Vicente smiled as he warmed to his story. "He pulled back! You see, this forced the enemy to chase him. He went closer to where his supplies were located and made the enemy come to him. Meanwhile, the enemy supply lines grew farther and farther away. And all this time the enemy was growing weaker because it did not know the territory. They had to go through swamps while General Washington knew the way around them, so his troops were dry and happy and not bothered at all by the flies."

"Flies?" said Miguel.

"Oh yes! YES! There were a great many flies in the swamp, you see, big insects that flew and would bite the enemy, causing them terrible pain, And snakes too, poisonous creatures that would swim through the water to sink their fangs into the enemy's flesh and inject their venom into them. Many of the enemy died in this way."

Vicente stopped his talk and waited, staring off into the distance, a look of wistful contentment on his face.

Miguel stared with open mouth at his father. A moment passed. Then another. Miguel finally could not contain himself further and exploded: "Well, what happened? Did Washington charge them? Did he win the battle? Father, please tell me!"

"Well, yes, of course he won the battle! He led his troops into the hills surrounding a valley, and when the enemy came into the valley, like sheep, he killed them all, every one! Well, he may have made captives of a few, but that is not important. Of course, it was not much of a battle, for the enemy was tired sick and by this point very few in number. But there is a lesson here, Miguel. A very great lesson can be learned." Vicente paused for effect. “A great general always chooses his battles, and when battle is not the right choice for a given moment or situation, well then, he must not be too proud or afraid to choose not to fight.”

“It was a wonderful stor—history, Father,” Miguel said.

Vicente tousled the boy’s hair, saying: “Yes, it was. Now go fetch your mother. Rosa will have dinner nearly ready.”

Miguel bounded for the door but caught himself up before he left the room. He turned slowly back to his father. His face had fallen. “Mother has said she will be staying in the cottage with the girl. Rosa is to bring her supper out to her.”

“Very well, go and wash yourself. You and I shall dine alone.”

“Perhaps after dinner, we could have another history, Father?”

“Yes, all right, now go, and, Miguel ...”

“Yes, Father?”

“You are a good boy. You have proper manners. It is evident to everyone.” Vicente hesitated and cleared the emotion from his throat. “So ... I do not insist you call me Father all the time. You may call me Papa.”

CHAPTER NINE: MARIA AND KATE

Weeks passed in this fashion. Always Maria and the woman Kate went riding. Always Rosa brought their meals to the cottage. Maria was afraid every day that the priest would come again. But he did not return. The man of the main house visited the cottage a couple of times, bringing beautiful flowers, but Kate would send him away without taking them. The words she said to him were angry ones, and on these occasions she would cry for a long time after he left. Sometimes Maria saw the man come out from the main house and get into his magical carriage, the one that moved with no horse and made strange noises with smoke coming out of it. He left and returned later in the evening. Once she saw Miguel go with him. She wanted so much for Miguel to come to visit the cottage, but he never did. Still, some things were wonderful. Kate had given her a pony to take on their rides and showed her how to make the animal turn around or stop or go fast. Maria had ridden a burro before but the horse was nothing like that. It could almost fly when it ran and this excited Maria so much that she laughed out loud for the first time since she had arrived here.

Kate looked so surprised when she heard Maria laugh. Then she laughed too, and for one happy moment they laughed together. Maria's heart was growing fuller with feeling for this woman, Kate, and she knew she must hold on to the feeling of these moments. She would remember them when the bad times returned, and she hoped that the memory of them might give her strength. She was beginning to understand some words of this new language, English. At first she only understood "yes" and "no," but more words became clear every day. Kate helped her very much by pointing to things and telling her their names. Horse. Pony. Trousers. Dress. Window. Door. Maria desperately wanted to give Kate back something. This woman was so kind to her. It made Maria feel wretched that she could give nothing in return.

So one day when they rode along the beach, Maria showed Kate her special place near the three palms. Kate's eyes grew wide, and she looked at Maria with great surprise on her face. Maria showed Kate the things she had salvaged from the boat, her little sleeping place, and the storeroom. Kate held the old canvas sail for some time and looked toward the beach. Maria wanted to tell her about the boat and the doctor, but she didn't dare. Things must remain this way. There was enough trouble already. She thought about showing Kate the pearl she had buried but did not want the bad luck to return. She remembered the signal Kate had first given her and put her finger to her lips. Kate laughed at that but then her face grew serious and she nodded. "Your secret's safe with me, my love."

Kate seemed very worried. Although the priest had not returned, it didn't mean he wouldn't come later. She didn't dare go to Sunday mass, much less bring the girl. She had watched out the window many Sunday mornings now and she knew Vicente had not gone to mass either. This was shocking to her. He had always shown such devotion to the church. Rosa had grown sullen and taciturn when she brought them their meals, and Kate suspected her standoff with the church was the reason. She was right.

Word was spreading throughout the hacienda, and the servants and workers were beginning to grow more somber and fearful. The word had spread quickly, the rumor that perhaps this was no longer a place blessed by God.

Kate's resolve, once made of steel, was beginning to be shaken. Things could not continue this way and she began to wonder if some understanding could be reached. Her fury at her husband was beginning to be tempered by her understanding of the situation. He had been kind to her in all things, but now his reputation would be suffering. In spite of this, he had been patient. After all he could have called the priest back and forced the girl's removal. He had nothing to lose by this as Kate had already withdrawn completely from him and he had no other weapons to fight with. Instead he had brought her flowers and she had thrown them back in his face.

What if the girl could be sent to the convent during the day, and she, Kate, allowed the sisters to teach her, provided the girl could return to the house in the evenings? Kate detested the thought of the girl being indoctrinated by the sisters, as she had detested the indoctrination she herself had endured as a child in Ireland. She wasn't opposed to giving something of herself to God, but was bloody well determined to keep the rest. Ah, but the church was never content with that. *Give yourself over to God. He will provide.* She was tired of the stupidity of it all. Her mother had almost starved as a girl during the great famine. Where were God's provisions then? Give yourself to king and country. Her father had given his life for king and country and left his family at the mercy of the Black and Tans.

As to her hopes, would this compromise work? She knew it was a fool's bargain; the church had no reason to give in and she had already infuriated the priest. She was sure of that. All she had left was to plead with him, and it was not pride that prevented that from happening. It was her knowledge that such pleading would not work. But she missed her son. She was losing everything. She didn't want to give up the girl. This strong, wonderful, mysterious girl. Still, what else was there to do?

It was possible she could hide the girl once more, she thought. Tell her husband and the priest that she had run away, disappeared as suddenly as she had come. Perhaps she had drowned in the sea. The girl's hiding place was a clever one and perhaps ... but no, it was of no use. She couldn't carry the lie, and besides, they would not be likely to believe her in the first place. They would search and eventually they would find the girl. Kate was not thinking clearly. The desperation grew in her with each passing day. Another Sunday was closing in on her.

On Saturday afternoon there came a knock on the door.

CHAPTER TEN: AN ARRANGEMENT

So they had finally come! Kate motioned for the girl to hide under the bed and Maria quickly obeyed. Kate steeled herself, crossed to the door, and opened it to find Miguel. Her breath caught and she snatched at her son, holding him in a tight embrace. Miguel thought his mother might never let him go although he was very glad to see her. At last she released him, holding him out to brush the hair out of his eyes. "My beautiful boy," she said, her voice trembling.

Miguel smiled back at her sheepishly. "Father is asking if you would see him at the house. He said you were not to worry. There will be no one from the church there. He gives his word."

"Tell him I will come. But before I go to him, you must return here and stay with Maria. Make sure no one comes in."

"He wants to see her too."

Kate wondered at this. But something had to be done. "Very well, tell your father I will see him in a few minutes, and bring the girl." Miguel nodded eagerly and dashed off toward the main house. Perhaps, Kate thought, they could come to some kind of arrangement.

Maria crept slowly out from the under the bed. She was glad it was Miguel's voice that she'd heard. But she had heard him say the word "church," and this frightened her. She had to trust herself to Kate.

But no, Maria thought, she could no longer do this. She had brought trouble to Kate, and she would not bring more. This was a dangerous time. But she had her small horse now. And Kate had taught her how to saddle it. If it came to it, she could run, and with the pony to carry her, she could be far away quickly. Maria told herself that once she got hold of her machete, she could fight if she needed to. Miguel's voice had sounded excited, not with fear but with happiness. Perhaps it might be something good. The good luck and the bad were all mixed together and it was very confusing. Maria would be prepared in any case. It would be difficult to run away, though, because Kate was insisting she wear the cursed dress and the uncomfortable shoes. And much sooner than she would have liked, Maria was being led across the yard once more to the main house.

Kate walked in the door with Maria, but there was no Rosa to greet them. She made her way cautiously to the library, but it was empty as well. Vicente's voice came to her from above. "I am upstairs, Katherine. Come, I have something to show you." His voice was even and betrayed no emotion. It was like he was reading from some damned newspaper. Kate's fear was growing inside her and that made her angry. What was he playing at?

"Miguel?" she called out.

"Miguel is with me, come up." Kate looked all around her, but nothing seemed to be amiss. The house looked normal, everything in its place. But she could tell that something strange was going on nonetheless.

"Why don't you and Miguel come down here?" Kate didn't want to relinquish her position close to the door.

"I can't come down because what I have to show you is up here."

The man was infuriating. Holding tightly to Maria's hand, Kate warily made her way to the staircase, looking up, but there was nothing to see. She hesitated, listening, but the heavy ticking of the grandfather clock was the only sound she could hear.

"Come, Mama." Miguel was up there. Well, all right, damn him, thought Kate, and she made her way upstairs with Maria's hand in hers. Thinking Vicente and Miguel to be in the study, she swung open the door. The room was empty.

"We are over here, Katherine."

In one of the guest rooms? Kate had had enough. She marched Maria down the hall, around a corner, and there, standing outside one of the guest rooms, Vicente and Miguel awaited them. It was a strange place to meet, Kate thought as she held the girl in front of her and regarded her husband. A shy smile played at his lips, the kind of smile she remembered from when he first courted her. She felt strangely formal and so she said to the girl: "Darling, this is my husband, Vicente Enrique Sandoval. Vicente, this is ... this is the girl I was telling you about." Kate had stopped ten feet from her husband and son but Vicente quickly crossed to Maria, bowed his head quickly, and then knelt before her.

He said to her in Spanish: "I am charmed to make your acquaintance, my dear, I have heard so much about you and it gladdens me to hear you have decided to stay with us. I understand your journey has been a long one, and it is my pleasure you to offer you our humble hospitality."

Maria could not look at him, such was her fear. She bowed her head, but this time did not seek the shelter of Kate's dress. Finally she looked up, off to the side, and caught Miguel wearing the playful smile he wore when she understood something he had been trying to teach her. Summoning her courage, she looked back at Kate's husband and saw him clearly for the first time. He has kind eyes, she thought. So much was happening and so quickly. Even though this man had spoken to her in her language, she understood only a little of what he had said. He was welcoming her, that was clear. She should have looked to Kate to teach her how to act. But it was up to her now. She made a big decision and gave Vicente a little smile to acknowledge his welcome.

Kate was thunderstruck. She had envisioned a thousand different outcomes, none of them like this. Even as a child, she had mistrusted surprises. She would be cautious and wait to see what her husband planned for the girl. For now, though, the girl had smiled at Vicente, and Kate knew that the child had good instincts. The two of them were coming to rely on each other. She looked up at her husband, her eyes searching his. His beautiful brown eyes, once so full of passion, were a mask to her now. They looked weary, yet somehow a twinkle remained. She had to remind herself that his eyes could no longer be trusted.

CHAPTER ELEVEN: SEALED WITH A KISS

"Come. Look." Vicente gestured to her and swung wide the door to the guest room.

Kate was struck dumb by what she saw. The room had been completely transformed and refurnished to accommodate a twelve-year-old girl. Its hideous gray walls were now bright pastels. The high, massive four-poster bed, of the darkest and most intimidating mahogany, was gone from the center of the room. The room looked enormous without it. Placed in a corner, near the window, was a much smaller bed with a frilly canopy. Stuffed animals, a bear and a unicorn, were set against the pillows. The bedspread was a soft pastel adorned with tiny roses. Under the window the sun streamed in on a small desk with fresh flowers upon it. The blood-red curtains on the window... replaced with white adorned with lace. Next to the desk a globe of the earth, and next to that a bookcase full of volumes obviously selected with care: *Little Women*, poems by Emily Dickinson, anything that might possibly be of interest to the girl. Maria could not read, of course, but perhaps Vicente did not know that. Nevertheless, the room spoke of ... a future for the girl.

The large closet stood open, filled with brightly colored new dresses. There were many pairs of newly bought shoes too. The heavy dark carpets had been replaced with ones of light blue, covered with intricate yet delicate patterns. Everything had been completely transformed. The artwork had been replaced. The large ugly picture of the bullfight was gone, thank God! The smaller framed hunting prints were missing as well. In their place was a variety of scenes. The larger picture was of a boat at sea, under full sail, painted on a glorious day with bright sun and sparkling blue waters. The smaller ones were of a circus; a clown in one, a ringmaster and elephants in another. Still another picture showed laughing children on their way to school, swinging books bound by a belt. Everything Kate's eyes touched upon had been carefully chosen with a young girl in mind.

Emotion choked at Kate but she kept it from rising to her face as she turned to Vicente. "What is it you want, husband?"

Vicente Enrique Sandoval could not and would not find it in himself to plead with his wife, or any woman, no matter what was in his heart. A man such as he must always hold himself with dignity. A man of stature, who could be counted on to be a reasonable man. He had practiced many times what he would say. One had to be prepared for any eventuality, and he felt himself on solid ground as he now spoke.

"It is in everyone's interest to put this painful time behind us. Nothing is to be gained by continuing this struggle. My son is in need of his mother, I would like my wife to return to the ways of respectability, and I suspect that you, Katherine, want to be a mother to this unfortunate child. There is much to be resolved. Rosa has been of very much help but she has a loose tongue. The servants and the workers are unhappy and production has suffered. More important even than this is that this house is no longer in the good graces of God. The priest has said as much. But I do not believe the priest speaks for God in this instance. I have long studied this situation and prayed to find an answer. So this is what I propose. I am prepared to go against Father Gregorio's wishes in return for us all to go back to the church and beg God's forgiveness. Father Gregorio has no doubt denounced me in his sermons, but it is my feeling that I am still able to command respect from many. To win back the others we must start attending mass again. I will state our intention to make the girl a part of our family, and give the promise she will be brought up with God. This return to the church will require courage from everyone. We have long been away and are the subject of much talk. I wish us to become one family with God's blessing."

Kate held the girl close and embraced her tightly, kissing her on the top of her head. She was silent for a moment while she looked around the room once more. She longed for this interview to be over and she knew now that it could not be unless they worked together. Did her husband mean what he said about becoming one family?

"That priest is too proud," Kate said. "He will never consent to give his blessing to this."

Vicente's eyes glittered. "I am sure God will give his blessing in the end. Father Gregorio is not God. He sometimes thinks he is, but believe me, I know of people who are closer. The bishop for one."

Kate took the girl's hand, led her to the desk, and had her sit. She walked up to her husband and faced him. "You are a good man, Vincent. You make me furious when I can't reach you, but inside, you are a good man. So how do I talk to you in your terms, my husband? What can I possibly say to such charming sweet talk as that? I agree to your proposal, Vicente Enrique Sandoval. I will—oh, I'm just bloody glad for this standoff to come to an end. So what is it to be, then? Shall I shake hands with you in agreement? Shall we congratulate ourselves over brandy and cigars in your study? Perhaps hold our glasses high in a toast?"

Now it was Kate's eyes that held a twinkle. Vicente caught the twinkle and the beginnings of a smile. He swiftly gathered her in his arms to hold her tightly, and it was sealed with a kiss.

Maria looked to Miguel in wonder. Miguel looked back at her with a bright and mischievous smile. They were now a family.

CHAPTER TWELVE: A PLACE TO KNOW, A TIME TO GROW

The new family attended mass the next day. They sat very near the front in church and stood erect and proud for the hymns, although they could feel everyone's eyes upon them. Father Gregorio very studiously ignored their return. Instead he spoke in his sermon of the sin of pride and how putting one's self before God was to forsake God himself and a sure way to damnation. The priest took his customary place after the mass, touching hands with each of his flock as they emerged from the church into the bright sun. The new family was among the last to emerge. Father Gregorio took many extra minutes to inquire about each of the families and their health, and this caused the new family to wait a long time before they could greet him. When it came their turn he suddenly remembered he must put out the candles, and brushed past them without a word.

So this is how it was going to be. There were many who had lingered outside the church, eager to see what would happen. Vicente turned to his wife and pitched his voice low. "Father Gregorio always knows what to say. He gave good advice in his sermon today. He should perhaps take this advice himself." Vicente was glad he had chosen the horse-drawn carriage instead of the automobile for the return to church. It was a fine day for a coach ride and Kate even sang to them on their way back to the hacienda.

The first time she was left alone in what was now her room, Maria was very still and as quiet as she had been in church. This room did not feel so much different. It was like a holy place. She remembered how she thought she was in heaven when she first came to this house. She remembered how her sense had returned to her and told her that it was not heaven after all. Now she was not so sure. She began with a great shyness to reach out and touch things, let her fingers gently trace their shape and form. The stuffed animals particularly fascinated her. She remembered having a small doll in her native village. By now it had to be many years old, while these creatures must be newly born. The bear looked at her with golden shiny eyes, neither happy nor sad. Its fur was very soft. The horse too had fur, much the same, but a horn grew from between its ears, poor thing.

The room reminded her of the sea, both light green and blue. Her new bed was like heaven's boat. Her eyes went to the big picture on the wall. The ship reminded her of her journey but the vessel in the picture looked so much bigger and stronger, like it could sail on the sea forever. She wished she could feel as big as the picture boat, but the room was large and made her feel small. She felt she might disappear at any moment. This is what it is like not to know, she thought.

She looked at the globe, touched it, and was startled when it began to turn. I did not know it did that, she thought. She looked at the little pictures and didn't know what to think about them. Her eyes traveled to the books. Miguel had explained to her about books. He knows what is inside them. I do not know. There are too many things I do not know, she thought. Again her sense came to her, to tell her that she wanted to know about these things. If she didn't want to know, her sense told her, she would always feel small.

When she had made her special place, everything was familiar to her and she began to be certain about her place in the world. There was no one to help her, it was true, but also no one could tell her what to do or hurt her. It had been good to be alone. She could do whatever she pleased and that made her feel big and strong.

You can feel this way when you know things, she thought. It was strange. You could not see knowledge, it was invisible. It was just there. It was like happiness. Knowing and happiness had come hand in hand. Perhaps they were the same. Not really, her sense told her, they were not the same at all.

Once you knew something, it was impossible not to know it. It could never disappear. It was a constant companion.

But it was possible to forget happiness. And happiness could disappear in the blink of your eye. So what kind of companion is that?

But to have knowledge by your side? The more things you knew, the stronger you could be. And her sense told her too that she could never be happy unless she was strong.

She was no longer alone and she knew it was impossible to go back to how things had been. She looked around again at her new room. Then, she thought, if this was the way it was to be, she would learn what she needed to learn. Kate and Miguel would help her. She wanted to know more about what was in the pictures. She wanted to know what the round thing was that turned when she touched it. Most of all, she wanted to know about the books. She wanted to be wise, like Miguel. She wanted to be strong, like Señor Sandoval. She wanted to share with others the love in her heart and stand as a protector to them, like Kate did. She wanted all these things and was determined to get them.

She didn't want to feel this small ever again.

She left her room and all the things she did not know but did not close the door behind her. She made her way down the stairs to find Kate and Miguel. She was suddenly very thirsty.

CHAPTER THIRTEEN: A ROSE BY ANY OTHER NAME

Maria spent many afternoons with Miguel and his books. It was difficult, just listening. She had so many questions. And she would not learn quickly unless she could ask them. Yet she could not ask them without taking Miguel into her confidence. Maria had kept herself hidden and buried for so long, like the pearl. It would have to be something small at first for it was all she felt able to do. There was a thing her mother had taught her to draw and said it was for her alone. But she would share this thing.

Miguel was drawing a picture for her of the way that sugar was processed on their plantation. He was finishing a drawing of the boiling house when Maria suddenly grabbed the paper and pencil from him. She turned away, moving to another part of the table. With fierce concentration she wrote on the piece of paper the thing her mother had taught her to draw. As soon as she was finished, she wanted desperately to hide it away. But she did not want this to be a mistake. And so, almost insolently, she thrust what she had drawn at Miguel. He stared at it for what seemed a long time before he looked up at her and smiled his biggest smile, the one that was almost laughing. Then his face became serious again. “Hello, *Maria*,” he said softly.

Then Miguel wrote something on the piece of paper and passed it to her. She looked down and saw the markings. It was a word he had explained to her while pointing at Kate. The paper said the word “mama?” She also knew from Miguel the mark on the end was used for a question. She understood and nodded. She was no longer frightened. She felt lighter inside herself. It was hard to keep things in. A very small candle of trust had started to burn and she hoped with all her heart that the wind would not come and blow it out.

When first Miguel, then Kate, and finally Vicente started calling her by her name, she felt a warm feeling. Kate said it was a beautiful name. Señor Sandoval said it was a holy name and she should be very proud. When they were with her, they would say her name. Then one day Kate called to her from the kitchen when she was in her room. “Mariaaaaaa.” Maria felt very warm inside then. When she practiced drawing in her books, she drew her name over and over again. It did not matter if anyone saw.

One afternoon, Kate called from the library for Maria to come and introduced her to a “very special teacher” who would teach her to talk by using her hands. Although Maria was shy, the candle of trust she carried within her was burning brightly. She even had the confidence to shake the teacher’s hand. If she could do this thing, talk with her hands, she would be able to ask her questions and learn more quickly. Her sense told her this was a very good thing. Moving her hands in different ways and making different shapes with her fingers, Teacher was able to show Maria how to talk. And the very first thing Teacher showed her how to say was her name. She had come so far, she thought, only to find her journey just beginning.

Three years passed quickly, like birds taking wing. Kate was there for Maria as she made the change from child to young woman, so much so that Maria felt their closeness was the most natural thing. She was stubborn about not wearing the dresses in her closet and this was a disappointment to Señor Sandoval, whom she had come to call Papa. But this was a small thing, really, for he had come to love her very much and she knew it. She learned how to read from the biggest books and to write with a practiced hand. She learned about the globe, about their island home, and began to understand how big the world truly was. She was now able to say a great deal with her hands, and sometimes so quickly that Kate had to tell her to slow down. She loved most to learn of history, of kings and queens, and of the Great American Revolution. She drank up all the history she could of what she had come to call her own country and of its people. Her lessons included mathematics and she competed in this fiercely with Miguel, who was not happy his younger sister was better at sums than he. Maria was given duties to carry out after studies. She was to care for and groom the many horses in the stables. She came to love this best of all. She would begin by mucking out the stables themselves and laying down new straw bedding, then she would make a warm mash for the animals, and brush them while they ate until their coats shone.

Maria always started with her own pony, Soldier. He was so happy to see her, tossing his head up and down as if to say *yes!* Yes! She would save her papa's horse, King, until the last. She was a little afraid of him because of his great spirit, but she knew better than to let him know it. She had been taught well that some animals would take every advantage they could get, and after King snuck a few bites when she wasn't looking, she learned to stare him down and talk with a stern voice. When she talked in her stern voice it would often make Rafael laugh until he slapped his knees. Rafael was the Sandoval's coachman and had been kept very busy before the automobile arrived. Now he mostly took care of the automobile, cleaning it and keeping it running properly. Sometimes he would help her muck the stables and they would talk and joke together. They had come to like each other very much although Papa said it was not a good thing to be too friendly with the servants. She did not understand this. Rafael worked very hard. Even when there was little to do, he would polish the automobile over and over, never letting his hands be idle. Rafael was warm and funny and kind. Why should she not be kind in return? She would ask Papa about this.

CHAPTER FOURTEEN: A TASK FOR MIGUEL

One morning Vicente called his son into his study.

"Miguel, my son, come sit with me. As you know, soon it will be time for you to go to the university. You have made us very proud, and when you earn your degree we will be even more proud. But in the time remaining before you go, there is something I would like you to do for me."

"Yes, of course, Papa."

"There was a time, not that long ago, when I was unhappy with your ... associating with the workers. It was my thinking that it was a waste of precious time and that you would learn bad habits and laziness." Vicente held up his hand to quiet his son's protest. "I no longer think of it in this way. It is my thinking now that a good businessman must know all he can about everything that concerns his business. I have knowledge of all the aspects of sugar production, the intricacies of the machinery, how to maintain our crop so that it can grow larger, the minds of the buyers and how to get the best price ... many of these things, which I have taught to you as well."

Miguel nodded, listening carefully.

"But it strikes me now that I know little of the minds of the workers. It is in this regard that you may be of great help to me and to the business as well."

Miguel spoke. "Father, are you saying I—"

"I am saying your time spent with the workers was not a waste. Not at all. In fact, I would like you to spend more time with them. Get to know them well. Find out their feelings. What they think of their work here. In this way we may further increase our production." Vicente took a moment to reflect. "You see, Miguel, workers can be useful tools just as the press, or the plow, can be useful and can be made to suit our needs. Yet if we do not know them well, or ... are unaware of their sharp edges, they could cause us harm."

"I must go to the city and will be very busy with meetings in the coming days. There are Americans coming to Havana, and we will have much to discuss. So it is important to me to know I can leave this matter in your hands and that you will make the best effort on our behalf, Yes?"

Although Miguel felt very uncomfortable about giving it, he felt some formal acknowledgment was proper in this case, so he rose with solemnity and shook his father's hand. "Yes, certainly, Papa. You may trust in me and I will do as you ask."

Vicente pulled his son close and embraced him. "Excelente, Miguel, Excelente!"

Tristan Sedillo was the poor son of a poor man's son. Although short in stature, he was squat and powerfully built and bore the flat features and swarthy complexion of his people. He had been working Señor Sandoval's plantation for five seasons, since his seventeenth birthday. He was known among the workers for his skill with the machete. Tristan was able to sever the cane at the very bottom of the stalk, the most valuable part of the plant, throw it into the air, and cut it in half before it touched the ground. In this way he was faster and more productive than any other worker. For this reason he commanded much respect among the workers.

But it was not for this reason alone. He had become a friend to Miguel, Señor Sandoval's son. Miguel would often visit him in the fields and they could be seen talking and laughing together. Why this should be so was a mystery to the workers, for to be too well-known invited attention and this was not a good thing. A worker who became ill or was not able to work quickly could hide easily enough if he was one of the faceless ones. What was more dangerous by far was that Tristan sometimes entertained Miguel at his small hut and gave him rum to drink. None of these troublesome things seemed to be of concern to Tristan. So the workers did their best to look away and pretend they did not see. It was best that way.

It was on one of these afternoons, after sharing some rum, that Tristan allowed his tongue to loosen, perhaps a little too much.

He told Miguel that though he knew Señor Sandoval to be a good man, he could be more generous with his workers than he was. The pesos they were given were sometimes insufficient even to buy food. The workers were no longer happy and Sandoval enjoyed such plenty. Seeming to know he had perhaps gone too far, Tristan slapped Miguel on the back. "But let us talk of more important things, amigo. You are of the age to be looking at women, ahh? Is there one who has caught your eye?" He began to sing loudly; a racy song about a woman of loose morals.

Miguel turned his head away and was filled with thoughts about what Tristan had said. The rum had clouded his thoughts, but they were clearing now. It was true, his father had provided well for his family, but why should Miguel's family have so much while so many of those who worked so hard for the family had so little. He turned back to Tristan, who had finished singing and now wiggled his eyebrows up and down at

Miguel, full of mischief.

"My father should know of this, Tristan. Why is it that you do not see him and tell him of these things? Ask him for more pesos for the workers. He is a reasonable man and will listen."

Tristan's face clouded in sudden worry. He had been foolish to say these things in front of the boy and now the cat could not be returned to the sack. A worker, who made trouble, even if he were the best of them, could lose his living. Not only this, but wagging tongues would make it hard to make another.

"It is of no importance, my friend. The price of sugar will rise. Perhaps then things will be better ahh?"

Miguel left Tristan's hut, thanking him for the rum and promising to bring him some of Rosa's fresh-baked bread. At the moment Miguel might have been a little unsteady on his feet but his thoughts did not waver. If Tristan would not discuss what was happening with the workers, he, Miguel, would. For it was no longer a task that had been set before him. It was becoming a passion.

CHAPTER FIFTEEN: AN EXTRAORDINARY THING

The day after Vicente left for his meetings in Havana, something extraordinary happened.

"Maria, come quickly," Maria heard Kate call with much urgency. Maria dropped the book she was reading and rushed down the stairs. She found Kate in the kitchen with Rosa and one of the workers. "Maria, Rosa tells me Manuel here has come because his wife is with child. Her time has come and things are not well. I'll have need of you. Rosa is gathering things to bring. I need you to go to the stables. Have Rafael prepare the coach and bring it round. Quickly as you can, love."

Maria looked over at the worker who stood clenching and unclenching the hat he held over his chest, eyes wild with fear. His fear sparked her own, and she nodded quickly and rushed out the door toward the stable.

"Rosa," Kate said, "tell Manuel we will come at once. Tell him we need him to go back to his home as fast as he can and build a big cooking fire. Tell him as well to draw lots of water from the well, as much as he has pots for; we'll bring more." Rosa repeated these things to Manuel and he rushed out the door and flew like the wind toward his hut.

With Maria's help, Rafael had the team hitched to the carriage very quickly and brought it round to the back door of the kitchen.

Rosa beckoned Manuel and Rafael in and they rushed to load sheets, kettles, towels, and sponges into the coach. Kate ran downstairs clutching a satchel. Maria helped her into the coach. "Rosa, you're to tell Miguel where we've gone but he's to stay at home. Muy importante. Rafael, we must go to the workers' quarters ... Quickly."

The horses responded to the whip, breaking into a gallop, and it was not long before they reached Manuel's hut. Maria could hear screams and sobbing coming from inside. Instinctively, she drew back.

"Come, Maria, it's all right, I need you with me now." Kate made a grab for Maria's hand and together they entered the hut.

Maria could not see at first because they had come in from the bright sun, but there was a terrible smell and she could hear a woman's voice gasping and groaning very close to her. She heard Kate's voice, soothing: "There now, darlin', it'll be all right, all right now." After a moment Maria could see more clearly. The hut was very small. The woman was in a bed in the center of the room and there was blood all around her. Outside, she heard Manuel moaning softly and scrabbling to start a fire. Then Rafael came in, bringing supplies from the coach. Kate had crossed the room and put her hands in a bucket of water to clean them. Maria did not stop to think, but instead took one of the towels Rafael had brought in and gave it to Kate. She did as Kate had done and cleaned her hands.

"Maria, help me turn her on her side." Maria did as she was told, but the smell was very bad and the woman screamed again.

Kate put her hands on the woman's stomach as if searching for something. Then she began to press and the woman cried out again. Kate's voice remained kind, even soft, but with purpose: "Hand me that sheet and that sponge there. Then go fetch more water. Put it in everything you can find that'll hold it."

Then Kate yelled toward the door of the hut: "Rafael, you must help with the fire and get more wood."

Maria went quickly out of the hut to fetch the water. Chickens scattered before her, clucking their protests and running this way and that. She found the pump, and cranked it with all her strength. Returning with a bucketful of water, she saw Rafael's eyes were wide and carried fear in them. Still, he said nothing and quickly went in search of wood. Manuel had the fire blazing well now and Maria's sense told her what to do next. She took the poking stick out of Manuel's hand, made a flat place, and placed the bucket in the middle, where the flames would soon set the water bubbling. Manuel lifted his eyes from the flames to thank her. When another scream came, he turned away but Maria did not. She strode purposefully toward the sound and entered the hut.

It was then that she saw a most extraordinary thing. The woman on the bed had her legs far apart and something was coming out of her. Kate was sponging the woman's brow and saying, "Go on, go on, once more, and push . . . PUSH." The woman was working as hard as she could. Her grunting exploded into something bigger. Maria recognized the sound and the face the woman made. She herself had made that sound when she had to take the boat with the doctor over the breakwater. It had been the hardest thing she had ever done, but she had made it happen. This woman was trying to do something just has hard, and Maria was suddenly sure she would succeed. The thing between the woman's legs came out farther and farther . . . suddenly Maria's mouth flew open. It was a baby!

Kate had told her this was the way of things. But Maria had no idea! She had put it out of her mind and now ... this!

There was a final sound from the woman, the biggest one of all, and suddenly the baby was out. Kate moved quickly to grasp the child and put her finger in its mouth to clear it. She motioned to Maria to come but Maria could not move. Her eyes were as big as the moon, witnessing this thing that was happening before her eyes. It seemed suddenly everything was different, like Maria had gone outside from the inside of herself. There was no sound, and Maria thought she had perhaps fled to another world, when suddenly the baby started to cry. The crying sounded loud, desperate, and urgent. Far away she heard Kate call out to her. But something very deep inside Maria was moving and suddenly she wanted to reach out, to take this thing, this poor and naked thing, this thing so helpless. To protect it. To save it from fires and sightless eyes and the laughing men who enjoyed it all. She began to feel bigger and bigger, like a giant. She heard Kate call to her again, louder now: "Sweet Jesus, will you stay with me, Maria; get me some warm water, if it's too hot from the fire, put cold with it till it's just warm on your wrist." Maria broke from her dream and ran from the hut to get the water.

Kate knows this feeling too, Maria thought. And her sense told her that her own mother had known this feeling as well. This need to protect. A feeling that was like rage. Maria had tried so hard to put her mother out of her mind. Now it was as if a rope that was tied to her had been pulled with great force. There was a great emptiness within and she wanted her mother to fill it more than life itself. Tears sprang hot, flooded her eyes, and rolled with no shame down her face. Her mouth opened to cry but no sound came.

She could not let such things matter now. She scooped boiling water from the fire and added the cold. She was careful to get the water temperature just right. She roughly pushed the tears from her face and went back into the hut. Maria saw at once that Kate's face was grim. She had wrapped the baby, still crying, inside a blanket. Maria set down the water in front of Kate, who picked up the sponge, dipped it in the warm water, and began to gently wash the child.

Maria's eyes shifted to the woman, who was very still, her eyes looking into nowhere. Maria bowed her head, but there was no God to talk to. Nothing to say. No God now.

There would be candles lit and hushed voices. The working women would come and clean and bring food for Manuel. Maria would give him wildflowers she had picked. The baby girl would go to the next hut, where there was a woman to care for her. And Manuel would go back to work the very next day.

When God takes the mothers, Maria thought, he takes away our hope.

Maria felt she had learned more in this day than she had in forever. It was a most extraordinary thing.

CHAPTER SIXTEEN: A SURPRISE AND A VERY SHORT RIDE

After mass on Sunday, the day before Vicente was to return from Havana, was when Miguel thought it a good idea to fight the bull.

It was a day the workers had to themselves, and could rest from their labor. Most stayed in their huts, happy for the chance to be out of the hot sun and to have a well-earned siesta. As the chickens idly clucked and pecked in the yard, a little guitar music could be heard coming from the huts in the workers' quarter and a little singing too. But more than a few of the workers followed Tristan over toward the main house and gathered to see the curious sight of Miguel entering the corral with a red blanket that was fastened to a broomstick and approaching Señor Sandoval's prize bull.

As it happened, Tristan and Miguel had been talking earlier of bravery, and as these things sometimes go, the talk got bigger and bigger until some sort of action was called for. There may have been a little rum involved in this decision too. Still, Miguel was holding himself with confidence and even strutting a bit as he began to circle the bull inside the corral.

Maria at that moment was in the kitchen and was making a lunch for her mother as a surprise. She was not very experienced in the matter of preparing food, but how hard could it be? Rosa thought it would be better if she helped, but Maria dismissed her from the kitchen and insisted on doing this thing herself. I shall make hotcakes for mama, she thought happily, and set about putting all the things she would need together. She mixed flour with milk and added salt as she had seen Rosa do many times before. She added eggs, but they did not break very well and some of the shell disappeared into the mix. She tried to think if there was anything else. There must be, because the flour she had mixed with the milk was very sticky. Maria added more milk and this made the batter too watery. More flour, then. Maria was becoming very flustered and that made her spill some of the flour on the floor and on her clothing. She must not forget the salt. Or did she put some in already? She added more to be sure.

The bull was a prize specimen. Huge and black with massive haunches and horns that looked quite deadly. Vicente had acquired him from one of the best breeders in the province and was always very proud to show this most regal animal to his guests. But at this particular moment the bull looked much confused and not so regal. The beast raised his head at first, and seemed at a loss to know why this young man would walk around him in circles, and what his intentions were with the blanket. But bulls are not known for curiosity, especially when the sun is hot, so soon the animal went back to peacefully chewing his cud. This was provoking much laughter among the workers and one of them went to his hut and returned with a guitar. He began to play flamenco music, to the delight of the others. Miguel was becoming red in the face. He felt he had to prove himself as a man, but this bull would not cooperate.

In the kitchen, Maria got out the big heavy pan and put it on to heat. She knew she was supposed to put lard in the pan or the cakes would stick to the bottom. She didn't know how much, but she didn't want to have the cakes stick, so she reasoned more was better. Now I will make up the tray, she thought. She found the tray was stored in a high cupboard, and by the time she was able to get it down, other things came out as well and crashed to the floor. I will clean it later, Maria thought. On the tray she set a glass for the juice and a plate she picked up off the floor. The pan was beginning to smoke, so Maria turned down the heat a little and put some of the cake mixture in.

Meanwhile, in the corral, Miguel poked sharply at the bull with the broomstick. The bull turned his head to look at him, but that was all he did. Miguel poked again and again, but all the bull did was amble away to the other side of the corral. "This bull is very good-natured, Miguel," Tristan called out. "He will not talk to you. When you are big like this bull, you do not have to talk big." Miguel made a very rude gesture to Tristan and crossed to where the bull was standing. The flamenco guitar was reaching a fever pitch.

In the kitchen, Maria was just about ready. She decided she would put a flower in a vase to make the tray look pretty. She went out the back door to the little flower garden behind the house. She heard much laughter and guitar music and decided she had to find out what was happening. Holding the rose she had picked in the garden, she ran toward the laughter. It was coming from the corral. She crossed the yard toward the stables just in time to see Miguel standing on the highest rail in the corral fence.

Miguel made the sign of the cross in his mind, got up on the corral railing, and jumped onto the bull's back! It must be said that this got the bull's attention very quickly and the massive beast leaped away from the fence with Miguel astride him. Miguel, trying desperately to keep upright, grabbed for the bull's horns to hang on to. This proved to be a mistake. The bull jumped high and began kicking, and sent Miguel flying through the air and landing quite hard in the dust. He scrambled to his feet at once and ran as fast as he could. Tristan held open the gate of the corral, and as soon as Miguel cleared it he slammed it shut and they both backed off very quickly. The bull was forced to stop at the gate but was clearly very angry, snorting and throwing his head back and forth. His wild eyes tried to find Miguel, who was doubled over both with relief and laughter. That was when Maria came over to him and helped him to his feet. She handed him the rose. She too was laughing. "Why is it men are so foolish, my brother? Or is it just you?" Miguel's backside hurt him very much and Maria had to help him return to the house. From behind him Miguel heard Tristan call after him "That was quite a show, amigo! You should join the circus!"

Miguel turned and waved back: "It was very enjoyable, Tristan, you should try it sometime!" Suddenly he heard a shriek behind him and turned to hear Maria cry out: "My hotcakes!" Miguel turned to see his sister running very fast toward the back door of the kitchen, where black smoke was beginning to drift out and make its way toward the cloudless blue sky. Suddenly the door banged opened and Kate appeared. She had smudges of black on her face and was wearing thick oven mittens. She was carrying the smoking pan with a much-blackened cake stuck to its inside.

Throwing the pan to the ground, Kate glared at Maria. "What in the devil is going on here?"

"It was to be a surprise, Mama."

There was a long silence. Miguel extended his hand, holding out the rose Maria had given him. "For you, Mama," he said.

CHAPTER SEVENTEEN: YOU HAVE TO KEEP UP WITH THE TIMES

Vicente had much to think about on the train to Havana. He made his way to the dining car, where he drank strong coffee and read his newspaper. There were bad signs everywhere and he was worried about this meeting with the Americanos. The price of sugar had fallen dramatically since Zayas and his liberals had come to power. Things had been so much better under Menocal. *There* was a man who knew how to make accommodations. And he was a friend to the Americanos. But he had been unable to win the election despite the fighting and now Zayas was trumpeting all his anti-American talk. To make things worse, the Americano general Crowder was sticking his nose in and putting a higher tax on sugar. Vicente could feel himself longing for the better days of the past.

He finished his coffee and threw down the newspaper, turning his attention to the passing countryside. He remembered his arrival in this beautiful land, recalling with pride how his father had shown him the way to turn bad times into opportunities. When Vicente was a young man not much older than Miguel, his own father had been nearly ruined during the fighting of the Spanish-American War. But he was wise in seeing opportunity with the independence of Cuba. Emigrating there with his young family from Galicia, he toiled to build the plantation that had made them rich. He had brought Vicente into the business early and it was just as well. Both his mother and father had been taken from him, dying of the smallpox before they could see their first grandson.

Vicente's thoughts were brought up short by the train pulling into the station. He stepped off the coach and into the grand old city of Havana. He had taken rooms at the Hotel Inglaterra for his meeting with the Americanos. Cabs were lined up outside the station, but he made the decision to walk. The exercise would clear his head for the business at hand. Still, as he made his way through the central park, memories took him away yet again and made it hard to think of business. Vicente had brought Katherine to this very spot when they were newlyweds. The two of them had admired the lights of the city. They had stayed overnight at the Inglaterra. Vicente was certain Miguel had been conceived there. Smiling to himself, he passed the grand pillars and entered the hotel.

"Mr. Sandoval, it is always such a pleasure! Your rooms are in readiness; Paulo will take your case and show you to them."

On the way up in the lift, Vicente was able to focus more clearly on the business at hand. The Americanos had called this meeting. They were not scheduled to meet for two weeks yet, but they had pushed up the time. It was not a good sign. He was to meet them for dinner in two hours and then they would adjourn to his suite for discussion. It would give Vicente time for a short siesta and to refresh himself.

The steaks were done to perfection. The great dining room was alive with the tinkling of crystal, the beauty of fine china, and the warmth of conversation. The wine too was excellent. The Americanos seemed jovial enough. "How is the family getting along, Mr. Sandoval? How is that young son of yours, hmm? What's his name again ... Michael? And that horse we presented you with. Enough spirit for you?" Vicente smiled politely and traded pleasantries throughout the dinner, but he had a sense that something was different. There was a tension in the Americanos that hadn't been there before. Their laughter was a little too hearty. Well, he would find out the reason for this soon enough. The dessert came: strawberry shortcake. Vicente left his untouched, although his guests seemed to relish every mouthful. After coffee, he spoke to them.

"Gentlemen, I trust you found the food to your liking. If I may, let us move our conversation upstairs, where we can speak of more confidential matters. I have a brandy you must try. It is of a rare vintage, and also I have brought with me a box of our finest cigars for each of you."

Ten minutes later the Americanos were comfortably seated with cigars lit and the brandy had been decanted. Now, Vicente thought, we will see. There was silence for a time that was not without tension. It is well-known that the one who breaks the silence of a negotiation is the one who holds the weaker position. The spokesman for the Americanos, the one who insisted he be called Bill, spoke first.

"We called this meeting a little early, Vicente, because we have concerns. I'm sure you know that news about this fellow Sanquily has been making the papers."

"Yes, yes, I know of him. Another liberal." Vicente almost spat the word.

"Yes, well, all his talk of making it harder for us to buy land in your country, making it harder for us to do business here, is being listened to, and we are afraid of what might come of it. Especially with this man Zayas in power."

"Señor Bill, we have enjoyed a mutually beneficial relationship for almost ten years. During this time, it is true, there has been much unrest, yet we have both been unwavering with our trust in each other."

"It is not a question of trust ... in you, Vicente. It is a question of politics. Right now, things are good. But our concerns rest with the future. The United Fruit Company wishes to act now while the climate is still right."

"The climate ...?"

"The political climate, Vicente. Now, you've been a loyal and valuable partner to United. And now it's time to secure our interests and to make sure both parties profit from the arrangement. So look here. The United Fruit Company is prepared to make you a very handsome offer."

"I'm afraid I do not quite understand." Vicente grew uneasy in his chair and set down his brandy glass.

"We would like to purchase your plantation, Vicente. We would, o' course, pay top dollar, and you'd be in complete charge of operations. The hacienda would continue to be your home. Nothing really would change except the size of your bank account. As I was sayin', we are prepared to pay handsomely."

Vicente felt his heart sinking, but before it could sink further he turned it to stone. He looked at each of these men. These Americanos seated around him. Every face blank, impassive, waiting for him to hand over his birthright.

"Señor Bill, gentleman, I have no interest in selling what my father worked so hard to build. The price is not important. The land is not for sale at any price. But I hope this will not affect our agreement. It is still a profitable enterprise for us both to enjoy, no?"

"The offer will stand, Vicente. Take time to think it over. Perhaps you will decide to accept it in the near future. Meanwhile, there is another matter to discuss. The price of sugar has dropped again. Kinda dramatically, I'm afraid. O' course, this means less money for both parties. If we are to continue our agreement, production will have to be increased. This is gonna involve implementing certain 'efficiencies.'

"Efficiencies? What does this mean?"

"Harvesters, Vicente, Mechanical harvesters. We're all kinda excited about it! These're machines which can triple production and bring our profits back in line with what they should be. You'd be responsible for purchasing and maintaining them, o' course, but we have a line on someone who can sell and ship them to you for a good price."

"These harvesters, how do the workers use them?"

"That is the beauty of these machines, Vicente. They're like automobiles, operated by one man, and one harvester can replace a hundred workers. You'll find these things'll pay for themselves very quickly."

"But what does this mean for the workers? I have many and they have families."

"Times change, Vicente. You have to keep up with the times."

Later, on the train, Vicente thought about what the Americanos had said. The rocking of the coach and the clicking of the rails was peaceful, but Vicente could find no peace. He found himself between a rock and a hard place. The new harvesters would mean the loss of livelihood for many of his workers. Perhaps some he could train to keep the machines in good working order, but ... many would go hungry. Vicente was angry. What could he do? It's true, he thought. You must keep up with the times. He drove an automobile now. The telephone was coming. He worked hard to keep up, and because of this, he was successful. He felt bad for these people but ... Why is it they did not care for themselves? Why did they accept whatever life gave them? Why could they not try to better themselves? For them, he thought the answer to everything is that it must be God's will. Well, perhaps God would help them. Because as far as he could see, there was little he himself could do.

CHAPTER EIGHTEEN: ANOTHER SPECIAL PLACE

Some days pass so quickly one hardly notices them. Others are very singular in nature. A single day can seem to last forever and burn itself into your memory. Today was to be such a day for Maria. She wanted to be alone with her thoughts for a time, so she had taken Soldier from the stable and, after a good brushing, saddled him and gone off riding.

Sometime earlier, Kate had taken her to the top of a small hill overlooking the plantation. Now Kate agreed to join her and together they went to the hill. It was a glorious morning, the air smelled sweet, and the sun washed the countryside with warm golden light. On the very top of the hill there was a small white picket fence surrounding two of the most beautiful statues Maria had ever seen. The statues were of two angels together, both looking toward heaven. They stood between two marble gravestones and together, they held a heart, which they lifted toward the sky. The angels were very tall and Maria had to look up a long way to see their faces.

Kate was laying flowers at the angels' feet. She smiled up at Maria. "These are the graves of your papa's mother and father.

'Tis their anniversary today and we remember the day by always bringing flowers for them. Your papa is away or he would be here too."

Maria signed to Kate: "How did they die?"

"They died of a terrible sickness. Many others died as well. You could catch it yourself, you see, just by being near someone who had the sickness. Those were hard times."

"But you and Papa never got sick?"

"No, child, your father was out of the country at the time. Attending university, just like Miguel will be doing next month. It was back when I first met your papa."

Maria looked around her. The white picket fence was freshly painted, and all around the grass was very green. Again she signed to Kate: "It's a very beautiful place."

"And you are a very beautiful girl. Now come, Rosa will have lunch ready."

Now she was riding along the path that would take her to the beach. She sometimes still visited her special place, but today her thoughts were set on exploring. Vicente had shown her a map of the plantation and today she had decided to ride her pony around to parts of it that were unfamiliar to her. On the west the land was bordered by the sea and to the north the main road that led to the city. It was a pleasant ride along the sea, and the gentle breezes played at her hair as she rode along. Still, it took her almost two hours to reach the road and turn eastward. The cane had grown tall and stretched along as far as she could see. As she rode beside the cane she could see the tall poles strung with wires that were being put in alongside the road. This would soon bring them the telephone.

Maria was very hot and dusty by the time she reached the edge where the Sandoval land began to turn south. Here was where the workers' quarter was located and the land was much rougher and there were many stones underfoot. She decided to walk the pony for a bit, for if the animal were to stumble, it could injure itself. In the distance she could make out the huts of the workers and some smoke coming from their cooking fires. There was a pathway leading toward the huts and she followed it.

Maria wondered why it was that some people had so much and others so little. The workers' huts were little better than the shelter she had made for herself in her special place and they did not own land such as this. They did not own any land at all. It did not seem right. They worked very hard, she had seen them toiling in the fields. They did not have new clothing or fine food or ponies. Maria began to feel a great shame grow in her. The workers had no time to read or learn from books. They were never given fine presents tied with ribbon and wrapped in tissue paper.

It was when she was thinking these things that she came upon a cleared place among the rubble. She stopped in her tracks and gazed about in wonder. Spaced out before her were perhaps two dozen crude unpainted wooden crosses. Leaving her pony, Maria walked very slowly among them. Some of the graves had pebbles in front of them, marking out a plot, and some had nothing at all. Some of the crosses were bound together by hide, others by a few nails. No winged angels. No picket fence. No green grass. Around the clearing, nothing but scrub weeds covered in dust.

When she reached the end of the row, her heart stopped. The cross she looked at was no different from the others, but the stony ground had recently been turned, the mound marking the plot still fresh. There were a handful of wildflowers scattered at the foot of the cross. She recognized them. They were the same collection of wildflowers she had picked and given to Manuel after that terrible day when his wife died. Maria knelt down in front of the grave, and tried to gather the wilted flowers, but her fingers were shaking. Soon her whole body began to tremble as the memories came flooding back. The bad smell, the blood, the woman's eyes looking into nowhere, and most of all the longing for her own lost mother and the rage she had felt.

She felt it again and she dropped to her knees on the grave, and as her tears fell and grew hotter her mouth opened and a long low moan came out. The moan grew louder and lasted a long time. When it stopped, part of Maria was gone but the other part of her knew that she had made sound come out of her mouth. She was silent a moment and tried to make the sound come again. It came again, and Maria put her hand to her throat and felt the tickle there as she practiced this new thing. She made a promise to herself to never forget this woman, Manuel's wife. Or these people who lived with nothing. She would return here, to this very spot. This would be her other special place.

CHAPTER NINETEEN: VICENTE RETURNS

Vicente's homecoming was bittersweet. Kate sent Rosa away after deciding that she would meet him at the door herself, looking forward to his lion-like embrace, his whispered words of love, and a time of intimacy. But when he arrived and was holding her in his arms, she sensed both tension and weariness in him. Usually, he was in very high spirits and full of stories when he returned from the city. Things must not have gone well in Havana, Kate thought.

"My darling, I will be happy to join you for dinner, but first there is a matter I must attend to. Could you please see to it that Miguel comes to my study? It is important I speak with him."

Kate refused to let the worry show on her face and tried to be playful. "Certainly, m'dear, and what would your lordship care to have for his supper?" But her husband was plainly distracted and did not answer. Instead he quickly climbed the stairs to his study.

Kate called for Rosa. "Rosa, Señor Sandoval has returned from the city and I was thinking of making a special dinner for him. Perhaps you could make us your paella. That'd be a grand thing. I'm sure Maria would help if we dare to let her in the kitchen again."

"Sí, señora, but Maria is no come back from riding."

Kate wondered at this. It was growing late. "Well, you tell her to wash herself when she gets back and help you with the dinner. I've a few letters to write. If you need me, I'll be in the library."

Upstairs, Vicente tried to busy himself with the plantation accounts, but he found himself thinking of how he was going to handle the workers when they learned of this harvester machine. Miguel could perhaps help him in this. He was growing close to the workers and might be able to make them understand. He would take his son into his confidence and together they would—

The study door opened and it was not just his son Miguel who came into his presence. He had brought one of the workers with him.

"Papa ... Father, this is Tristan. He has come to talk with you about the workers. He comes on their behalf."

Tristan found his mouth was very dry and he was very nervous. No, more than nervous. He thought himself to be a brave man but now he was frightened. He gripped the hat he was holding across his chest more tightly, swallowed, and found his voice sounded small in his ears.

"Señor Sandoval, it is a great honor, I ..."

Vicente ignored him and spoke directly to his son. "Miguel, I will be happy to speak to ... Tristan, but this is not the time. And it is most certainly not the place. This is our home, Miguel. You should not have brought him here."

Tristan swallowed hard again, his voice almost a whisper. "Forgive me, Señor Sandoval. I will go—"

Miguel spoke over him. "Father, Tristan wishes to speak with you of the conditions under which the workers must labor."

Vicente glared at his son. He bit his words sharply. "Does he? Then perhaps it would be as well if he spoke for himself." He glanced over at the worker and could see the man was plainly frightened. This harsh tone had not been helpful. He reconsidered and let the anger leave his voice.

"Tristan, I would be most ... agreeable to speaking with you of these things, and we will choose a day to do so in the near future. But I will speak to you at the place where I address all of the workers. It will be at the usual place by the stables. I am glad this matter has been brought to my attention. Miguel will go with you to show you the way out and then he will return here to me, as we have matters to discuss. He will advise you when a day has been set for our talk. Miguel, if you would be so kind ...?"

Miguel was furious, but there was little he could do. Tristan had already turned and was leaving. Miguel followed him into the yard. Tristan whispered to him, "This was a very bad idea, Miguel."

"The discussion is not over, my friend. I will come tomorrow and we will plan for the meeting. You must take heart. All will be well. I will go back and talk more with my father."

Tristan looked at Miguel with tired eyes and said nothing more. He walked away toward the workers' quarters shaking his head.

Vicente gazed down from his window on his son and this man Tristan. Things were coming to a head much more quickly than he wanted. How could Miguel have done this? He had asked the boy to get close to the workers to find out what they were thinking; he had certainly not asked him to take their side! He had wanted to take the boy into his confidence, to have him as an ally in helping the workers understand the new reality of the harvester, but now . . . ?

He would put off the delivery of the harvester for a month. By then Miguel would be at the university in Havana. He would find out from his son what was on the workers' minds. They were unhappy, he knew. It would be necessary to give them something.

Then, in a month, when the harvester came, he would tell them the truth. What was it the Americanos called it? "Efficiencies." Efficiencies would have to be implemented. The price of sugar was down, so wages would have to be reduced. Perhaps enough of them would quit, so that he would not have to tell them he had no work for them. It was not much of a plan. But it was better than nothing.

When Miguel came into the study and began, "Father, you must understand—" Vicente interrupted him, his voice loud and angry.

"Miguel, why did you not first come to me? Why have you mistrusted your own father and placed your confidence in these peasant workers over the interests of your own family? You have disappointed me today. I had wished to take you into my confidence, for you to take part in the family business, but this has shaken my faith in you. In time, perhaps at the university, you will learn what true priorities are."

Miguel's voice rose, shaking with anger, as he said, "Priorities, Father? You think these people's lives are not a priority? You think living with rats is a priority?"

"Miguel, there will be no more discussion. Go!"

Miguel angrily stormed out of the study, but before going he turned to his father and said, "This is not over."

Vicente turned back to the window and looked up at the sky. Clouds were blocking out the sun. No, my son, he thought to himself, this business is far from over.

CHAPTER TWENTY: TENSION

Dinner was a somber affair that evening. Kate had heard the argument between Miguel and her husband. She couldn't make out what they were arguing about, but a coldness grew between them now that she could feel. Maria too was withdrawn and nothing seemed to lift her spirts, not even Rosa's paella. Kate thought Maria's and Miguel's moodiness might be because of their ages. Adolescence was a mysterious and vexing time and she supposed it had always been this way.

But the final few weeks before Miguel left for university were no better. Maria saddled her pony every day after her chores and went off riding to God only knew where. Kate offered to go riding with her like the old times, but Maria said she would rather go by herself. And Miguel seemed to have such anger in him. It was of no use talking to Vicente. He refused to discuss the children's behavior. Kate would just have to be patient. But these times were affecting her too. She no longer sang during the day as was normal for her.

Miguel had met with the workers and tried his best to get them riled up, especially Tristan. "When my father meets with you, you must not act like before, like a cobarde, a gallina!" He spat the words out. All the anger he felt toward his father, he let out at Tristan. Tristan's eyes had grown ice cold. Miguel's words had cut deeply. Coward! Chicken! Miguel had gone too far. It was just as well that he was going away, thought

Tristan. Their friendship was at an end. He began to have meetings with the workers himself and did not invite Miguel.

"A Sandoval is not to be trusted," he told the workers.

One of them spoke up and challenged Tristan. It was Manuel. "It is not true! The girl brings flowers to my wife's grave! And the woman tried to help my wife! She delivered my son safely!"

Angry now at having his authority questioned, Tristan said, "The girl is not one of them. They took her from the sea. You have all heard the stories. And the woman does not matter. Since when do women matter? It is the father that must not be trusted! He works us like dogs and pays us nothing! We do not have enough to eat! You all know we are not to go near the big house. It is like we bring him shame! Now he goes to church. But you all remember the time when he did not. I tell you he is not to be trusted. The son said he would help us, but now he runs away to the university like a cobarde! I say again, they are not to be trusted. Neither the father nor the son!"

"And listen to me well. I am to meet with him soon. And I, Tristan, will see to it we get better treatment. Tristan is not afraid of Vicente Sandoval. If you want to put your trust in someone, trust God and trust me, Tristan. I will make things better!"

The workers began to nod in agreement. If they had to choose a leader, they would choose Tristan. Perhaps with God's help he could get them better pay, or more food, at least.

An excitement was washing over Tristan. He felt his chest swell with great power. He, Tristan, was no coward! Now he was a leader. He could feel the strength rising in him. The Sandoval's would know more than his name soon. They would show him respect. If they did not, they would be sorry.

Maria was not idle during her time alone. She still rode her pony along the beach, but now she practiced making noises in her throat while she rode. Her voice still sounded strange in her ears and she intended to keep this new thing a secret. But she remembered that day long ago when she had seen Kate come riding along the beach, her long red hair flowing behind her. She remembered the magic of Kate's singing and how she had memorized the words to Kate's song. And so, as she walked the pony down the beach, she practiced using her voice, singing softly:

"'Twas hard the woeful words to frame
To break the ties that bound us.
But harder still to bear the shame
of foreign chains around us.
And so I said the mountain glen
I'll meet at morning early.
And I'll join the bold united men
While soft winds shook the barley."

Maria stopped her pony at her special place and went inside. She had come here more often of late, bringing things that would not be missed to fill up her storeroom. She had improved the surrounding area as well. She had cut the palm leaves and used them to construct two little palapa huts that were well made and, better still, waterproof.

She had brought books to her place too, and sometimes spent her afternoons reading. She read a book by a man named Daniel Defoe, *Robinson Crusoe.* He was like I am, she thought, a castaway. But I need no slave to help me. And anyway, sometimes it is better to be alone.

She read parts of the Bible too. Jesus seemed to her a good man. What a marvel it would be to heal the sick just by touching them. But she didn't understand what he meant when he said the poor will always be among us. Had he just given up? If he could heal the sick, why not save the poor? And what he did with the loaves and the fishes. Why did he not make enough so everyone could eat?

But today was not a reading day. Today she had work to do. She went to her storeroom and got out the paint and brushes she had brought from the stables. Today she would ride to the graveyard. And then she would paint each cross a bright white so it could shine in the sun. She would place stones around every plot. And while she did this work she would sing to the gravestones. They would not be forgotten any longer.

CHAPTER TWENTY-ONE: EDUCATION, ENTITLEMENT

The day Miguel left for the university; the goodbyes were stiff and formal. Kate put her arms around her son and tried to hold him tight, but he pulled away. He shook hands with Vicente, neither man looking at the other. Only with Maria did Miguel speak. He embraced her for a long time and whispered to her: "You and I are of the same spirit. You must not let them take it away from you."

The trip to Havana was long. But it was exciting too. Miguel was a boy when he entered the train, and would be a man when he returned. He smiled at the passing villages, at his people out working the fields. I will soon make life better for them, he thought. These were good thoughts to have as the rocking of the train lulled him to sleep.

At the hacienda, the time had come for Vicente's meeting with Tristan. As he walked to their meeting place Tristan was nervous. But he was also inflamed with energy and rum. The rum gave him courage. This time our meeting will be different, he told himself. Tristan Sedillo will stand straight and tall! I will tell Señor Sandoval what is to be. There must be an increase in pay. There must be more time to rest. He must do something to rid us of the rats that run around the huts.

Arriving at the meeting place a little early, he paced back and forth, practicing what he would say. But early became late and still Señor Sandoval kept him waiting. At last Tristan saw him riding up on the great stallion, the one the Americanos had given him. Tristan stood up as straight as he could and did not take his hat off. But still his legs shook a little. Vicente rode up to him but did not dismount. Tristan looked up at Señor Sandoval. It was difficult to see his face in the bright sun. He started to say what he had practiced but Vicente cut him off.

"Tristan, I am a busy man. I understand you have concerns about the treatment of the workers. I am sure I know what these concerns are. I make it my business to know. So I will make clear my position, Tristan. The price of sugar is down. There is new equipment I must pay for. Also, the crop will be smaller this year than in the past. Now let me make clear to you your position. You and your people have work. Enough money to buy food. The entire Sabbath to rest. So you can see that while I have less, you have what you have always had. But that is not to say I do not listen or understand your concerns. Miguel tells me you have a problem with rats."

Tristan bowed his head, wondering what he could say. This meeting was not going as he had planned. He was angry, but he could not think quickly enough to say what he needed to say. "Sí, Señor Sandoval. It is true." He silently cursed himself for sounding so defeated.

"Very well. I shall fix this problem. The rats will be gone soon. We do not want them to spread sickness. It is good you have brought this problem to my attention, Tristan. It shows that you are a mature man. There may be a brighter future for you here. Changes are coming. I have purchased a very big piece of equipment. It will help in harvesting the cane. This machine can cut much cane in a day because it is motorized like my automobile. Do you understand?"

Tristan squinted up at Vicente. The horse under him was

becoming impatient and was pulling at the reins. "Sí, Señor Sandoval, I think so."

"Good. I will need someone to operate this machine. It may be that you can learn to do it. This might be a real opportunity for you. Does this not please you?"

"Sí, Señor Sandoval. You are very kind."

"Never let it be said that I do not listen. Tell the workers things will get better in time. I expect next year the price of sugar will go up. And I am a man of my word. Tell them also that they will soon be free of the rats."

"Sí, señor, I ..." But Tristan did not get to finish his pitiful thank-you, for Vicente had wheeled his horse around and was riding away. "Andele!" Vicente galloped off in a cloud of dust that coated Tristan in a blanket of shame.

Tristan Sedillo kicked at the stony ground on his way back to his hut to finish the bottle of rum. He would have to think of something to tell the workers. To convince them they had won a great victory. Perhaps with the rum's help he could even convince himself.

At the university, Miguel had made new friends—. Reuben Villena, Julio Mella, and many others. They shared his passion to bring a better life to the people. They held meetings in secret. They became involved in protests against the government and Miguel felt honored to be asked to join them. Waving signs, they denounced Zayas and his corrupt government. He read all the literature he could on socialism and Julio introduced him to *The Communist Manifesto*. The way to bring about real change would be to divide the land equally among the people. There must be a central bank which would make sure everyone shared in the wealth. Miguel thought of little else besides these sweeping changes. His studies were suffering, but it mattered little to him.

He was very excited about the meeting he had attended last night. He had gone to the main hall to hear Alphonso Riesgo speak. Riesgo was calling for an immediate reform of the curriculum of the university. The teachings, Riesgo said, had to focus less on law and philosophy and more on science and economics. Only in this way would the workers be able to free themselves from American colonialism. He told the students to listen to the teachers and ignore the meddling priests. Last night Miguel had yelled out his approval and before the evening was over had joined the First Revolutionary Student Congress. Now he had somewhere he could put his anger to constructive use. He and his friends were of one mind, one purpose. There would be hell to pay.

CHAPTER TWENTY-TWO: A PROMISE MADE, A BROKEN DREAM

There was something burning inside Maria. She was spending more and more time in her special place. She had taken to wearing workers' clothing and no longer wore the new clothes that were in her closet. She knew this was making her mother very angry, but no amount of scolding changed her mind.

Now she wanted something more but was unsure of how to get it. Her papa was the one to ask, but he had not learned much of the sign language. She would have to ask her mother for help, but hesitated because Kate had been angry with her about her clothing. Still she would try. She found Mama in the library writing letters. The sun streamed in on Kate sitting at her desk. Maria thought again how beautiful her mama was and wished there was not such a distance between them now. It would make what she had to ask more difficult. Maria signed to Kate the question: "Miguel goes to the university. I want to go too."

Kate put down her pen and turned away from her letter writing. Her voice took on a tone of gentle warmth and she smiled a little. It was the first time Maria had signed to her in a long time. "Maria, the university is for men. There is no place there for women. You're a smart girl, heaven knows you'd do well enough, but it's no use. Besides, your father would never allow it."

Maria signed furiously, "But you could talk to him."

"It'd be of no use, Maria. There are a thousand reasons, but all you must know is your father will have his mind made up about this matter before it's even brought up."

Maria signed again: "You have stood up to him before. You have made him change his mind. I want to go to the university and be strong in the mind like you."

Kate was losing patience. "Book learnin' has nothin' to do with the strength o' my mind, darlin'. Now there's an end of it!" She was immediately sorry for losing her temper, but there it was. Then she thought of something. Maria had angrily turned and was leaving the library when Kate stopped her.

"Maria, wait. I'll make a bargain with you. If you put on some decent clothes and start wearin' them, every day, mind you ... I'll talk to your papa. See if it'll do any good."

Maria crossed over to Kate and crooked out her finger. Kate reached out her own crooked finger and they interlocked the fingers in a sign of agreement.

"Right. There's a girl. Go up now and get those rags off you." After Maria had gone, Kate turned once again to her desk and looked out to the blue sky over the distant hills and gentle waving palms.

God knows what I'm lettin' myself in for, she thought.The next morning there was no sun. Dark clouds moved across the sky and the wind had risen. Kate looked down from her bedroom window to see an automobile approaching. They were still a strange sight, these carriages with no horses, and the workers stopped to look as it passed. From the markings on the side,

Kate knew it was a government car. She heard Rosa open the front door and could hear muffled voices. She was about to go downstairs when she heard her husband's voice invite the men he was with into the library. She was curious, but kept back. Perhaps Vicente would tell her later. But for now she would have to practice what to say to him about Maria. She had to see that he was in a good mood before broaching the subject. Perhaps after a good breakfast. She must make sure to lead up to it gradually. God knows there had been tension enough in the house long enough without adding to it.

She met up with Rosa in the kitchen. "Did the men say why they have come, Rosa?'

"No, señora, they say only that they must speak to Señor Sandoval."

"I see. Well, let us have soft-boiled eggs, Rosa, for breakfast. They are my husband's favorite. With the thick bacon and the special coffee."

But the special breakfast did little to put Vicente in the mood Kate was hoping for. He was brooding and avoiding conversation.

"What did the government men want, darling?" she asked tentatively.

"It is something for me to deal with, Katherine. It is not something I wish to discuss at present."

"Are the eggs done properly? I know they are your favorite."

"The eggs are fine. What is it, Katherine? You have something on your mind. I know this thing you do. You are trying to prepare me. You want to ask a favor of me. What is it?"

Well, so much for that, thought Kate. There was no going back now. She would try her best. "Well, Maria's been getting letters. From Miguel; he talks of life at the university."

"Does he?" Kate didn't like the tone of her husband's voice. It held a quiet ugliness. Still she pressed on.

"Maria would like with all her heart to attend the university. She has her heart set on it. Just for a year perhaps. We could see if—"

"So Miguel writes to Maria, does he? Tells her all about life at the university? Tells her about his radical ideas?" Vicente was speaking with clenched teeth, his eyes like glittering stones, and Kate felt like his words had begun to cut like knives.

"The men from the government were here to discuss Miguel's 'ideas.' Did you know that he is under investigation? That he has joined some revolutionary group? That he reads subversive literature? Are you aware our names have been put on a list?"

Kate sat stunned, at a loss for words.

"And now you tell me he has been spreading his filth to Maria? Poisoning her mind so that now she wants to go to join him in this foolishness?"

"Maria only wants to learn. To have a chance to—"

"There will be no more talk of this. I have assured the government officials this will end. Miguel's insolence will end. I have ordered that he be sent home at once. There will be no further talk of the university in this house! Our names! On a government list!" Vicente swept the plates from the table, sent them crashing to the floor, and quickly strode out of the room. Rosa moved quickly to clean up the mess.

As Kate knelt to help her, her last reserve of strength gave out and she reached out to Rosa. "Oh, Rosa, there's nothing but hurt, and for the life o' me I don't know what to do." Rosa held her close and they rocked together in silence among the broken china for a long time.

CHAPTER TWENTY-THREE: OCHO LOCOS—THE FIRST LESSON

Maria found the house with the yellow door. She hitched her pony to the rail outside, wondering if the old man would really be able to help. Earlier that afternoon, Kate had come into the stables where Maria was tending to her papa's stallion. She had pushed a note into Maria's hand.

"Maria, there is trouble. Serious trouble. 'Tis to do with Miguel. There will be no university, Maria, and you mustn't ask about it or show any further interest in it to Papa. There is an old man in the village. He used work at the university. He may be able to give you lessons. Anyone in the village will help you find his house. This is a note asking him to help if he can. I'm sure the man won't understand if you sign to him." She handed Maria a few coins. "Here's some money, not much, but you can offer it to him."

Maria began signing to Kate, but Kate grabbed her hands and held them still. "No questions, Maria, go now. And your father must not know of this. Do you understand? Tell me, for the love o' God, that you understand!" Kate's own desperation silenced Maria and she nodded quickly. "All right, love, go." Maria did as she was told. She saddled her pony and rode to the village. The villagers said the old man's house was one of the last ones at the edge of the village and she would know it by looking for a yellow door.

She went to the door to knock but he must have seen her from his window for he opened the door at her approach. He stood squinting at her, his hand to his brow, trying to shield his eyes from the bright sun. Maria saw that he was very old and frail, with lines on his face that went very deep. His white hair was thin on top but he had very bushy eyebrows. Maria did not think she could learn very much from a man like this but stuck the note out at him anyway. He did not take the note but continued to look at her, so Maria shook the note closer to his face. Finally he took it.

"I am sorry, I cannot help you," he said after reading it. As he was turning away Maria touched his arm to offer the coins. She felt something go through her when she touched him and she thought that he had much strength and energy for one so old.

He looked down at the coins in her hand. "It is not much but I suppose for you it is a lot. I have not taught in many years." He smiled sadly and touched her cheek. "Keep your money, child. I am afraid I can be of no help to you."

Maria did something then that she had promised herself she would not do. But there was something about this old man that her sense told her was very important.

She trembled as she opened her mouth, and after a moment words came: "Please. I want to learn."

The old man looked at her again closely, as if he had missed something. He gave a very small nod to her and said softly, "My name is Wilfredo."

Maria tried to smile back but she was very nervous suddenly. She had not spoken actual words to anyone in as long as she could remember. Suddenly time seemed to slow down and she felt as if she were in a dream.

Wilfredo spoke again. "Well, now that you know my name, it

would be a courtesy if you would tell me yours."

"I am Maria," she said.

"Maria, it is good to meet you. Maria, do you know this game? Ocho locos?"

Maria shook her head.

"It is a game played with cards. The Americans call it 'eights are crazy.' Perhaps you would play a game of it with me. I will show you how."

Maria was growing angry. "I want to learn the truth. N-n-not to play games."

"Who says you cannot learn and have fun too? Come inside. Or if you prefer, we can play at this little table outside. I will get the cards."

"No, I want to learn real knowledge. Here is the money. Will you teach me or not? I have n-n-no time for games."

Wilfred studied her for a moment, then said: "Keep your money, child. I am an old man. I have no one to play cards with. If you want me to teach you, you must play ocho locos with me. That is my price."

"Very well." Maria sat down at the little table outside while Wilfredo went into the house. He came out with playing cards and a mug of coffee. "Would you like some water?" Maria shook her head. "How about some lemonade? I could make some for you."

"No, please, let us play this game so it will be over and then you can teach me."

Wilfredo explained the rules of the game and they began to play. He smiled as he noticed Maria's growing impatience. Still, she picked up the game quickly, and before long they had played several rounds. Maria began to show her temper. "This is a silly game," she said, banging down a card on the table.

Wilfredo drew a card for himself and let her talk.

"If you are such a good teacher, you must be wise." Maria looked at the cards on the table, made her decision, then banged down another card. "I cannot see why a wise man would play such a simple, foolish game." She drew a card, and then banged another on the table. "Perhaps you are not so wise after all. I will play only one more game and then we must go on with the lesson. As you can see, I have won four times already."

Wilfredo dealt out the cards. "Very well. But you must answer a few questions before the lesson. The first question is very simple. Getting to this lesson is very important to you. Is it all you can think about?"

Maria nodded.

"And yet you played your cards very well and won many games. So perhaps the lesson was not all you were thinking about."

"It was. But to get to the lesson I had to put my mind in a different place for a time."

"So if you want something very much, you can put your mind in a different place? Think of something else? Even when you want this first thing so very much?"

"It is only because you make me play at this card business."

"But I cannot put your mind in a different place. It is only you who can do that."

"Yes, I—I suppose that is true."

"Will you think about this some more?" he asked. "About placing your mind in a different space? Even when it is difficult to do?"

Maria thought about it. Finally she said: "Yes, I will think about this." She looked over the little table to see Wilfredo smiling at her. His eyes held a sparkle in them. He looked younger, Maria thought.

"Then the lesson is over. You have done very well."

CHAPTER TWENTY-FOUR: THE HARVESTER

Tristan could not believe how big it was. The machine that was to cut the cane had arrived in the early afternoon and was driven to the plantation from the railway station. It was as tall as three men, as long as twenty horses, and was painted a bright red. A man was showing Señor Sandoval how the big machine worked. He had to climb high in a tower on the machine, and when he turned the motor on, Tristan had to cover his ears. He had never heard anything so loud! He moved along the line with the other workers, pretending to be cutting cane, but he was keeping an eye on the machine. Señor Sandoval had said he might be the one to run it one day.

After Señor Sandoval climbed into the tower, the machine started to move, turning toward the workers. They were badly frightened by this and ran to get out of the way. Tristan was curious to see how the machine worked. There was a sort of plow on the front that stood the cane up straight. Then the big blades on the bottom started to cut the cane. The machine was doing two rows at once! There was much blue smoke and the air was filled with dust and pieces of leaves. As one row was being cut, a piece of metal that looked like a big arm came out and stripped the second row to prepare it for cutting. The workers sometimes looked at the machine and sometimes looked at each other. They did not speak, for their voices could not be heard over the noise of the machine. Besides, what there was to say? After the two rows had been completed as far as the drainage ditch, Señor Sandoval got down from the machine and waved at Tristan to come to him.

"This new machine is called a harvester, Tristan. What do you think? It is very impressive, no?"

"Sí, Señor Sandoval, it is very big. A very big machine, like you said."

"There are other supplies that have come. I would like you to bring five or six workers to the storeroom by the boiling house. There are barrels of fuel that are needed for the harvester and oil too. They must be unloaded from the wagons and put into the storeroom. A space has been cleared for them in the corner. You will see it."

"Sí, Señor Sandoval, I will do this right away."

"Good. I will be there shortly to make sure it is done properly. And, Tristan, there are also boxes that contain traps for the rats. I will show you how to use them."

"Sí, señor." Tristan hurried over to the workers and began selecting six to accompany him to the storeroom.

Vicente was well pleased with the morning's work. It helped to take away some of the bitterness he had come to feel when thinking of his son. The harvester had worked well and would be able to accomplish more in a day than he had thought possible. When he was doing his accounts this morning, it hadn't taken long to realize that with the machine, there would be a very large cost saving. The Americanos were right in this. Soon he would have to tell the workers that some of them had to go. He would start with fifty at first; then, if the harvester continued to work well, he could let another fifty go. This could save him almost five hundred American dollars per day!

If Miguel had not stirred up the workers, letting so many go would not be so worrisome. But with Miguel gone, this Tristan seemed to have become their leader. As he made his way over to the storehouse Vicente decided that Tristan would be the first to go. He would not be allowed to cause trouble.

Soon his thoughts turned to Katherine, and he thought that he had behaved badly in front of her. His temper had gotten the best of him, breaking dishes and demanding to be shown the letters written to Maria. He had to make things better. He was not sure quite how to do this, but wait ... Kate had wanted him to give one of the workers a job as a gardener. This Manuel person. She had told Vicente the story of Manuel losing his wife in childbirth. No doubt she felt sorry for him. Vicente would not go so far as to create a job for a gardener when, in fact, he had no need for one. But perhaps Manuel could be taught to maintain the harvester. Vicente could tell Kate he was giving Manuel an important job and perhaps that might help to make up for his bad behavior. Well, he would have to see.

When Vicente got to the boiling house, Tristan and the workers were already rolling the barrels of fuel off the wagon and putting them in the storeroom.

He walked over to the front of the wagon and beckoned Tristan to follow. He reached into the wagon and lifted out a wire cage.

"You see these cages, Tristan? These are going to fix the rat problem. Let me show you. You place the cage on the floor or near anywhere you see droppings from the rats. I have brought bacon as well. You put a little piece of bacon here ... the rat will come to get it, thinking what a fine feast he will have! But as the rat gets close he sets off this trigger here. The little gate will close and now the rat cannot get out. You see?"

Vicente tripped the trigger and the gate fell. "There are snap traps that would kill the rats right away but they could hurt children or anyone who steps on one by accident. This way is much safer. Once the rat is in the trap, you take the cage and put it in the water trough and this will drown it. Do you understand?"

"Sí, Señor Sandoval. I can do this this thing."

"Good. This will be your responsibility, then. Set these traps and soon there will no longer be a problem with the rats. But listen to me, Tristan. You must wear these gloves when you handle the rats. Rats often carry sickness and this will make sure you aren't bitten."

"Sí, Señor Sandoval. I will do this thing. Perhaps you will have other jobs for me as well?"

"If you are successful in this, Tristan, then we will talk of your future."

Tristan Sedillo was in very high spirits on his way home. Señor Sandoval had given him much bacon for the traps. There would be plenty for the rats. And what was left over he could take for himself. It would be he himself who enjoyed a fine feast! Tristan thought his future was looking very bright indeed.

CHAPTER TWENTY-FIVE: OCCUPATION

Julio Antonio Mella was not a patient young man. The formation of the University Students Federation was still in its infancy and already they had staged many protests. But the protests were going nowhere. Now more action was needed and it would be up to him to lead it. Miguel and the others had listened well, the items on the checklist enumerated, and all the supplies they would need they carried with them. At eleven o'clock they took over the administration offices of Havana University, forcing everyone out. They locked the doors and unfurled banners, rolling them from the windows for all to see. Miguel was with three other students occupying the library. There had been pushing and shoving but no one had been seriously hurt ... yet. The protesters barricaded the entrance so no one could enter. Now the administration would have to listen. The students' demands would have to be met: newer textbooks, student representation, and free tuition for all. And they would occupy the university until they obtained what they wanted. They had food and water. They were prepared to hold out for a week.

It took only a matter of hours for the news to spread to the capitol building. President Zayas was not in the mood to hear it and angrily put the phone down. Who was this Julio Mella to issue demands? It was outrageous. This idiot had actually managed to shut down the university. Still, he thought, I must handle the situation carefully. Too much force would make a martyr out of this boy rebel. He called in his chief of staff. "Have a platoon of soldiers sent to the university. There is to be no shooting. They are to cover all the entrances and exits, and no one is to be permitted inside. Nothing permitted inside, no food no water. If anyone wants to leave, they are to be allowed out, and then arrested. I want a list of everyone known to be associated with this action. Those who are not already in the university are to be arrested on charges of conspiracy. This must be stopped before it can go any further."

Miguel was eating a sandwich when he saw the army trucks pull up to the campus. So, the government had sent soldiers instead of negotiators. His stomach started doing little flips as he saw the soldiers take up posts by the entrances. He had been given a revolver but he had never used one before, and besides, it was very old and Miguel was not even sure it worked. He checked it by opening the barrel. There were only four bullets.

He wished Julio was here. Miguel told himself if he remained calm and waited, Julio, who was a powerful speaker, would make the government see reason. Still, he began to sweat a little. After what Julio had said about corruption in the government, he was no longer so sure that they would be open to negotiating. The government cared about nothing except money. If you had enough of it, accommodations were made for you. Even here at the university there were corrupt professors who would sell a degree if the price was right. There had been money for new textbooks, Julio had said, but it went into other pockets. The idea of free tuition was a noble one. If the poor could become better educated, they would be able to better themselves. But there were too many in government who were friends to the Americanos. And the Americanos had no interest in his people bettering themselves. They treated his people like slaves and wanted them to stay that way. Even the richest landowners could sell to no one but America. But the rich landowners treated the workers no better than the government. His father was one of them. He was against helping the workers and didn't even want them too close to his house. Miguel wondered if Tristan had met with his father and if things had changed. He had told Tristan and the workers they must be prepared to stage a strike. If their requests were ignored they must turn them into demands. Give us what we want or we will not work!

He regretted his harsh words to Tristan when last they had met. Together they could have made things better. But he knew too that when you take away a man's pride as he had taken away Tristan's, calling him a coward, there is no turning back. Just as now there was no turning back. Miguel looked out the library window to see what was happening. The soldiers seemed in no hurry to enter the building or start to fight. They just stood at the entrances, but Miguel noticed their guns were held at the ready. He sat back down on the floor to finish his sandwich. He had a drink of water too, but he had to be careful how much he drank. The water might have to last a long time.

He thought again about his father and how angry he had been. Well, that is nothing compared to what he will feel when he finds out about this, Miguel thought. It was almost funny but he didn't feel much like laughing. The truth was Miguel missed his father. He should have talked with him about making things better for the workers instead of going behind his back. His father had told him many times about the importance of trust. Miguel knew he had betrayed the trust his father had in him. Well, now it was too late. And anyway, his father had also told him that you must fight to get ahead. And that's what he was prepared to do. To achieve something you had to focus on that thing and nothing else. Then you must fight to get it. Or, Miguel thought bitterly, if you are corrupt like the others, you only have to pay for it. And if you are rich, then you just take what you want. So if you don't want to be like the others, he thought, what choice is there but to fight?

CHAPTER TWENTY SIX: OF KITES AND FLAGS

Maria spent time in her special place thinking about her first lesson. Trying to get her mind to go a different place was no easy thing. But it was easier in her special place somehow. She was very troubled about the situation at home. Her papa and Kate hardly spoke to each other, and because of this silence, noises seemed louder somehow. The closing of a door, Rosa moving things around in the kitchen, even the sound of Kate setting down a glass on a table seemed to echo through the house. Maria tried to put her mind in a happier place. She remembered the telephone and tried to put her mind there.

Yesterday, the man who installed the telephone had tried to teach Rosa and Kate how to use it. It had made Maria laugh to see their faces. "One part sits on this cradle, as you can see," the man said. "This is called the receiver. When you hear the ring, you pick up the receiver and put it to your ear. Then you speak into the other part. You say something to let the person on the other end of the line know you are there. Then you will hear their voice coming through the part you have held to your ear. It is very simple. Señora Sandoval, would you like to try? I will go to the other telephone in Señor Sandoval's office and make a call to you. You remember what to do when you hear the ring?"

Kate and Rosa had looked at each other and their eyes were very wide. Kate had nodded very solemnly to the man and he left to go upstairs. A moment later, everyone jumped when the black thing made a ringing sound. Kate moved slowly toward the thing they called telephone as if it might bite her. She moved so gingerly you would think the thing was going to jump up and bite her. Kate's eyes grew very wide and even across the room Maria could hear sounds coming from the earpiece. Maria covered her mouth so Kate would not see her laugh. She made her face as serious as she could and said, "Mama, you are supposed to speak into the other part. Remember?"

Kate looked sideways at her daughter and Maria could tell she was very nervous. "What do I say?"

"You need to say something. Once you say something he will say something back and you will hear his voice. That is what the man said."

Kate did not want to get any closer to the telephone. "All right, then," she said in a loud voice toward the telephone, "g'wan away!"

"No, Mama, you must go close and speak right into the black thing that looks like a bell."

Kate frowned. "I'll not put my mouth near that thing, it's not clean."

After a while the man who'd brought the telephone went away, shaking his head. He said they would need practice. The first time Rosa had tried to use the telephone and she heard a voice through the earpiece, she dropped it as if it were on fire and ran back into the kitchen. "The man says the telephone is the way of the future, Mama" said Maria.

"Some kind of future it'll be! The next thing you know, everyone will be frittering away time on the telephone instead of doing something useful."

I had a good lesson with the old man, Wilfredo, thought Maria. Putting her mind in a different space had made her feel better. She was to have her next lesson that afternoon, but this morning she had taken time to begin making a flag for her special place. There was a very grand flag in the courtyard of the hacienda and she remembered once helping Rafael attach it to ropes and move it up to the very top of the big pole. When it caught the wind it opened up and flapped and she thought it very beautiful. The flag had blue and white stripes and a sideways triangle of red with a single white star in the middle.

That afternoon, when it came time for her lesson with the old man, Wilfredo, she told him about the flag in the courtyard, how beautiful it was and that she was making her own flag. "Perhaps, that is a good place to start the lesson," he said. "Have you ever flown a kite, Maria?" She did not know the word and shook her head. "I have done this and I think you would like it very much. Today I will show you how."

The old man went into a room and came back with a big sheet of paper in the shape of a diamond and attached to a ball of string. "It is a fine day for kites because there is a good breeze." They went outside into the sun and Wilfredo showed her the skill of kite flying, how she must run until the wind caught the paper diamond and it went soaring into the air. "You must do the running," he said. "I have become too old to run. It is for the young to do." He showed her how to let the string out and when to bring it in. She kept her eyes on the kite as it went higher and higher. She was very careful with the string and soon she was mastering the skill.

"Tell me, Maria, how does it make you feel, to look at this kite so high in the air?"

"It's wonderful! I feel as if I would like to be the kite and be up high in the air too."

"Yes, it can make you feel very happy to fly a kite, Maria. It is like a flag perhaps?"

"Yes! Yes. It is like a flag."

"Perhaps, Maria, this is how flags came to be. Who can say? Children, when they are young, receive much joy from flying a kite. They imagine as you do, how they would like to be like the kite, flying so high in the air. But as they get older, they are told by ignorant ones that flying kites is for children. That there are far more important things to do. But I think they do not forget the feeling of flying the kite. So perhaps they make a flag and put it on a pole so they can look at it and try to feel that happiness again."

"Yes, that seems right. It would be a good reason to make a flag."

"But it is important to know, Maria; there is a difference between flags and kites. When people look at a flag they can feel happiness, yes. But often when people make a flag they begin to think of things differently. They think to themselves, this is my flag and no one else's! You see when a country makes a flag, it is saying many things to other people. It is saying we are proud people and we make this flag to show our pride for the place we live in. Everywhere in the country the flag is flown to remind people of this, and for many, it changes them. The first thing they feel is that because they now have this flag, the land becomes theirs alone."

"But the land should belong to the people!"

Maria turned to the old man with anger in her eyes. She dropped the ball of string; quickly Wilfredo grabbed it and put it back in her hands. He helped her to gain control of the kite once again. He thought a moment, and then continued.

"But which people, Maria? We are all people. You know from your geography it is a very big world. And it is filled with people. Yet once a country makes a flag, many people in that country think of themselves as different from all the others in the world. And because the flag makes them feel proud, sometimes they begin to think that they are better than people who live under other flags.

"Let me ask you something. Do you notice when you fly the kite that your mind gets bigger and you begin to imagine things?"

Maria's tongue came out of her mouth in concentration as she tried to steer the kite. "Yes, it is a good way to say it."

"Yes, well, it is sad but when people fly flags, many times the opposite is true. Often their mind gets smaller and smaller until it can only fit inside the flag and then the flag is the only thing that matters to them. Many people kill because of a flag. Many people die for the sake of one."

This puzzled her and she asked, "So, you say to me the flag is a bad thing?"

"No, Maria, flags are just bits of cloth, as kites are bits of paper. They are neither good nor bad. It is people who cannot grow their minds that can cause many problems."

They were silent for a time, both looking up at the kite as Maria steered it across the blue sky.

Wilfredo smiled. "Well, Maria, we have completed our second lesson. And you see? I told you lessons could be fun."

CHAPTER TWENTY-SEVEN: A PRICE MUST BE PAID

Vicente was well pleased with himself. Almost one square of cane had already been cut. The harvester was working well and the cane was of excellent quality. He rode his great stallion along the perimeter of the field where the workers toiled away. The harvester had stopped just ahead of them, leaving them to bring the cut cane into the big wagons and stack it in piles. But there were far too many workers now for this task and Vicente could see them performing the work much more slowly than usual. He saw some workers exchange furtive glances and he knew the time had come. He must tell seventy-five of them to go. He had been delaying this for too long. It was an awful thing to have to do, but what choice did he have? It was the way of things. It was the future. But at least there was something he could do for Kate. Perhaps then things would be better between them.

He rode over to where Manuel was gathering the cane into bundles to stack on the wagon and called to him. "Manuel, come here."

Manuel dropped the cane as if struck. He was suddenly very frightened. It was never good to be singled out by the jefe. Always better to be one of the faceless ones. It was worse still to be called by name. He did not know how Señor Sandoval could know his name. He badly wanted to run but he could only do as he was told. He approached Vicente as he sat astride his horse, took off his hat, and bowed his head. Sí, Señor Sandoval?" He stared at the ground.

"I want you to go ahead to where the harvester sits. The operator is having his lunch. You are to tell him you are to be trained in the operation of the machine. You will also be responsible for its maintenance. Do not worry. The operator will show you everything and you will have a week to learn. Do you understand?"

Manuel nodded.

"Look at me when I speak to you, Manuel." Manuel lifted his head and looked up to Señor Sandoval, but in the bright sun all he could see was the shape of a man silhouetted on a grand horse.

"My wife speaks highly of you. She says you have lost your wife recently. Yes?"

Again Manuel nodded.

"It is a hard thing. I could not imagine having to live without my wife. But this will be a great opportunity for you. If you learn to do this job and show promise, you will be well rewarded. Now go. Quickly!"

Manuel hurried through the stubble and past the big dusty carts toward the harvester. As he moved among the workers he could feel their eyes on him as they moved aside to let him pass. He knew they were as surprised as he was. One worker did not step aside. He stood as if made of stone. It was Tristan Sedillo. Tristan looked past Manuel to Señor Sandoval with a look of pure hatred on his face. Manuel scurried around him.

When he reached the harvester he gave his message to the operator as instructed and the operator showed him how to climb into the big tower on top of the machine. Manuel looked back toward the workers, back to where, only minutes ago, he had been loading cane. The workers looked so small from up in the tower of the machine. It was if God himself had lifted Manuel up.

Vicente reined the stallion in and rode back to the hacienda. He thought to himself of how it would be. He would order a huge bouquet of the finest roses. He would knock very gently on her door. He would present himself as humbly as he could. Give her the flowers. Tell her what he had done for Manuel. Kate would look at him sternly for a moment, then laugh and step into his arms. All would be well again.

As he rode into the courtyard, Rafael came running out to meet him. "Señor Sandoval, there has been a call on the telephone for you, from Havana. It is from the Ministry of Defense. They have left a number. They say it is urgent that you contact them at once."

Vicente dismounted. "See to my horse, Rafael."

"Sí, Señor Sandoval."

In his study Vicente took his time dialing the telephone number he was given. Whatever this was about, it was not good news. It took what seemed forever to get through to the right person. He had to identify himself over and over again. Finally, an authoritative-sounding voice came on the line.

"Señor Sandoval, you are speaking with Raul Nevarez. I am with the defense ministry. This call was placed to you as a courtesy. It is in regard to your son, Miguel Sandoval. You should know he has been arrested."

"Arrested?" Vicente felt fear clutch at him. I must remain calm, he thought. I must think carefully. A moment passed. "Has this to do with these protests going on? Miguel is just a young boy. He did not know what he was getting into."

"Señor, your son was among a group of students who occupied the university using force. The situation has been resolved but your son stands charged with sedition. Señor Sandoval, it is a capital offense."

Vicente's mouth worked at saying something, anything, but words would not come. The fear had taken firm hold now and was closing off sections of his mind. He felt light-headed, dizzy. This could not be real. It could not be happening.

"Are you still on the line, señor?"

Vicente found his voice at last. "Yes. Yes, I am here. But there is some mistake. My son—"

"There is no mistake, señor. I tell you again, this call was made as a courtesy. It is merely to inform you. Justice will be carried out swiftly . . . unless ..."

Vicente grabbed on to and held the last word as a drowning man reaches for a hand extended to him. He knew now where this was leading and that there might be a way to win a reprieve. He tried to keep panic out of his voice.

"Yes. Yes, I understand. I believe you were saying . . . ?"

"I was saying that it might be possible that accommodations can be made. Still, the charges are most serious."

"Of course. You will find in this matter that I am prepared to be generous."

"It is my understanding you can afford to be. But you understand the situation. It would require a great deal of generosity on your part."

They came to terms. Vicente's son would be released with a stern warning providing a bank draft was delivered to the proper authorities. Although not in a position to bargain, Vicente was able to gain assurances that his son would be provided with a train ticket home upon his release. As he put down the phone, relief washed over him and he felt weak. It was a trait he despised, weakness, yet there it was. He sat a long time thinking, and as he recovered he was able to push weakness aside and replace it with bitterness and anger. This strengthened him. At day's end Vicente had Rafael saddle his horse and rode off to the workers' quarters.

CHAPTER TWENTY-EIGHT: TRISTAN SPEAKS OUT

The sun was setting on the Sandoval ranch, giving out one final blaze of angry red that lit up the horizon and seemed to dance in the fine particles of dust that hung in the air. The workers filed slowly back to their huts like a defeated army. Not a word was spoken. They were all lost and walked as though asleep. It had not been a good day for any of them. It was true that their workday was done, but tonight there would be no rest even though they longed for it.

Tristan Sedillo, however, did not long for rest. He had gotten word to all the workers that a meeting was to be held at the pump where they drew their daily supply of water. He would have something to say about the day's events. Vicente's words had cut them all to pieces. Señor Rich Man sitting on his big horse.

The day's events played themselves over and over in Tristan's brain until he felt like he was falling and there was no bottom. He went through every detail, looking for something to hang onto, something to save himself.

Late that afternoon Vicente had ridden up to the workers. They labored as if in slow motion in the hot dry heat, trying to appear busy. But there were too many of them to bundle the cane and they looked at each other in silence and fear. Vicente blew the whistle that told them they were to line up to receive their orders. He walked his horse into the middle of a group right at the place where Tristan was standing, dividing them into two halves. They drew back in fear as white flecks of foam flew from the stallion and he stamped and lunged at his rider's cruel tugging of the bit in his mouth. Vicente ignored the group around him and addressed his words to Tristan. There was a roughness to his voice and a callousness the workers had not heard him use before.

"Tristan, you and the people with you in this group: I have no more work for you. No more work, you understand? This has been your last day. You will have to go and find work in some other place. Your houses belong to me. You will have to leave them. But I am not without compassion. I will give you one week to gather your belongings and perhaps find other work. You can gather your last payment from the paymaster. I have provided an extra three hundred dollars to be divided among you. This is to help you until you find work."

Tristan felt strangled and light-headed but managed to find his voice. "Señor Sandoval, I am not with these people, you said to me that—"

Vicente cut him off. "You are definitely with these people. What I said to you, Tristan, was that you showed leadership. These people will have need of your skills in helping them find other work."

Vicente tuned to the group behind him. His violent tugging on the reins caused his horse to rear up, but he easily maintained his balance and brought the horse under control.

"The rest of you, go to your homes. You will report to work tomorrow at the usual time. Get good rest because I think you will find tomorrow there will be no more loafing. Adios!" With that, Vicente rode off, leaving them with their heads bowed with sadness and hopelessness.

The communal pump was the rusty centerpiece of a small clearing near the edge of the workers' quarter. Beyond it was the drainage ditch and the railway tracks on which supplies were brought in and out, ferried by wagon to the storerooms near the boiling house. Nearby there were stacks of fuel drums which Tristan began arranging in a circle. Next he set four drums near the water spigot and placed boards on them to create a platform from which he would speak. The workers would have to crowd in tightly to fit within the circle. If this made them uncomfortable, so much the better. Tristan wanted the workers angry and the tight circle would make sure everyone heard him clearly. Tristan soaked rags in kerosene and nailed them to cane stalks to make torches. He fixed these to each corner of his speaking platform. Soon he was ready. Tristan stayed away from the rum except for a little to give him courage. He would need his head clear for what he had to do.

The workers ambled slowly into the circle. Some held their heads high, and were looking around, openly curious. Some whispered to one another as they came. The ones who no longer had work mostly shuffled in with heads down. They didn't see any reason for this meeting. Their fate had already been decided. But mostly they came so they could feel they were still with the others. So they could feel as if they were one with their comrades.

Standing on his platform, Tristan was an impressive figure. He jutted his jaw out and he rolled up his sleeves so his powerful muscles would show. The firelight from the torches was reflected in his eyes as he began to speak.

"So, amigos, you have seen today with your own eyes. It is what I have been telling you all along! The Sandoval's are not to be trusted! You see now what has happened. Don Vicente takes the food from our mouths! He takes half of us, and throws us away like garbage with no thought except for himself. You see the machine he brings to take our places? This machine is like him. A greedy pig! It eats everything in its path and leaves nothing for anyone!"

Tristan paused. There was not a sound. He had his audience in thrall! He paced upon his stage and paused for dramatic effect.

"I know of your sinking hearts. I know, for many, your bellies will soon be empty with no promise of food. I know you feel there is no hope. But I swear to you on the lives of your hungry children, and the graves of the ones who have gone before us, there is hope! Tristan Sedillo is telling you there is hope!"

Tristan heard the talk among the workers, the urgent whispers. It was exactly what he wanted to hear. He was awakening something in them.

"This pig Sandoval wants half of us gone and half of us to work like dogs. So we will all stand together. We will strike! There will be no one to work for him tomorrow! Unless all of us work, no one will! Think on this, amigos. The cane is ripe. It must be harvested soon or it will rot. Who will pile the cane the greedy machine spits out? Who will bundle it and put it on the wagons? Who will boil it?"

Tristan paused again before asking his final question. He could sense the workers' anger now flowing toward him in waves. He could sense they were ready. He reached behind him for the machete he had carefully kept out of sight. As he raised it high above his head, it blazed in the reflected torchlight. His voice became a roar in the workers' ears. "Who is with me?"

The chorus that came back at him was music to his ears. He cast his eyes at the crowd. They were with him. Still, more than a few seemed to be standing back, aloof, as if in doubt. Tristan needed them all. He spoke again.

"So, amigos, we will strike tomorrow. But we will strike not only for the half of us that were robbed today. We will strike against what will happen to the rest of us. I have told you of my meeting with this pig Sandoval. What I didn't tell you, I feared to tell you. This son of the devil told me his plans to buy more machines. More and more machines so that he would need no one! He swore me to secrecy about these plans and tried to bribe me with a job of maintaining the machines. My fear kept me from telling you until now. But my conscience has won out over this devil. Tomorrow we strike. So tell me once more, Are you with me?"

The workers roared their agreement this time. Tristan looked them over carefully. This time he had them all.

CHAPTER TWENTY-NINE: FREEDOM'S PLACE

"Today is such a lucky day for you, muchacho." The voice seemed to come from nowhere. Miguel's cell was pitch-black, but he could hear a man was talking and getting closer to him. The jangling of keys reached his ears. He heard the echoing of a key in the lock and the release of the bolt. The solid metal door swung open and Miguel was blinded by the sudden light. The guard pulled him roughly to his feet and shoved him out of the cell and into the concrete wall in the narrow prison corridor. Miguel almost fell but something told him to keep moving. He began to see shapes as his vision slowly returned. When he slowed for a moment, unsure of where he was supposed to go, the butt of a rifle crashed into his back and propelled him clumsily forward, but again he managed to remain upright. He sensed it would go badly for him if he fell. The door was open at the end of the corridor and Miguel shuffled with tiny steps into the dust of a large square. It was the prison yard, the walls high and topped with rusted barbed wire. Miguel stood wavering on his feet while the guard undid the shackles that bound his hands and feet. He squinted to bring things into focus. "Have a seat." The guard pushed Miguel to the ground. "There is something you need to see, muchacho."

As his vision cleared Miguel wanted suddenly to be blind

again. In the center of the prison yard stood a wooden post with a man tied to it, blindfolded. Miguel's stomach heaved. He tried to look away and the guard hit him with the rifle. "You will watch or be next. Choose!"

As Miguel looked up, an officer approached the man tied to the post. The officer removed a pistol from a leather holster at his side, pressed it to the man's forehead, and fired.

The guard pulled Miguel to his feet and pushed him forward across the yard to an iron door. Miguel could not help looking back at the slumped-over body tied to the post. "You pissed yourself, muchacho." The guard pointed to the growing stain on Miguel's trousers. He laughed and spat tobacco juice.

The officer holstered his weapon and approached Miguel and the guard. "That will be enough, Corporal." He spoke to Miguel. "You are a very fortunate young man. Your father has made an accommodation. You are to be released. Your release, however, comes with a warning. If you decide to make any further trouble, it will be you at that post. Do you understand?"

Miguel moved his head slightly.

"Very well. The corporal has papers for you to sign. You are to be given a train ticket so that you can return to your home. Go!"

On the train, Miguel tried to make sense of all that had happened, but it was of no use. Earlier, at the university, everything had seemed to be going the protesters' way. The government car, the officials, the paper signing—first by Mella, and then by the chancellor of the university. The students had won! Miguel himself had shaken Julio Mella's hand! But then an officer had come to him saying he wanted to ask "just a few questions, purely a formality." Once Miguel was out of sight of the others, he had been badly beaten and thrown into a cell. And now he was being sent home like a dog with its tail between its legs ... They had succeeded in frightening him, bullying him, and humiliating him. Miguel realized he was very tired. But as sleep came for him, he thought to himself there was one thing they had not been able to do. They had not yet broken his spirit.

With the late afternoon sun streaming into her bedroom, Kate held her husband closely as he slept, his head on her lap, running her fingers through his hair. He had come to her earlier as she was sitting in bed reading. She remembered the growing panic in his voice.

"Katherine ... I need you, Katherine. I need you now very badly. Things are crashing down all around. I have done all I can but I cannot hold this inside myself any longer. There is so much trouble. I feel ashamed. There is so much you don't know." He sat on the bed next to her, his shoulders sagging in defeat. "I have tried as much as I can Katherine but now I ..." Kate reached for him and took him in her arms. They rocked back and forth for a time. And then he told her everything. Kate listened, and when he had finished there was a moment of silence.

"It doesn't matter," Kate finally said. "None of the rest matters. Here's the only thing that does matter ... sure you've saved our son's life. Let your heart have a bit of a rest, love."

Maria was in her special place. Her next lesson was scheduled for tomorrow and she wanted to be ready. What the old man had said about flags and kites went over and over in her mind. It made sense and had given her much to think about. She went through her books trying to think of questions she could ask, for she now believed Wilfredo truly was a wise man and there was much to learn from him. But each lesson seemed to deal with only one question. And there were so many going through her mind. Well, she must determine the best question. Perhaps she would ask him how she could become wise. Could a person do that without becoming old? Did she have to wait that long? How did he become so wise? Had he been wise when he was her age?

Suddenly Maria giggled. She was going too fast. That was already five questions. She made her mind up to just ask the first one. How could she become wise? That seemed a fine question for a lesson. Maria closed her books and went down to the sea and let the cool water cover her feet. She put her mind in the other space for a time. Then she set off for home. She would pick some wildflowers on the way to give to Mama.

CHAPTER THIRTY: TRISTAN SOLVES HIS PROBLEM

Tristan Sedillo was a leader of men! Now Sandoval would have to listen to him. When the workers failed to report to the fields in the morning, it would be he, Tristan, who Sandoval would have to come to. As he thought of the way it would be, he saw himself astride the big horse and Sandoval who would have to look up at him. The rum was making things look better and better. The meeting with the workers had gone better than expected. Oh yes, his speech to them had been glorious! And because he was careful, they were behind him to a man. They had even entrusted him with the three hundred dollars of severance pay. He told them it would be used as strike pay. All the workers looked up to him now. All except the fool Manuel, who had not come to the meeting. No doubt he was thanking God and Sandoval for his good fortune.

It was then that a seed of doubt planted itself in Tristan's mind. He took another big swallow of rum to chase it away like an unwanted guest at a party. But it only grew in his mind. What if Manuel decided to make trouble? Manuel would lick Sandoval's boots now that he had been given this big promotion. The promotion that had been stolen from him, Tristan! What if Manuel were able to sway some of the workers? Get them to turn against Tristan. The workers were like sheep.

They could easily be led. What was worse, they were easily frightened. If Sandoval discovered he was the cause of these problems, what would happen then? These kinds of thoughts were now making Tristan a little frightened himself. He must think of another plan. Just in case that ... yes, a wise man must consider all possibilities. What if ...?

Tristan looked over at his work belt hanging on the chair by his rickety little table. The machete in its scabbard, the little food pouch that was now fat with three hundred dollars. He took another big drink, set down the bottle, and took the money out of the pouch, letting the feel of it make his fear small again. He had never seen this much money before, let alone held it in his hands. It was two months' worth of pay. Two months of backbreaking work. Two months in the fields was a lifetime.

If he were to just disappear tonight, the money would be his. The workers had been foolish to trust him. He had no confidence in them anyway. He was sure now that they would back down and not strike. He would be identified as the troublemaker. But what of that? If he were to leave now, there would be no one to punish. And he would be three hundred dollars richer. The sheep would be sheared.

Tristan thought some more while he finished the bottle. Yes, that is what he would do. But then his fear crept back, tugging at him, while he tried to plan.

What if Sandoval took up the workers' cause and tracked him down? If he was caught, he would be imprisoned. For years. Perhaps even shot. And Tristan was sure he would be caught. Where is the justice for a poor man?

Rich men steal and are rewarded. Poor men steal and they are punished. It is the way of things.

Tristan was now feeling trapped. Trapped, just like the rats he had been collecting in the cages.

There were perhaps two dozen of them in a cage in the corner of his hut. Tristan had thought it too much trouble to drown them one at a time. So he saved them up.

And now an idea loomed up at Tristan through the fog in his brain. What if Sandoval could not chase him down? What if he had bigger things to think about? Tristan stumbled outside his hut for some air. There was a good breeze blowing and it did much to clear his head. He judged the wind and the direction of it, and came to his decision.

The setting sun was washing the land in a soft golden light. It washed over Tristan Sedillo as he stumbled away from the workers' quarter for the last time. He made his way downwind to the cane field just behind the hacienda. By the time he got there, it was quite dark and he was sure he was hidden from view. With him he carried the rats in their cage and a gallon tin of kerosene. Tristan set about his task in a slow and deliberate fashion. He put the cage on the ground and found himself a long stick. With this he would be able to open the door to the cage at just the right time. Then he poured the can of kerosene over the rats, soaking them completely. Next, he lit a match and threw it inside the cage. The cage exploded into flames with a whooshing sound. Tristan used the long stick to open the door. The flaming rats scattered in all directions, running for their lives into the cane field.

The cane caught quickly and the wind helped enormously. Tristan watched, fascinated as this fire child of his grew high and tall. What had Sandoval said? That he was able to solve problems. Well, he was certain that he himself had solved this one. He walked away from the fire reluctantly as there is always something hypnotic in flame. Once he was far enough away, he moved quickly. He made his way across the drainage ditch. He moved, crouching low across a field, to the railroad tracks. The slow-moving freight train came into view as he knew it would. As it did every night at this time. Tristan was careful to hide from the engine's spotlight, and when the train was passing he saw his chance. It was simpler than he thought. He barely had to run. He hoisted himself up into an open boxcar and hid himself in the corner. There was even hay to sleep on. The train blew its whistle for the upcoming crossing, and then rounded a corner.

Tristan Sedillo was gone.

CHAPTER THIRTY-ONE: FIRE!

It is said that fire makes a good servant but a poor master. A master filled with greed that takes all it is able to reach. It is a cunning thing that can feed itself as it moves so it can grow steadily larger. Deep within the wall of flame now approaching the hacienda, little circles of air began to form, creating little chimneys through which the fire could feed itself while sending burning embers high into the air to be spread by the wind. The burning embers flew everywhere. Many reached the hacienda. They found places to hide under the clay tiles of the roof. Some came to rest on the thatched roof of the stable. Others made it as far as the storeroom. The fire itself leaped and grew. It jumped from one cane field to another. Everything that could fly, walk, or crawl was on the move, trying to get away. The fire itself was no longer walking. It was running.

It was running toward Kate, who was helping Rosa set the table. It was running toward Vicente, who was shaving. And it was running toward Maria, who was coming up the path from the sea with her bouquet of wildflowers.

Kate and Rosa agreed they smelled smoke. Vicente noticed light on a windowpane and turned to see the giant wall of flame approaching, pouring out a dense black smoke. Maria heard horses neighing shrilly in panic. She dropped the flowers and began to run toward them. As she rounded a corner she saw the stable roof ablaze. Already the black smoke was making it difficult to see. Everything seemed to be happening all at once. Vicente charged down the stairs and out the kitchen door. Rafael had made it out of the stable trying to lead Vicente's stallion to safety. The horse was kicking and rearing up. Maria ran toward the stable in a desperate attempt to rescue her pony. She made it as far as the door, where the heat hit her like a wall and she could go no farther. Kate looked out the window to see the blazing stable and Rafael fighting with the horse. Then she saw Maria on her knees by the stable. Kate cried out in relief. She turned to Rosa. "We're safer in here for the moment, Rosa. Gather wet towels as quickly as you can. Put them under the door. I'll fetch Maria."

She ran to the front door, and as she threw it open there was a great crack and one of the flaming beams above the entrance collapsed, barring the door. She ran to find Rosa. They would have to make it out through the kitchen.

At that moment Vicente rounded the corner of the hacienda. His face and clothing were covered in soot. He held a machete in one hand and the other was covered in blood. "Rafael, go bring the workers. We must create a firebreak. Go quickly. Take the automobile."

He went over and pulled his daughter to her feet. "Maria, you remember where the graves are, on top of the hill? Go there now. You will be safe. Mama and Rosa will join you soon. When Rafael returns with the workers, he will take you into the village to the train."

"Maria!" Vicente took her arms and squeezed.

"Maria, you must listen to me. Miguel comes tonight on the train. We will need his help. He is to come directly here. Mama will buy tickets and you will all go to Havana. Do exactly as I have told you. Do you understand?"

Maria's tear-streaked face was smudged with soot and the look in her eyes was dazed and far away. It was all coming back. It didn't seem possible, but it was all happening again. The fire, the smoke, people running, the blackness of burned things all around her. The taste of ashes in her mouth. Just like before. Part of her heard what her papa was saying, and part of her was a little girl from long ago.

Vicente shook her firmly. "Maria, please! I need you to understand. Do you understand?"

Maria's eyes suddenly came back to the present and once again she saw her papa's face, his eyes filled with deep concern. She nodded fiercely.

"Then get the horse and go now."

With each passing second, the flames grew. As the automobile sped away toward the workers' quarter, the cane on both sides of the road was beginning to smolder. Maria approached the jumpy stallion without fear and stroked his forehead. Her touch had a great calming effect, and she was able to quiet him. She gripped the stallion by the halter and started toward the hill.

Inside the hacienda Kate made it through the growing smoke and into the kitchen only to find Rosa lying on the floor.

"Aiiieeeee, señora, I hurry with the towels but my foot turn around on me." Kate knelt down to her.

"It's all right, Rosa. You've sprained your ankle. D'you think you can get up?" Rosa was coughing and shaking her head. "It's all right, love. I'll help you. Just put your weight on me and we'll do it together, all right?" Rosa was not a slender woman, but Kate was able to get one arm on the kitchen table and somehow found the strength to lift them both up to standing. Both women were coughing now with tears in their eyes from the smoke. The heat was becoming unbearable. Rosa's eyes were wild with fear. Kate grabbed a wet towel from the table and said,

"Put this over your mouth, Rosa. It's going to be all right. Just a little way to the door now, love, just a few more steps. Lean on me. That's right."

Suddenly there was a high groaning sound from above. Kate looked up.

Vicente heard the groaning sound too. He made a sprint toward the kitchen door. He was too late.

With one last groaning cry the entire roof of the hacienda collapsed in on itself.

CHAPTER THIRTY-TWO: A HELPING HAND

What does a man do when his heart has been ripped from his chest? What does he do when the door to his life is slammed shut in his face? Vicente was crazy with grief. Katherine, sweet Katherine, my darling, my love, my very life. He wanted nothing more now. Nothing but to run into the flames. But this did not happen. Vicente began to see himself from a distance. His mind seemed to have left his body and he looked down to see a man step back from the incredible heat and flames. He saw the man run in circles as a chicken will sometimes do when its head is severed. As he looked down on himself from above, he thought perhaps God had come for him. No, he thought, God is punishing me. He looked down again and saw his hands and realized he had returned to his body. The man running in circles was him. The sins, all the deadly sins, he had committed them all: pride, greed, lust, envy, gluttony, wrath, and sloth. And now the price had been exacted from him.

Through the smoke Maria came running toward him. Their child, this wondrous child of the sea. Vicente felt his heart start to beat again. This is why he would go on living.

Maria had seen the roof collapse too. She knew, just as she knew years ago, that Mama was gone. First Mother and now Mama. She ran to Vicente, great sobs racking her body. He clutched her to his chest and held her tightly. He turned her face away from the flames and felt her tears on him. He gently stroked her hair, and they walked away a few steps as the sparks rose behind them and rose into the night sky.

Through the smoke and cinders, Vicente saw the automobile speeding down the road toward him, shimmering in the waves of heat and ash. He closed his eyes and held on to his daughter until he heard the car brake to a sudden halt in front of him. Rafael jumped out and rushed to his side.

"Señor Sandoval, they are coming, the workers ... some of them, they are coming."

Vicente tried hard to bring his mind back to the present. "Some of them?"

"Yes. Manuel has talked to them and he comes now with perhaps twenty. Perhaps more."

"Twenty? What do you mean twenty? Rafael, tell me what is happening?"

"The workers make a strike, Señor Sandoval. They say they will not come. They say you must talk with Tristan Sedillo. He is leading them. They say they will not come until he says to come."

Suddenly Vicente felt Maria violently pull away from him. The tears scalding her cheeks now were tears of rage. The horse stood not far from where she had dropped his reins. She took them up and tugged the horse over to the automobile. She climbed onto the fender of the car and leaped onto the horse's back. Maria kicked at the stallion's flanks savagely and he quickly sprang to life. As Manuel and a group of workers came running into view, Maria flew through them and past them at a racing gallop. The workers scattered to let her pass and looked after her wonderingly as she disappeared into the smoke.

Vicente let her go. She needed to be alone and he was of little comfort to her. She would return when she was ready. He must try to save what was left.

"Manuel, get these men to form a line with their machetes. We must create a firebreak in the cane so it cannot reach the boiling house or the storeroom. Rafael, I am going to the boiling house to attach a hose where the water line comes in. We will use it to wet down the buildings. I want you to pull a horse trough over to the hand pump and fill it." Vicente turned to the workers and picked out two. "You and you, go with Rafael. There are metal buckets in the storeroom. Bring as many as are there over to the pump."

Feverishly the men set to their tasks. We are fighting a losing battle, Vicente thought. He had counted about thirty workers. It would not be enough. They were slashing through the cane very quickly but there was fire on two sides of them now and soon it would be three. All they could do was delay. But if that was all they could do, then they would do it. They would fight!

Vicente brought coils of hoses out of the boiling house. Three hundred feet. Not enough. Still, better than nothing. He attached the hoses to each other and then attached one end onto to the incoming water line. He scrambled over to the pump house to turn on the water. The faucet handle was hot when he turned it. They were running out of time! But the water came bursting out of the hose and Vicente said a small prayer of thanks that there was still water pressure. He set to work hosing down the pump house first. Then he turned the hose to the boiling house. He turned to look at how the workers were doing. The firebreak they had created was working for now, but he could see high flames on the other side. The fire seemed to be waiting. The crackle of it sounded to Vicente's ears like laughter. The fire was laughing at him as it waited, just beyond the cane break. Waiting until one of the flying embers made a successful jump. This ugly, evil thing was just waiting until they grew tired or slowed down enough so it could take away what little remained.

Vicente's worries about Maria tore at him too. He desperately hoped she had gone to the hill where his mother and father were buried. The fire would never reach her there. He thought bitterly of the time he wanted to send her away with the priest. What kind of man was he back then? What kind of man was he now? To let her ride off like that without going after her. She had brought such joy to him and Kate. And now ... He forced his mind back to the present. The two workers were filling buckets from the trough and rushing them out to the cane break. If only he had all his workers with him. He could stamp out this ugly fire that laughed at him. He wished now he had treated the workers less harshly. He wished he had treated Tristan less harshly. But, he thought with great bitterness, if wishes were horses, beggars would ride.

And someone *was* riding. When Vicente saw who it was, his heart filled up so much he thought it might burst.

The someone who came riding was Maria. She had brought workers and they were running beside her. If this were not miracle enough, she had brought all the workers with her. Every single one.

CHAPTER THIRTY-THREE: MIGUEL RETURNS

Miguel awoke with a start. The crying sounds were gone. He realized the sounds had been coming from him. The train was still chugging softly through the night, the shades in its cars pulled down and the coach in darkness. He looked wildly around him; gripping the arm of his seat finally reassured him that he was safe and on the train. It had been a nightmare that had awoken him. The pistol firing, the man at the post slumping over, it had all come back to him in his fitful sleep. The nightmare kept repeating itself. He kept seeing the officer's expressionless face. First in his cell, then in the square, then at the university. Always the same blank expression on his face. No anger, no remorse, nothing. And the officer had placed the pistol on Miguel's forehead and cocked the hammer.

"Just a formality. I can assure you, just a formality." Miguel tried to remain still and let his breathing return to normal. The man who had been seated next to him was gone, and as Miguel carefully looked around in the shadowy light of the coach, he could see the man was still on the train, but had changed seats. Miguel couldn't blame him. He was aware of his own body odor and it was bad. He still wore the clothes he had worn when he had been taken at the university. They were badly torn and there was blood on them. He had not shaved in days and he knew he looked, and smelled, repulsive. The conductor had not wanted to allow him on board, but the soldier at the station had informed the conductor who he was and where he was to be let off. Miguel had had been dreading going home but now he realized he wanted to do so very badly. He would not fight with his father. He would save that battle for another day, when he had recovered. I have learned an important lesson, he thought. Nothing that school could ever teach me.

He had trusted too easily. He had been too easily fooled. He would not make that mistake again. But for now he could let his mind calm down. He relaxed and even smiled to himself as he indulged in thoughts of a shower, a shave, and a bowl of Rosa's wonderful soup.

The train must be getting close, Miguel thought. He lifted the shade and recognized where he was right away. They were passing through the little village close to the hacienda. He saw the casas outlined clearly, but that could not be. It was late night and none of the little homes were lit from the inside. The light was coming from the sky. It was almost like the sun was rising. Then horror came over him as one by one, like dominoes, the realizations toppled into one another. The sky was lit up because there was fire. The fire had to be a huge one to light the sky like that. Then the final realization hit his heart and it began to hammer in his chest. The fire came from the cane fields. The hacienda!

The train was already slowing to let Miguel off at the place where the supplies were unloaded. But it was too far ... Miguel rushed, panic stricken, to the door of the coach, threw it open, and stepped into the open space between the cars. He took an instant to judge speed and distance and leaped from the train. He landed almost in the exact same spot Tristan Sedillo had stood while waiting to jump onto the passing freight hours before. Miguel had run across the small field and the drainage ditch in seconds and entered what was left of the cane field behind the house. He saw only small patches of fire because here there was nothing left to burn. Smoke and ashes rose all around him.

Miguel's eye was caught by the reflection of something metal in one of the little fire patches. He briefly looked toward it and what he saw made his blood run cold. Lying on its side in the cinders was an empty one-gallon kerosene can. He tried to pick it up, but it was still very hot and burned his hand. He dropped the can, looking around him as if the person responsible for the fire might still be there. When he looked up toward his home, there was no home. Only a smoking silhouette, a blackened skeleton. He let out an anguished wail. He ran toward the skeleton. He ran toward his lost childhood. He ran and ran and ran.

The battle was not over. Although by now almost two hundred workers had joined the fray, the flames had jumped to the third square and it would take all they had to contain it. Vicente was hosing down the storeroom, running from one end to the other, and his face, highlighted in the firelight, was sweating, soot covered, and grim. Miguel's flight had taken him to the courtyard. His eyes searched frantically and found his father. He ran to him screaming, "Papa!"

Vicente heard Miguel's call and dropped the hose. He turned and rushed to meet his son. His darling boy whom he wanted to protect more than anything. If such a thing were even possible anymore. He grabbed Miguel in a fierce bear hug that lifted him off the ground.

Miguel was surprised at his father's strength. His father had not lifted him in the air since he was a boy. And now Maria was running toward them. But where was Mama?

Vicente put his son down and clasped him by the shoulders. "Miguel, it is good you are here. But as you can see, there is no time to talk now. We will talk soon. But now you must help me get the fuel barrels out of the storeroom. Roll them over to the courtyard. Quickly!"

Vicente led the way to the storeroom and Miguel followed. Maria had caught up with them and moved toward the storeroom too. Miguel looked over at her and tried to smile, but what he saw on her face frightened him. There were no words to say.

There were six barrels to be moved and Vicente emerged from the storeroom rolling the first of them. "Miguel, we will form a chain. Stay here, outside, with this barrel. Maria, go to halfway between here and the courtyard. Miguel, you will roll each barrel to Maria. Maria, you roll the barrel to the center of the courtyard and come back for the next. Understand?"

Maria quickly nodded and ran to her position. Miguel rolled a barrel to her and came back for the next one that Vicente was rolling out of the storeroom.

The chain was working well and soon they would win another small victory. Vicente moved quickly into the storeroom for the last barrel, but in his haste he did not notice that the screw top on the barrel was open. Only when he tipped it on its side did he realize from its lightness that he had made a mistake. Gasoline poured from the barrel as it began to roll. Vicente grabbed at it as it rolled, to set it back upright. The gasoline splashed on him as he managed to get the barrel on end again just outside of the storeroom.

Outside, the fire was being beaten back. The laughing, ugly thing would soon be no more. But one final ember fell from the sky and found its way to the little path of gasoline leading from the storeroom. The path became a line of fire, the line of fire led to Vicente, and as quickly as a thought, Vicente was part of the fire.

Vicente hit at the flames on his body to put it them out, but his hands were on fire too. He only had time to look down to realize that all of him was on fire. He tried to run toward the horse trough but a searing pain stopped him, and all he could think to do was change direction. The fire has won and will consume me, he thought. Then he was hit from behind and thought no more.

Miguel hit his father with a flying tackle, knocking him to the ground. In an instant Maria was at his side, and while Miguel rolled his father over and over, Maria poured dust on him to smother the flames.

After the flames were extinguished, Miguel rolled Vicente onto his back as gently as he could. Maria lifted his head and placed some rags under it for a pillow. Vicente's eyes looked up at his children. There was great fear and pain in their faces, yet he made not a sound. Maria and Miguel both saw this look in their father's eyes but had to look away for what the fire had done to him was unspeakably cruel. So instead of looking at their father, they lifted their heads and looked at each other, and somehow, in each other's eyes, they found a little comfort. The son and the daughter knelt on either side of their father as he lay in the dust of the courtyard.

The birds flying overhead could only see small dots on a sand-colored square. Each of the three squares around the sand-colored square was black and smoking. Beyond them lay the sea. The birds would simply fly away to a better place.

The fire had taken all it wanted and left. All that remained was either broken or blackened. And of what use is a broken thing? How can black ever become white again?

CHAPTER THIRTY-FOUR: A RAT ON THE MOVE

Tristan Sedillo was feeling sleepy and lazy. And why not? There would be no work for him in the morning. And with three hundred dollars in his pouch he could take his time to look for something that would suit him. The railcar cradled him, rocking back and forth. For something to do, he leaned out of the boxcar and looked down at the railroad ties passing by. They are like steps, he thought. Someone had to put down each tie and spike it in. So they would not move. So they could not move. So they would know who was boss. All those ties bore on their backs the big nameless one who rode over them. Tristan had once been like those ties. Now that he saw them pass by like this, losing count of them quickly, he realized how unimportant they were. He was now on the big nameless beast riding over them. He was part of it. Like the big man and his big stallion. Sandoval. Riding over everyone. Well, now that Tristan saw what it was like to ride, why not enjoy the journey?

After a while he looked up from the ties and saw a small campfire among some palms grouped close together. He looked toward the engine and saw the lights of a town approaching. It would be better not to be seen for a time. Who knows? A rich man like Sandoval could have spies everywhere. Tristan was a man who thought ahead, ah? He jumped from the moving train but it moved so slowly he didn't even stumble. He felt very good about himself. He made his way toward the group of palms and the campfire, and nearing it, he called out:

"Amigos? A beautiful evening, ah? Perhaps you would share the warmth of your fire? Some companionship?"

As he stepped cautiously into the firelight he could see there were perhaps ten men, sitting around the fire, dressed in military uniforms. And Tristan, dressed in the clothes of a simple campesino, was suddenly very busy trying to keep his face from looking frightened. His heart was racing. Perhaps Sandoval's men were already looking for him?

"Sí, Sí, come, come, we have wine, amigo, and we will share."

Tristan could not refuse now, so he sat where a man had indicated. They looked very merry, these men, so perhaps it would be all right. A bottle of wine was passed to him and he drank a little and passed it to the person beside him. One of the men, closest to the fire, regarded him with curiosity. But his eyes seemed kind enough when he spoke.

"Your clothing, amigo, speaks of the fields, yet here you are with us, and after dark too. Perhaps you are an adventurer?"

Tristan's mind went as quickly as it could. "Sí, perhaps it is so. I am on a journey."

"A journey, yes, yes, we are all on a journey, amigo. I am Roberto and these people around you are soldiers of the new order. We are going to change things!"

"I am Tristan, Roberto." He silently cursed himself for revealing his name. Perhaps the fire had already been talked about. He would have to be careful.

But just then the wine bottle came around again and Tristan drank a little deeper this time. He knew from Roberto's careless and grandiose way of talking that he was drunk, and so were his compadres. They seemed to pay little attention to the new arrival and most of them seemed to be in a stupor from the wine. Tristan relaxed a little more. One of the soldiers began to play a harmonica and another began to sing to the melody. It seemed a good thing to do while sitting around a fire. Roberto, if he was their leader, didn't seem to mind. But he was looking intently at Tristan and it made him nervous. Finally, Roberto spoke.

"We had a good leader in Zayas, Tristan, a good leader of our country, you understand? You understand how important it is to be the leader of a country? But now this lying dog, Machado. He was all right at first perhaps; they are always all right at first. But now he does not wait for the will of the people. He says we need him and he takes a second term! No vote! He takes our voice. He kisses the Americanos asses. The ones that are taking away our jobs! We—that is me and my compadres —we will take this rooster off his perch. So what do you say, adventurer? Will you join us or will you spend the rest of your life in campesino rags? We can supply you with fine clothing, like we wear, and food for your belly instead of starving like a rat. And when we win, there may be a higher place for you still. We need people, compadre. We need adventurers. What do you say, amigo?"

The wine had gone around now many times and Tristan could feel himself warming to it.

"It is true what you say. The Americanos take our jobs. But it is not only them. It is the landowners too. They buy the machines from the Americanos. The machines come!

"I was on a job and they brought the big machine they call the harvester in. Suddenly half of us are told to go. With nothing! I tried to stand up for my people and call a strike. But when they find it was me? I was lucky to escape with my life."

And now Tristan said loudly, the wine giving him courage: But my people stood with me! We were as one!"

He took another gulp of the wine and finished with a flourish: "Because I am a leader of men! "Roberto nodded gravely. "You are the sort of man we need, amigo. You could be an officer!"

Tristan considered this. "Yes, but you must know what my adventure, as you say, is about. I only come this way because my sister is very ill and will not live long. I must see her first, because she is my only family. She must have respect paid. But when this task has been seen to, I will gladly give myself up to this cause."

Roberto considered gravely. Finally he said: "Then go, and when your sister is with God, you will find us training in the hills north of Vinalles. We keep a lookout at a farmhouse close to the base of the tallest hill. It has a weathervane in the shape of a rooster. When you knock on the door, knock once, count to ten, and knock only once again. You will hear an old man's voice say, 'Go away. Let me sleep.' You will respond, 'The only good sleep is in death.' Only if you say these words will the old man answer the door. He will see to it you get to us."

CHAPTER THIRTY-FIVE: DECISIONS

With Rafael's help, Maria and Miguel were able to get Vicente to the village and the train station. They ripped the cloth roof off of the automobile and made a makeshift stretcher that was supported on the front- and backseats of the car. While Rafael drove, Maria and Miguel followed behind on the horse. There was a woman in town that looked after the medical needs of the village. She was summoned and hurried to the station to help. She was very gentle. She bandaged Miguel's hands, which were badly burned. She squeezed cloths filled with cool water over Vicente and prayed. She had an herbal salve, but Miguel would not let her apply it. There was no choice but to wait for the next train to Havana.

Seeing that Miguel was grief-stricken and seemed almost delusional, Maria said, "Take the train to Havana, Miguel. See to Papa. I will return to the workers. I will save whatever I can."

Miguel turned to her, thunderstruck. His mouth and lips worked strangely, like he was a fish out of water. His sister seemed to him to have spoken, but he thought the words she uttered came from his own mind.

"You speak?"

It should have been a moment for a brother and sister to comfort each other. But all Miguel felt was anger. All that had happened had taken him by surprise and made no sense. He could no longer trust his instincts. His loyalty had been betrayed. He could no longer trust that things would turn out as they should. He had sought comfort with home and family, only to have them disappear in flames. And it seemed now that his sister, whom he had come to love with all his heart, had been keeping secrets—from him, from his family. An unreasonable anger flared in him. He spat at Maria's feet and turned away from her. It was as if an iron door clanged shut between them.

In the days that followed, Maria moved about like a girl in a fog. She and the workers had put out the last of the fire and began working to save what they could of the cane crop.

Together with Rafael, she exhumed the bodies of Kate and Rosa from the rubble. The workers made a solemn line on either side, hats in hands. The remains were carefully borne to the graveyard at the top of the hill. Under a sky heavy with thunder clouds the two women were buried. Blackbirds in a nearby tree swept into the sky and disappeared from view. As the last shovelfuls of dirt were put in place, large drops of rain began to fall.

Maria thought that God had sent in the rains. They came and they pounded down in sheets for three days. The earth was hard baked and could not absorb all the water, and Maria and the workers were often knee-deep in water as they salvaged as much of the cane as they could. Even burned cane has value, if it can be processed in time. Maria had learned the value of time in the crushing and boiling process. The workers responded to her urging and the machinery of the mill still worked. There would be a crop.

Miguel had taken up temporary residence in Havana. His father would live, the doctors had said, but he had suffered permanent damage. The burns would require extensive skin grafting, a skill the doctors had not yet mastered in Havana. Tendons had been damaged and he had lost the use of his right arm. Vicente's lungs had also been scorched. The best Miguel could hope for, they said, was only a partial recovery; Vicente would remain a frail man for the rest of his life. Miguel felt bitter and helpless, reduced to holding a glass of water with a straw in it for his father to sip at as he lay covered from head to toe in bandages.

After a month had passed, Maria received a wire telling her of Miguel's return. With nowhere to stay, she had moved to the workers' quarter. She shared a hut with Manuel, and nothing was thought or said about it.

When Miguel arrived at the station, there was no one to meet him. On his own solemn journey he made his way to the only place he knew to go, the only thing that remained. The little graveyard at the top of the hill. Just behind the great marble statues and off to one side, he found them. He looked down at the two little mounds of earth outlined by stones and marked by crude white wooden crosses. He finally found the tears he had needed to shed for far too long.

Maria found him there. She saw his body shaking and reached to touch him on the shoulder. There was no surprise. There was no bitterness. He simply turned and fell into her arms, sobbing. They held each other and she stroked his hair and soothed him. After a time he stopped crying and still they held each other. The stillness encircled them.

Miguel finally drew away from her and looked up at the sky as if asking God for help. None came and he looked down at the ground as he spoke. His voice was low and there was shame in it.

"Maria, I am flying with Papa to London. To the doctors there. Specialists, they call them. They can do this thing called skin grafting. It is necessary that Papa have this done or he will die. Maria, I—"

"Miguel, my brother, of course you must do this! You must not worry about anything else. Papa is everything now. I can care for the plantation. The workers are with me. We will rebuild. It will take time but ... Miguel, you will not look at me; there is something wrong. Tell me."

"Maria, Papa has signed a paper. It gives me the power to ... sister, I have sold the land to the Americanos."

Maria's breath caught in her chest. She wanted to be sure she had heard right. But there was only silence. Only the sight of her brother, who kept staring at the ground in shame, told her what he had said was true. She felt light in the head. So this is what a bullet feels like, she thought. She felt as if she had been shot in the back. Behind her she heard crows calling out with their crude voices. Mocking her. Laughing.

"It is not a good price, but it is something. We can all sail to London together. We can begin again ..."

"You have sold the land, Papa's land, our land?" Maria was having trouble drawing breath and her voice sounded hollow to her own ears. She felt a pounding in her head as the blood rushed back to it.

"Sister, there was no choice. We needed the money. For Papa's operation. For all of us to go on living. In London we can—"

Maria at last found something to hold on to to keep her balance. And that thing was rage.

"Miguel, you are a traitor. A traitor. You sell your birthright, your people, and all the things you tell me you believe in. And who do you sell to? The people that take from everyone and leave nothing behind. The people that come to this land like the fire came to our plantation and steal all that is good, leaving only scraps and ashes behind."

"Maria, please, I had no choice."

"You had a choice, Miguel. You could have chosen to struggle, as all our people do. But you chose to take thirty pieces of silver instead."

There was silence for a moment. They looked in each other's eyes and found no refuge there, only pain.

"You have made your decision Miguel, and I have made mine. You will go to London. I think if Papa had known what you would do, he would not have signed any paper. I will stay with my people. I will struggle, I will fight. I will fight the Americanos. They may have a piece of paper, but I will fight to hold on to this land."

"Maria, please, come with us to London. I am begging you."

"Traitors beg, Miguel."

And with that, Maria turned and left him. With tears blinding her, she went back down the hill to her people.

CHAPTER THIRTY-SIX: A RAT PLANTS A TRAP

Tristan Sedillo sipped his coffee at the Hotel Inglaterra. What a fine gentleman he had become! He now wore a white duck-cloth suit tailored just for him, and not unlike the one Señor Sandoval had worn. Fine leather boots on his feet. The suit alone would have cost him two months' wages, but with three hundred dollars to spend, it did not seem like much at all. Still, the money would not last forever, and if he was to live in the manner of a gentleman he would need more. Quite a lot more.

His mind worked over what the rebels had said at the campfire. It was an opportunity to be sure. To have good clothes, food, and perhaps women who would find a rebel's lifestyle romantic—why, that was something, to be sure. But these kinds of insurrections never seemed to gather any steam, and Tristan knew he could be shot for even consorting with these men. As far as he was concerned, nothing ever changed. There had always been someone with all the power, all the riches, while all he could hope to do was break his back to get enough to eat. He did not want to go back to cutting cane and living like a dog, but he did not want to risk being shot either. Perhaps there was another way.

Tristan began to think. The government would be very happy

to have information about the rebels. Tristan knew where they were hiding. And he knew how to find them. Perhaps the government would be grateful enough to pay for this information. But what if the government knew what he had done? Señor Sandoval would be looking for him and would seek police assistance. Maybe his name was already known to the government. If this was the case, he would be walking into a trap. He thought perhaps he could use another name. Going to the government carried risk, true, but it was either that or join the rebels. He was sure he could not go back to cutting cane, in any case. He would be found. No, the government was the better choice.

Tristan drank a little rum to give himself some courage even though it was very early in the morning. And just before noon he entered the capitol building and approached a desk where two men in military uniforms were talking. He was frightened but it was too late to go back. He did not interrupt but waited till one of them noticed him standing there and spoke to him.

"And what is your business here, señor?" the man asked,

They had called him señor! And how polite they were. His new clothing seemed to change his status. Suddenly he was a man to be respected! Still, Tristan was wary. He did not know how to speak the high-class talk of the ones above him although he had heard it used often enough by Señor Sandoval. He cleared his throat and summoned courage.

"It is very important. I must see someone in charge. It is about people who want to fight the government."

The officials looked at one another and the first one spoke again.

"I see. That would be the Ministry of Defense. I can tell someone you are here, señor...? What name shall I give, señor?"

Tristan paled. He tried to keep his voice steady. He spoke using what he hoped was an educated tone in his voice. "Señor

Garcia."

"I see. Señor Garcia, please come with me."

Tristan fought the urge to grab his new panama hat and hold it to his chest but instead did not remove it at all. He was frightened, yes, but the rum and his new clothing were giving him confidence too.

He was led into an outer office where a young woman was tapping her fingers on a machine that seemed to be fed with paper. He was told to sit and did so. He began silently praying that he had done himself no harm. The young woman looked up only briefly and went back to feeding more paper into the machine and began tapping away again.

After what seemed hours, a military officer came out of the inner office. His uniform was new looking and many medals were on his chest. He did not smile, but silently beckoned to Tristan to follow him into the inner office and sit in front of a huge desk. His eyes seemed to be burning into Tristan Sedillo, who shrank into the chair. The officer sat himself in a great chair behind the big desk and studied Tristan as if he were looking for something. Finally he spoke.

"You have said you have information regarding possible rebel activity, Señor Garcia. It is a good thing when citizens such as you come forward. Now, perhaps you could tell me the nature of this information and how you came to acquire it?"

Tristan had never addressed a military officer before and was not sure how to, but he answered: "It is only by chance, my general, but while I was traveling, I overheard some soldiers talking. I thought they were government soldiers. But they talked of fighting the government!"

"You flatter me, Señor Garcia, with the title of general, but I must ask you to address me as capitan. I am most interested in where you overheard this talk. Also you seem quite nervous. May I get you a glass of water?"

"No, thank you, capitan. It was on the train to Havana, capitan. These men, they talk against our leader, General Machado. They say they will put an end to the government. They ask me to join them, capitan."

"Really . . . and why do you suppose they would confide these things in you, Señor Garcia? I must tell you it is quite humorous to me. If this concerns rebel activity, perhaps you are one of them trying to lead us into a trap, yes?"

"No, no, my capitan. I am just—"

"You wear the suit of a gentleman, but your manner is laughable. You are a campesino, no? Still, I will humor you. Tell me what you know and be quick."

Tristan was sweating freely now. How could he have been such a fool? He must attempt no more lies. Perhaps they would show mercy.

"Capitan, it is true. I am a campesino, as you say. But what I tell you of the rebels is true. I did not hear it on the train but around a campfire. These people, they were drunk and wanted me to join them. It is true they wore uniforms, yes, and carried guns! So I came here. I regret to say I thought I might be paid for my information. You see, my sister is very ill—"

"Enough! If you tell me something useful, you will be sent to a cell while we verify the information. If you do not tell me something useful right now, you will be taken out and shot. Does this help to free your mind of nonsense?"

Tristan wanted to go back to the fields where he was king of the machete. He wished none of the events of recent days had ever happened. He wished he could be a little boy again and have his mother beside him to ease his fear of lightning and thunder. But it was not to be. He could feel his sweat growing cold as it soaked him. He looked to the captain with pleading in his eyes.

"Capitan, their leader is named Roberto. He and his men are training in the hills north of Vinalles. They keep a lookout at a farmhouse near the base of the tallest hill. The weathervane is in the shape of a rooster. I was to knock on the door, knock once, count to ten, and knock once again. When someone answers I am to say certain words ... the lookout will bring me to them. But if you—"

"Enough. You will lead us to these men. You will knock on this door. If your information is correct you will be rewarded. If it is not, this place north of Vinalles will be your grave ... do you understand?"

"Sí, mi capitan."

As he was led out of the office to a cell, Tristan looked over at the woman still tapping away at the machine. She did not look up. It was strange how every day, someone's fate is being decided, and other people just go on as if it is another day.

CHAPTER THIRTY-SEVEN: REUNITED

Miguel found Maria in Manuel's hut. She was stirring the great cooking pot in the center of the room and had her back to him, so did not see Miguel enter. Manuel did, though, and his eyes filled with fear. The two men looked at each other for a moment, then Manuel gave a brief nod and left the hut. Miguel spoke.

"Maria." She did not turn but he could see her back stiffen and she stopped stirring.

"I know you will stay here. I have not come to try to change your mind. It does not matter what you think of me, but there are things you should know."

Maria turned to him angrily and started to speak but Miguel cut her off.

"If you want to have an enemy, you should start with Tristan Sedillo and not the Americanos. He is the one who burned down our home. But there are other things too. Is there somewhere we can speak in private?"

Maria dropped the spoon, wiped her hands, and strode past Miguel out of the hut. After a few steps she stopped and beckoned him to follow her. They walked in silence, with Maria leading the way. After a few minutes of walking, she spoke. "We will go to the sea. My thoughts come easier there." For the rest of the walk nothing was said.

They both tried to understand each other during the silence.

As they walked along the beach, Miguel told Maria about all that had happened with him at the university, how he had returned to find the empty kerosene can behind the hacienda, and how he understood her anger and wanted to help her.

"I am no traitor, Maria. And I have not given up. But it is important to choose your battles. This is not the end."

Maria suddenly felt tears coming and she turned her face away so her brother would not see them. He reached for her and they held each other tightly before speaking.

"Rafael is driving me to the train station and will come with me to Havana. You take the car. You will find it useful. Also, there is money from selling the crop. It is not as much as it should be because of the quality of the crop, but it is still a lot of money. It is yours, and if you need more I will wire it from London. You are my sister and I am your brother. We will take care of each other. Together we will win."

"I am sorry I did not have more trust in you, Miguel. I ..."

Maria took Miguel's hand and led him away from the beach, saying, "Come. I want to show you something."

She led him to her special place, the one she had kept secret all these years. The place only Kate had seen. She showed him the old machete, the bits of sail, as well as all her books and items she had hidden away. She brought out two cigars and offered him one. He looked at the cigar and then up at Maria. They both burst out laughing. It was the first time they had laughed in a long time. Then they sat in silence and smoked. It felt good. It was Miguel who finally spoke.

"We must make a plan."

They talked late into the afternoon, each having their own ideas and putting them together so they fit perfectly. They swore each other to secrecy, but then Maria hesitated.

"I must share this with my teacher, Wilfredo. He is a wise man and may be of help."

"Do you trust him with your life, Maria? Because that is what you would be doing."

"You talked to me of trust, Miguel, and how we must be careful. How it must be earned over time. But am I not careful? You knew nothing of this place until today."

Miguel smiled. "Our hearts beat together now, Maria. Yes, all right. I wish I could meet this Wilfredo, but we must go now. Rafael will be waiting."

"We?"

"You will need a driving lesson if you are to take the car. And besides, will you not come and see me off safely?"

"After what we've talked of Miguel, I think others should be worried about their safety, don't you?

After they reached the station, Maria had her driving lesson. It was impossible to remember so many things at once. There were so many pedals and levers and buttons. First advance the spark. Then set the accelerator. Turn on the magneto. Set the gear and press the starter. Maria's face became red with concentration, but after several tries she was able to guide the car around the rail yard despite. Still, much of the time the car jumped and heaved like a cat bringing up its lunch. She forgot to turn down the spark advance so that when she turned the car off it backfired louder than a gunshot. Many people at the station ducked and took cover. Raphael was shaking his head and Miguel was looking up at the sky and blowing softly. The jet of steam from the arriving train brought the lesson to an end.

"Maria, you will get the hang of this after some practice, but you must stop now, the train is about to leave."

Later, Maria would remember the day as one in which time

either slowed down or sped up. The driving lesson had flown by like Chaplin in the moving pictures. But her goodbyes with Miguel seemed to last forever, as she held him and rocked back and forth. The drive back was speeded up again, with Maria trying hard to remember the pedals and what they did and how to steer in a straight line.

But now the day was coming to an end and time had slowed down again. As the sun set Maria stood atop the hill in front of the little white cross where Kate was buried. She felt so many different things at once. She felt a great loss that nothing could replace. She felt a great anger that made her want to grind her teeth. She felt a powerful yearning inside to be somewhere far away. She tried, as Wilfredo had instructed, to go to another place in her mind. For a time it worked and she felt calm and peaceful and was able to empty her mind of thoughts. When she came back to herself, she was still looking down at the little white cross. A voice rose in her throat that she was powerless to silence. She found herself singing the words Kate had taught her so long ago.

> "'Twas hard the woeful words to frame
> To break the ties that bound us.
> But harder still to bear the shame
> of foreign chains around us.
> And so I said the mountain glen
> I'll meet at morning early.
> And I'll join the bold united men
> While soft winds shook the barley."

CHAPTER THIRTY-EIGHT: THE TRAP CLOSES

Tristan Sedillo had given up hope. For two weeks he had rotted in a cell. He knew the number of days only by the scratches he had made on the wall. His grand white suit was filthy and he could smell himself. It was not the good smell of work, but the smell of rot. If only he could go back in time. Had a chance to do things differently. But he had been stupid and now he was feeling very sorry for himself.

But then he heard the sound of a key in a lock! Someone was coming. Please, he thought, anyone. Perhaps a guard with a priest. Let it be so . . . someone to kill him and put him out of this misery.

When his cell door opened two guards dashed in and grabbed him from the floor and roughly stood him on his feet. A third officer waited outside the cell.

"Today you have a chance to live. You will take us to this rebel camp. If you have spoken the truth, the general will see you. If you have lied you will die. Do you understand?"

Tristan searched one face after another. There was nothing but stone in the eyes of his captors. He nodded meekly.

The officer spoke. "Clean him up. Give him something to eat.

Try and make him look like he could be worth something."

An hour later Tristan was brought outside into the early morning darkness. The wind was cruel and the rain whipped around in angry sheets. He was led toward a line of trucks filled with soldiers and placed in the back of one of them, under guard. Tristan found himself trembling violently. The faces surrounding him seemed to be set in stone with eyes that did not blink. At a shouted command, the trucks started up and began to snake down the dirt roads toward Vinalles.

The movement of the truck over the rough road pitched and jolted Tristan and he thought he might lose the small breakfast they had given him. He had to try to remain calm. There might be a chance to escape later and he must be ready. Perhaps, during the fighting, he might slip away unseen.

The sky was beginning to lighten a little when the trucks came to a stop. But still the rain poured down. Tailgates swung down and the soldiers jumped out of the trucks, making very little noise. Tristan was given his instructions.

"The farmhouse you told us about is down this road on your left. Go and try to enlist in this group. We will be watching and following. If we hear one wrong word or this turns out to be shit, you will die."

The walk to the farmhouse was the longest of Tristan's life. The rain had soaked him through within seconds and he prayed someone would be at the house. When it finally came into view it looked abandoned. No light shone from within. This is how it will end, he thought. When he got to the door he knocked once, then, shaking in the rain, he waited. For ten seconds. For the shot that would end his life. After ten seconds passed he was so relieved to be alive he nearly forgot to knock again. A thin voice came from within. "Go away' let me sleep." It was the sweetest sound Tristan had ever heard. He took a deep breath and closed his eyes, concentrating on keeping his voice steady.

"The only good sleep is in death."

After some shuffling sounds a door opened and an old man stood on the threshold, first looking him over, then around him to what else might be there. The old man cocked his head, motioning to someone behind him. A younger man in army fatigues came out of the house and stood in front of Tristan. The old man went back in and closed the door. The younger man looked Tristan over in silence and didn't seem to think much of him. Then he suddenly lifted his head to the sky and called out a bird sound. A grackle. After a few seconds the call was returned. The man beckoned Tristan to follow and they started into the dense undergrowth and began to climb the hill.

For a time there was only the sound of their passage through the jungle. Tristan's heart began to beat normally. Perhaps in a few moments he could slip away and make his escape. The swish-swish of the passing ferns lulled him. He began to have thoughts of a warm fire, a bottle of rum, and a beautiful woman looking down on him with gentle eyes, stroking his hair.

The thoughts of the warm fire seemed so real. He could hear it crackling. But in reality, it was gunfire he heard. The man leading him squatted down and motioned for Tristan to do the same. But in the next instant the man was hit by a bullet and lay still.

Near him Tristan noticed an explosion that threw up dirt and burning leaves. He fell to the ground and crawled to a nearby banyan tree. Hugging the ground like a lover, he closed his eyes. After a time the sounds of the guns moved up the hill and became distant. He would be safe now. He could make his escape. His breathing slowed and he felt heavy. Perhaps just a little sleep first.

He awoke when an officer kicked him with his boot.

"We return now. The general will want to see you. Don't

worry. He has a fondness for snakes."

The trip back to the capital was a very different one from the somber trek to Vinalles. The sun had broken through the clouds and the soldiers in the truck were laughing and joking. Some even nodded and smiled at him. It seemed he was no longer a prisoner. Already Tristan's confidence was returning. Why shouldn't the soldiers smile at him? They were wise to treat him with respect because he was on his way to see the general. These soldiers would do well to keep on his good side. He was again a leader of men.

When they returned Tristan was led into the general's office and told to wait. He took in the surroundings. The huge desk of polished wood. The great high-backed chair behind it. There were comfortable seats of leather in front of the desk, but Tristan did not dare sit. His eyes moved to the furled flag by the window. A grand place indeed. And why should he be frightened ... He had helped his country in its time of need.

The general strode quickly into his office and took up position behind his desk. He frowned as he sorted through some papers in front of him, seemingly oblivious of Tristan. Finally he found what he was looking for and seemed satisfied. He did not look up from the papers but barked out in a loud voice: "Send him in."

Tristan could now afford to be amused. He thought to make the sound of clearing his throat to let the general know politely that he was already in the room, but the sound was strangled within him.

For into the general's office, his eyes burning with knowledge and hatred, strode Miguel Sandoval.

CHAPTER THIRTY-NINE: CHOICES

Wilfredo finished his morning meditation and went into his tiny kitchen to make coffee. He looked out his window. Maria would come soon. For two weeks she had come for lessons every day. They went to the field nearby, and together they flew the kite. Maria had shared with him all that had happened. He was very concerned for her and kept her in his prayers daily. She had many questions and it was a challenge for the old man to answer them, because in all his life he had never heard of such troubles as Maria had endured. He had never encountered such a wounded soul. Wilfredo knew he had to be very careful, for he wanted very much for Maria to find peace and let go of her hatred, but he would need to keep her respect if he hoped to accomplish such a thing.

She was able to go to a place inside herself, a place of detachment, easily enough. The rule was no talking while the kite was in the air and to keep her eyes on the kite at all times. She even practiced breathing the way Wilfredo had shown her. That took a kind of patience that was rare in one so young. Afterward he would listen as she told him of the injustice she saw everywhere. Why was the world such a place? Why did evil have such an easy time of it? Did he believe in God? How could Jesus forgive? Why was he not angry when she told him of all that had happened to her? Did he not believe evil should die?

Wilfredo did his best to answer.

"Let me say this: The world is a place that offers us choices. The choice to do what we believe is good or to do what we believe is evil. You must face these questions. Consider what you do, the choices you make. It does not matter if I believe in God. Answer first for yourself. Do you believe in God? I am very concerned for you, because of all that has happened and what choices you will make because of it. These choices will be very important.

"Let me give you an example. This fire took many things you loved away from you. Yet fire itself cannot be good or evil. It can provide warmth, cook our food, and give us comfort. Just as easily it can take our home away, our loved ones, or even our own life. This is the nature of fire. Good or evil lives in the choices we make. So we can see the fire as good or evil. But that is because we choose to.

"The fire cannot make a choice."

"The man who started this fire at your home made a choice to do so. Because he made this choice, he will now have to make others. This is his path."

"You can see, then, the importance of the choices we make when we talk of good or evil. Before you make your choice, it is good to fly the kite, to breathe with it, to be quiet and listen to yourself. It will help you in making the right choice. And to make sure your path is the right one for you."

Later, back at her special place, Maria thought about all that Wilfredo had said. Much of it made sense. Some of it did not. It would take time to consider it all. But Maria did not have much time. The Americanos would soon be coming, coming to take the land. Once they arrived, Maria and Miguel would have a chance to put their plan into action.

She lit a cigar and watched the smoke curl upward, thinking of what the recent past meant for the future.

Most of the worker huts were abandoned now; with no work available, the campesinos had left to roam the country looking for work. But a few remained—twenty-four to be exact. Many had volunteered, but only these few had been selected. Twenty-four workers to be turned into soldiers. They were to be trained, according to the plan, as revolutionists. Miguel had helped in their selection before leaving for Havana.

Living quarters would be constructed in the nearby hills, where the training would take place. Maria would use the money from the recent crop for this purpose and also for food and supplies. They had the car, which would prove useful. They also had the great stallion, which Maria could not bear to part with. Her papa had named him King, but from now on he would be called Soldier.

Maria wondered too about Manuel. She still shared his hut and he had been eager to join in the training of the new recruits. Miguel said he would make a fine soldier, but lately Maria had noticed him becoming more stubborn and less willing to hear what she had to say. She was angry too that among the others she was becoming known as "Manuel's woman." It was her money that would pay for this initiative, her plan; it should be under her direction. Would they listen to her? Why was it that men were so quick to assume ownership of what was not theirs? Perhaps this revolution should be about giving women the right to have their say too. She needed a way to claim ownership.

An idea took hold of Maria and she went to her storeroom and took out some cloth and paint and brushes. Wilfredo had spoken of choices. She would make those choices! She chose red paint to always remember the blood that had been shed. She chose blue for the color of the sky. She spread out the cloth on a driftwood table she had made. She would not be painting crosses any longer. Now she would make a flag! A flag to claim ownership of this new movement. A flag to remind herself and everyone else that she had made a choice. Her choice and hers alone. And on the blood-red linen, she drew a kite made of blue, the color of the sky.

CHAPTER FORTY: A DEAL WITH THE DEVIL

Miguel made a lunge to wrap his hands around Tristan's throat, but the general's guards were there to stop him. They pulled him away but not before he had violently spit on Tristan, hitting him in the face.

"This, then, is the man you told us about?" asked the general.

"This is the pig I told you about!" Miguel said.

"Well, this is good news. It will certainly save us the trouble of looking for him. You will have to swear out an affidavit. I understand you have booked passage to London for you and your father?"

Tristan's face had become almost gray and he stood frozen while the spittle slowly ran down his face. He now looked to Miguel with pleading eyes, which seemed to be full of contrition. Miguel's eyes had locked with Tristan's and they burned into him.

"Cobarde!" Miguel spat the words at Tristan. "I will not leave until I see this man in hell."

The general seemed mildly amused by Miguel's intensity.

"I think his journey may not be as pleasant as yours. However, the affidavit will be sufficient in this case. I understand you have been waiting here in Havana for some time and your father's medical needs are pressing. I do not wish to delay your passage any further. My personal guards will see you to the ship. If they can be of any assistance, no matter how small, you need only mention it to them. It is my hope your voyage will be a safe one."

"If you wish to make my journey bearable, take out your pistol and shoot this man now!"

The general smiled faintly. "There are procedures to be followed in these matters, señor. As I am sure you are aware. Adios."

The general motioned to the guards, who had to use some force to escort Miguel from the room. When the general was alone with Tristan, he walked to his window and gazed down on the capital below. Tristan shivered and did not know where to look. He could feel his heart pounding in his chest. Some moments passed in a heavy silence.

"So it seems your name is not Garcia after all, but Tristan Sedillo, is that correct?" the general asked.

Tristan's mouth was working but he was unable to find words.

"Take your time, señor, but I would caution you that the first words you utter should not be a lie. It would not go well with you if they are."

Tristan tried to get hold of his breathing. At last he spoke. "It is true, my general. My name is Sedillo. I don't know what Señor Sandoval has told you but—"

The general turned to Tristan and became very matter-of-fact. "He has told us that you deliberately set a fire that burned down the Sandoval family's plantation and are responsible for the murder of two innocent people as well as critically injuring another."

There was silence. Tristan had not noticed a clock in the room before but now he heard it loudly. It sounded like it was ticking his life away.

"Yes, it is true, I set a fire, but the young Sandoval, he ... he was telling the workers on the plantation to rise up against the government! Just like the ones in Vinalles I told you about. I wanted no part of it. I was very angry with them. How could they do such a thing? The government had been so good to them. I tried to convince them. I had great influence ... but this young Sandoval . . . he threatened them. He said whoever did not join his revolution would be killed and I—"

The general silenced Tristan with a wave of his hand. "You are quite the artist, Señor Sedillo. You paint such a picture! But I think the colors are a little too bright and you perhaps make things a little bigger than they actually are, no? I find the truth to be so refreshing. It helps to put things in perspective. I think that is what your painting lacks: perspective."

The general, with great deliberation, took a cigar from a box on his desk and with it a cigar cutter. He cut the end of the cigar and as he did so, he continued: "As an artist, what color do you think the truth to be? I find red is the color that best brings out truth."

Tristan began to speak but the general waved him off. He slowly lit his cigar and the smoke curled upward. He picked up the cigar cutter and placed it next to Tristan.

"This cutter is a most useful tool, Señor Sedillo. But you must be very careful when using it. It is very sharp. It is about the size of your finger, you see?"

Tristan saw. The look of fear in his eyes was unmistakable. The general continued his voice still soothing. "Perhaps you could paint another picture, one that contained a truer perspective, or perhaps we could use a little red to bring out more of the truth."

"Please, my general," Tristan said. "I ...yes. I set the fire. It was because we workers had been fired, me and all the others. Señor Sandoval brought in a big machine to do our work. I was angry, I—"

"Yes, of course. I can see how that would make you angry. But was there not also some money involved? Some three hundred dollars?" The general smiled and blew cigar smoke at the ceiling. He motioned for Tristan to continue.

"Yes, it was meant for the workers. But I took it. I confess. I needed it to make my escape. I needed it to—"

"You buy for yourself a white suit and become a man of importance, is that not so?"

Tristan hung his head in defeat.

"Yes, my general. It is so."

The general half sat on the edge of his desk and regarded Tristan for a time. "One is called upon to make decisions. You made yours and now I must make mine. It is a delicate art of balancing the elements of a case. On the one side there is the Sandoval family. A most respected family."

Tristan nodded mutely. He could feel his heart filling with dread.

"Still, this younger Sandoval has caused us a great deal of inconvenience at the university. In the past, before our current troubles, the senior Sandoval was most generous in offering assistance to the government of this island. But this assistance has now come to an end. And it has come to an end, my friend, because of you."

Tristan wanted to swallow but found he could not. The general continued, his voice even.

"Now, on the other side, we have you. A man who has lost his way. A man who has committed a great crime."

Hot tears came pouring out of Tristan's eyes. "My general, I—"

"But despite all that, this lost man, this criminal, has found his way to the truth. Shown himself to be a man of questionable ambition, but ambition nonetheless. A man who has helped his government, and if given the chance will continue to do so. A man who would be deeply in debt if he is given a small mercy and a chance to show his loyalty."

The general had crossed behind Tristan and now placed a hand on his shoulder. It was the touch of salvation. Tristan wanted to sob in his gratitude, but he did not. A leader of men must not grovel, but understand when fortune turns in his favor.

"Sí, my general, such a man would be foolish not to show a most holy loyalty."

"I think I have come to my decision."

The general crossed behind his desk again and began examining the papers on it. "You will work only for us from now on, Señor Sedillo. You will put away thoughts of yourself and your white suits. You are to go among the villages to find insurgents ... like the ones you directed us to in Vinalles. You will report any such activity at once. You will present yourself as a man in need of work. Do you understand?"

Tristan's voice came back strong and clear. The voice of a loyal soldier. "Sí, my general."

"Excellent." The general lifted an open cigar box to Tristan. "Cigar?"

Tristan thanked the general and helped himself to a cigar. But his hands were shaking when he did so.

The general smiled to see this. "Here, let me cut that for you."

CHAPTER FORTY-ONE: HOMECOMING

Vicente was back at the governor's ball. Dancing with this charming ... more than charming ... beautiful red-haired woman. She was laughing ... there it was ... it was her ... accent ... he was trying to ask her ... about her accent. She laughed and laughed . . . something about his sword. Ceremonial, it's just ceremonial . . . "Well, it's pokin' me" . . . more laughter ... getting lost in her laughter ... "Katherine," she was saying ... "If you must know, it's Katherine" ... laughing again, dancing, turning round and round. "Call me Kate ... call me Kate." . . . "I'm gettin' dizzy," she said. He remembered. Kissing her on the balcony overlooking the city. Such a kiss. So warm. "Too hot in here."

"We'll call him Miguel after his grandfather."

"He is almost as beautiful as his mother." He had said that. He remembered now... Miguel . . . he ... too hot in here, too hot . . .

Vicente opened his eyes. To what was the present. The pain made him shut his eyes again, but it could not erase the reality. He remembered waking up in the distant past. Those first moments of consciousness were always like trying to find your way upward. Now it was ... now it was just spiraling down, always down. He had been burned. He was in bandages. All of him in bandages. Everything he tried to move hurt him so much he abandoned trying and just used his eyes. Eyes looking out from the bandages. His eyes could not be fooled. He recognized the electric fixture on the ceiling and the colors. He was in the Hotel Inglaterra in Havana.

What about the fire? The fire! What happened to the fire? He began to panic and tried to call out, but he had no voice. His breath was like thin paper and it made him dizzy to try to yell like that. He would have to ... Katherine said the dancing made her dizzy. He must get back to that. To his Katherine, laughing. He heard voices in the next room; low ... He couldn't make out what they were saying. He moved his eyes as far to the left and right as he could. The bandages were like blinders on a horse! He grew angry and tried to move his head but it wasn't just the bandages that restricted him. His skin held him in place. His skin felt so tight it would not let him move.

Finally he was able to shift his head just a little. To see the bedside table. Bottles. His eyes began to close. He remembered when she sang to him. "You have a beautiful voice, Katherine." More of her laughing. "Can I touch it?" He remembered looking shocked. "Your sword ... your sword, g'wan wit you ... what did you think?" More of her laughter ... like music falling down from the trees! He wanted so badly to go there. But now there were voices in the room. A woman's voice. Someone beside him. A shadow to one side of him. "Señor Sandoval?" Eyes looking down into him. Another voice. A man's voice: "His eyes are open. Señor Sandoval? Can you hear me?"

Vicente did not know who these people were. Medical people. He did not care to see them or hear them anymore. The pain was pressing on him, making it hard to think.

"Señor Sandoval, I am your doctor. I want to examine you. I will just lift these bandages a little ..."

Shooting stars, hot stabbing pain. Oh, Katherine, please, my love. Make them stop.

"Give him thirty drops of laudanum. I'm afraid the infection has progressed. There is not much else we can do."

The spoon came again. Always the spoon. Such a bitter taste.

"You'll feel better soon, Señor Sandoval. Soon your son, Miguel, will return."

They talked to him as one talks to a child. Did they not know who he was?

Soon, spoon, soon, spoon...

Vicente reached for Katherine and she was there, her eyes so gentle and kind. But her eyes could be fiery too. Couldn't they be fiery, my love? Yes, of course. But not now, not with you. I will hold you. Yes, hold me. I feel cold.

Outside the hotel, Miguel asked the guards to kindly wait in the lobby while he saw to arrangements. The ship was to sail in just over an hour. There was an infirmary on board stocked with all they would need. The ambulance had arrived and was parked by the portico of the hotel. He tried to think if there was anything he had forgotten. Ugly images of the pig Sedillo kept running through his head, but he pushed them away. He must concentrate. Passports, currency, address book. Everything was in order. Two orderlies were stationed at the bottom of the stairs with a stretcher, waiting for him to say it was time. He nodded to them. They must be gentle with the patient as they carried him down. There was no wind. That was good. He did not know why he thought of that. But there was no wind.

It had been so frustrating... the wait. Day after day, waiting for the ship to dock while his father's life slipped away. In London, they would perform the miracles. Such things they could do in medicine these days! If Papa could just hold on till the end of the journey. It would take just over a week and the first of the surgeries would be performed within twenty-four hours of their arrival.

Miguel took the steps to the third floor two at a time and was breathless by the time he entered the quiet hush of the suite.

The doctor was just coming out of the bedroom.

Miguel tried to quiet his breathing and kept his voice low. "It is time. The ambulance is outside. They are coming now with the stretcher. How is he?"

"I am afraid the infection has spread señor. We have sedated him with laudanum but—"

"Is he awake? Can I talk to him? Everything will move quickly now. You'll see, I must tell him it will be all right now. Things are finally moving."

The doctor looked at the nurse and back to Miguel.

"He is conscious, but heavily sedated ... I..."

Miguel brushed quickly by the doctor and opened the door to the bedroom. "Papa?" He neared the bedside and to his relief he saw the top sheet moving up and down.

Katherine was tickling him. This little miracle wrapped in a soft blue blanket. Showing Vicente his toes. "Look at your son. Look at his tiny toes, love, have you ever seen anything so perfect?" Vicente smiled down at the two of them. What a fortunate man I am, he thought. I am a father! A father ...

"Papa?" Vicente was surprised to hear the voice come to him from above. Everything was so misty. Hard to see. Yes. Papa. He will call me Papa one day, Katherine.

"And you will make him a grand papa, my love." Katherine smiled up at him.

Miguel stood over him, looking down on him. But it was not the baby Miguel. His son was a man. How could this be? Miguel looking down. Katherine looking up. Down was up and up was down.

Vicente struggled to open his eyes wider. To see clearly that his son had grown into such a fine man. He seemed, though, to be worried about something. But what a handsome young man. His eyes filled with tears. Miguel touched his hand. He could feel it.

He sensed Katherine was behind him, very close.

Vicente opened his mouth to tell Miguel he was perfect. But no sound would come. The tears were blurring the vision of his grown son, so he went back to Katherine and the baby. Back. And then without a sound, on that early spring morning, Vicente Enrique Sandoval returned home.

CHAPTER FORTY-TWO: A DANGEROUS PATH

Maria's group was making progress. She looked across the clearing they had slashed out of the undergrowth. The encampment was slowly taking shape. High in the hills they had built a series of eight huts roughly in the shape of a circle. The huts had been kept as small as possible, to be used only for sleeping. At the center, construction was under way on a larger shack, which was to be used for meetings, planning, cooking, and if need be, a last defense. The first defense was the outer ring. Surrounding their encampment, they had dug pits, filled them with wooden spikes, and covered them with dense undergrowth.

It broke Maria's heart to see Soldier used as a common workhorse. The once proud stallion was reduced to hauling poles, yoked like a plow horse. Still, all must do their part.

One of the last things to be done was the removal of all Maria's belongings from her special place to her hut in the hills. As she was leaving this magical place for the last time, she remembered the pearl she had buried so long ago. Perhaps she should dig it up? It might help procure arms or food. But what if the pearl were bad luck as she had imagined? No, it would be better to leave it. Let it be a curse to the Americanos.

Maria and Miguel's plan called for the formation of three groups of eight. Ocho locos, after what had become Maria's favorite card game. Each individual in these groups would be referred to only by the number assigned to them. The groups would be kept apart and unknown to each other. Only the leaders of each of the three groups—Maria Miguel, and Manuel —knew of the existence of the others and their purpose. The first group, headed by Miguel, would be in charge of recruitment and would work out of the university. Miguel had a contact there and it was he who would head up the day-to-day operations of group one. Miguel thought it best that Maria not know the name he was using.

Group two, headed by Manuel, would be in charge of the villages—in gathering support for their cause and making sure they became "friendly villages." He and his group were to go from village to village to the north and to the south, helping the campesinos in any way they could. They would supply labor or food. Anything to curry favor with the locals and bring them onto their side.

Manuel sensed Maria had grown distant from him and did not object to the distance. In any case she had become impossible. He had tried to show her a better way, but she would not listen. This division into three groups would give him a chance to lead without interference. Perhaps Maria might even learn the lesson that leadership was best placed in men. And perhaps in one of these villages, Manuel could find a woman with softer edges than Maria. A woman who could make him feel more like a man.

Maria's group, group three, would be responsible for acts of sabotage. Strikes were to be made on any Americano holdings or on the government itself if it chose to intervene. The first strike was being planned for the next morning. Three harvesters had arrived at the rail depot and were to be brought out to the old Sandoval plantation and be put to work. It was Maria's job to see they never got there. She would send two scouts to the rail yard at midnight and report back about security and locations. The strike was to be carried out in the hours before first light. They would dispatch any guards as silently as possible and take their guns and ammunition for future use. Gasoline had been packed in bottles and strips of rags inserted to make firebombs.

Maria's thoughts went to her last meeting with Wilfredo. It had been a bitter disappointment. They had flown the kites as usual but Maria found it hard to concentrate and could find no peace in the activity. Wilfredo had been distant and afterward, during their talk, she found out why. Although she had told him nothing of her plans, Wilfredo seemed to sense that something secretive was going on.

As she drank coffee at the little table outside his home, Wilfredo tended to his flower bed. There was silence for a long time. Finally, Wilfredo spoke.

"I am worried about you, Maria. About the path you have chosen."

Maria set down her cup and an unreasoning anger took hold of her. "My path does not concern you, old man."

"Yes, I can see you have made that choice already. But it need not be a final one."

"You talk of choices. God chose my path for me long ago. You speak of getting to a higher place. And I tell you God sees no such place for me. All this talk about letting things go ... letting things pass through you ... it makes me laugh! I don't have to let them go ... things are taken from me! God has taken everything from me! I will have nothing to do with higher places or with God!"

A troubled silence followed her words. Wilfredo let it be. Finally he said: "You asked me earlier if I believed in God. Maria, what if ... what if God were nothing more than a convenient receptacle in which to place that which we do not understand. We can place our thanks there for good fortune or we can place the blame there for bad things that happen. We place hope there and call it faith so we don't have to be responsible for such a fragile gift."

Maria rose to leave. "All that is in you are words. I will listen to no more words."

Wilfredo shook his head sadly and looked up at the sky as if it were speaking to him. "You have still much anger. God has not taken that from you. I know you will leave now. But, Maria, will you think about something for me? Even if we never speak again, think of this one thing."

"Say it quickly and let me go."

"It is just this Maria: What if it is you who are God and God is who you are?"

CHAPTER FORTY-THREE: CONDOLENCES FROM THE ENEMY

Miguel sat by his father's bed. So now it was over. No need to rush anymore. His father was at peace. Miguel felt numb, a sense of nothingness growing inside him. He was aware of Rafael coming into the room, touching his shoulder. He heard his own voice as if from far off. It sounded strange and flat.

"Rafael, I ... I would like you to bring my father to the ship after all. I want you to accompany him and see that he gets to Spain, to Galicia. There, old friend, I need you to see he has a dignified burial. There is nothing here for him any longer. He would have wanted you, his oldest friend, to do this last thing. I will make sure you have the money you need. Will you do this last thing for the family?" Rafael nodded solemnly. "Good. That is good. I must go now and send a wire to Maria."

"Señor Sandoval?" the desk clerk called to Miguel as he was crossing the lobby of the hotel. Miguel paused, and a great tiredness descended on him. It seemed the outside world would not leave him to his grief. He made his way to the front desk.

"Señor Merrick of the United Fruit Company asks if you would join him for lunch. There is a matter of some importance he would like to discuss with you." Miguel's eyes turned to stone. He stared straight through the clerk until the smile disappeared from his face.

"Señor Merrick and I have concluded our business together. I have no further need to speak with him."

Miguel turned to leave.

"He said I was to tell you it concerns your father." Miguel stopped.

"He is in the dining room, señor."

William Merrick rose to greet Miguel as he approached the table. He offered his hand and Miguel pointedly ignored it.

"Michael, Michael, this is all so tragic. I ... well, all of us at United Fruit are so sorry for your loss. Your father was a fine man. A fine man. We were in business together for many years, as you know. He was a real friend."

Miguel gritted his teeth. "Señor Merrick, our business is concluded. You have the property. There is nothing more to do ... You wished to speak with me concerning my father. You said it was of importance."

"Call me Bill. Please. Michael, I know this isn't a good time, but just hear me out. Look, have a seat, would you? Would you like a coffee? Somethin' stronger maybe? At a time like this, you could probably—"

"Señor Merrick, please get to your point. If there is something about my father that I need to know ..."

"Well now, it concerns an offer we made to him. I'm sure he would have wanted you to hear this. But please, can we at least sit down?"

Reluctantly, Miguel took a seat across from Merrick.

"First things first. The gravesite ... that property will be separate from our agreement and ceded to you in perpetuity ... uh... that means forever. We would consider it a privilege to help with your father's interment. We could—"

Miguel cut him off viciously. He did not wish to be patronized on top of everything else.

"My father's remains are on their way to Galicia. That is in Spain, by the way." Miguel paused, and then continued reluctantly: "But I thank you for your kindness in preserving the sanctity of the gravesite. Now, if there is nothing further—"

"We would like you to manage the property, Mike. It is an offer we made to your father and we want to stick by it. Hell, it would be helping us out. You know the business. It makes good sense. We would rebuild the hacienda for you, better than before, and you would have complete control over operations."

Miguel was growing furious, but held his tongue as he glared into the shark-dead eyes of the Americano.

Merrick continued: "Now, it would involve you becoming your own company, of course, and as such you would become what we call an affiliate. So the money would pass through your company's hands first on its way to us. You would be well compensated, make no mistake about that. See, we're having a problem just lately with these antitrust people in Washington. But having you back on board could be good for everyone. These are exciting times, Mike. United Fruit is vertically integrated now. Now that's just a fancy-shmancy way of saying we control the product all the way down the line. From the harvesting of the cane to the refining to the distributing. And you could be our inside man, Mike. It's in both our interests. We can make some serious money here. This island is a gold mine."

It was at that moment that Miguel felt a great change overcome him. It was a curious thing. The old Miguel would have spit in the Americano's face and walked out. But this new Miguel surprised him. He seemed colder and more deliberate in his actions. He recognized that this was opportunity presenting itself. What was the old saying? Know your enemy and know yourself and you will be victorious. Miguel managed a tight smile.

"I will consider your offer, Señor Merrick."

"Bill ... please."

"Yes, well, I will consider your offer, Bill. But now, if you will excuse me, I have more pressing matters to attend to." Miguel rose from the table and Merrick rose with him.

"Sure, sure, I completely understand. Look, I know this is a hard time. But, I mean, we can help each other. That's what friends are for, huh? So, think it over, Mike. It's just ... we're gonna need to get going on this thing as soon as possible. Give us your answer by tomorrow and we'll go from there."

Miguel nodded curtly. "Until tomorrow, then, Bill."

"Okay. Sure. Until tomorrow, Mike."

Miguel started toward the lobby, his thoughts turning already to the sad duty of saying his final goodbyes to Rafael, and sending heartbreak through the telegraph wires.

Merrick called out behind him: "Oh and don't forget to pass on our condolences to that sister of yours too. What was her name again? Margaret?"

Miguel clenched his teeth at this and kept on walking. Thoughts of vengeance burned through him as he framed his silent response. Maria, her name is ... Maria. And believe me, you will come to know her well.

CHAPTER FORTY-FOUR: BLOOD HARVEST

Maria's scouts reported back by 2 a.m. They had done their job well and gave her a detailed account of the setup. There were two guards posted at the train itself: one at the engine and one toward the rear on the opposite side. Both were armed with machine guns and sidearms. Their patrol consisted of walking toward each other, meeting in the middle, and walking back. Three more soldiers guarded the station house along with the stationmaster, who was manning the telegraph office. There were two sets of double doors, one on either side of the terminal, and a single door on the north end. Four small windows, two on each side of the doors. As to the perimeter, there was one maintenance person who was sleeping in a tiny shack just off to the south side of the station house. There was a military truck equipped with radio parked off to the south side as well, facing away from the tracks. It did not have keys in it. Gas lanterns lit the station house and two electric yard lights stood on either end. One road provided the only access. It came in from the west. Their prize, the harvesters, rested on three open flatbed railcars behind the engine.

Maria addressed her soldiers. "Comrades, gather round and listen closely. Our attack will proceed as planned. You have all trained for this moment, and worked hard. On this day we will be rewarded with our first victory. You must follow the orders I will give you to the letter, because our collective success can only be accomplished if each man does exactly as instructed. Agreed?" She looked to the face of each individual as they nodded their assent. They were concentrating on her words, all of them of the same mind. This was good. This was vital.

"We will have one great advantage, and that is surprise. Surprise in our enemy leads to confusion and we will use this to our advantage. We are to remain invisible and silent whenever possible." She began drawing out her plan in the dirt with a stick. Each man's task was spelled out in detail and she had them repeat it so she could be sure that they fully understood what was expected of them.

At the appointed hour they approached silently from the north. They made their way slowly and carefully as there was no moon to guide them. They came on like ghosts, down the hill, close to the tracks. Each of them performed flawlessly. Number two took out the first guard at the engine with a rag soaked in chloroform. Number three did the same with the rear guard. Both guards were stripped of their uniforms and weapons. Their machine guns and pistols were passed to Maria. After this was accomplished, a nod was given to number four, who cut the telegraph and electric lines leading to the station house. Number five entered the shack to the south and quickly gagged and bound the maintenance man. Maria gave arms to number six and seven, and together they crept up to the station house. They burst in and caught the three unsuspecting guards in the middle of a card game.

"I am sorry to interrupt your game, gentlemen. Please be kind to your wives and children and do not move, even a little. Six, take their weapons. Seven, do you have the camera?"

"Sí, comandante."

"We must preserve this moment for posterity. No, gentlemen, hold the cards up here where we can see them. Just go back to your game ... pretend we are not here."

Seven held up the camera and the flashbulb exploded.

"This photo will be sent to your commanding officer. I am sure he will understand your need for recreation when you all work so hard. Now, if you all would be so kind as to remove your uniforms . . . ?"

The three soldiers exchanged urgent glances, and one of them nodded to another.

Maria fired a short burst from her machine gun into the ceiling. The sound was deafening in the enclosed room. Plaster rained down on the soldiers. "Please, do not mistake my generosity in sparing your lives as stupidity. Remove your clothes. Now!"

The soldiers hurriedly began to strip. "When they are done, tie them and gag them."

"Sí, comandante."

Maria made her way into the telegraph office and confronted the stationmaster. He looked up at her with a grim smile. She returned it and closed the door behind her.

"I thought perhaps you were not coming."

"We could not pass up the opportunity, Arturo. You have done well. No one suspects?"

"Perhaps my wife. But she has a jealous nature."

Maria smiled. "That is good. We need you here, but it is important that you remain safe. I will have to tie and gag you ... It may be a long time before anyone comes ..."

"That is nothing. But, comandante, I fear I have news that is not so good." Arturo opened one of his desk drawers and took out a sheet of yellow paper. "It came earlier this afternoon."

As Maria read the words the bottom dropped out of her world.

A great helpless sorrow filled her heart. She looked out the window at nothing. A black night. She closed her eyes and let the time pass.

Time passed but the feeling did not.

"Comandante ...?"

Finally Maria turned her attention back to the present. "I will always think of this night as a gift to my papa, Arturo. He went through the fires of hell before he died. And I promise that his death will not be for nothing. They want hell? I will show them hell!" She stormed out of the station house and hurried to the tracks. Number three was stacking boxes filled with the gasoline-filled bottles. She grabbed one of the bottles from a box and lit it. In a black rage she threw it with all her force onto the flatbed carrying the first harvester. The firebomb exploded under the machine and the flames quickly shot up into the night sky and began to spread.

Maria yelled to the machine as if it were a living thing. "No more will you take honest work from my people!" She lit another bottle and hurled it at the second harvester. As it too exploded, she cried out, "No more will you take the food from their mouths!" As the third bottle smashed and added to the flames, she screamed: "Now *we* will take from *you*!"

And indeed they took. The blood harvest had netted them a dozen weapons with ammunition, a military truck, and two radios with extra batteries along with five military uniforms. The damage they had done was designed to be remembered. All three harvesters were destroyed beyond repair. The controls of the train engine had been smashed, hoses cut and burned. Rails had been torn up and the road into the station house barricaded. Maria urged her comrades to hurry as they bundled their spoils into the truck. It would be driven down an abandoned road near the village and hidden in the brush, but it must be done quickly before dawn so they would not be seen.

Time was running out, but Maria entered the station house one last time. She crossed over to Arturo. “Someone will be keeping watch on the hill to the north. If no one has come by this afternoon, rest assured that they will eventually come with food and water. But, my friend, you must remain tied.” As Arturo was bound and gagged he nodded his understanding.

Maria’s final act before leaving was to take the flag down from the pole at the side of the station house. In its place she raised her own flag. It began to unfurl in the early morning breeze. It showed a blue kite flying against a blood-red background.

CHAPTER FORTY-FIVE: FREEDOM OF THE PRESS

William Merrick exploded into the general's outer office and pushed past the guards posted there. His face crimson, his blood pressure going through the roof.

He growled at the general's secretary. "The general in?"

"Sí, señor, but it is not a good time—"

Merrick cut her off: "Well, it's a goddamned good time for me."

He barged into the inner sanctum. The general turned from his window behind the desk. He raised a hand to stop the two guards who were moving in.

"It's all right. Mr. Merrick and I have things to discuss. Please leave us." The guards retreated reluctantly into the outer office and closed the door.

Merrick brandished a rolled-up newspaper in the general's face as if he were going to strike him with it. "Have you read this ... this ...?"

"Yes, Mr. Merrick, I—"

"'Rebels Catch Government Forces with Pants Down!' And there are pictures! Pictures, for chrissakes!"

The general gritted his teeth. "Believe me; I am very upset by this as well—"

"Upset? *Upset?* I've lost over a hundred thousand dollars' worth of equipment! I've got a stockholders' meeting in New York a week from now. They are expecting a dividend of thirty cents on the dollar. Thirty cents on the goddamned dollar! After this fiasco, they'll be lucky to see ten! But I'll be sure and tell them that you're upset. That'll help a lot. Our security people are ... UPSET!" Merrick spat the word out.

"Mr. Merrick, please. I will take care of this."

"You better goddamn well take care of it!"

"You may reassure your people that this matter has our full attention and I will handle it personally. It will not happen again."

"No, it will not happen again, buddy boy, because we put you here, and we can sure as hell take you out."

The general's eyes glittered. "Please do not attempt to threaten me, Mr. Merrick. We have enjoyed a profitable partnership. We both have interests in this matter."

"Okay. Okay. Look. You just better hope to hell I have some good news for my stockholders by the time of this meeting. They are going to be screaming for blood."

The general managed a small smile. "And they shall have it, Mr. Merrick."

Merrick regarded the general with uncertainty for a moment. "Well ... good."

"And now, if there is nothing further ...?"

"There is one thing. Those harvesters were on their way to the old Sandoval section. We'll be putting the son in charge of day-to-day operations. He's going to need people to get a new crop in. I want you government people to help in any way you can."

The general's eyebrows shot up. "Are you sure that's wise? The young Sandoval is known to us. He, along with some others, caused considerable trouble at the university. I'm not sure it is advisable—"

Merrick waved him off. "Wild oats, General. I did business with his old man for years. Michael's a pussycat."

Merrick threw down the newspaper with its lurid headline on the general's desk. He crossed the room and opened the door to take his leave. At the last moment he turned back to the general. "And, General ...? I hardly think you are in a position to tell me what's advisable when it comes to security."

After Merrick left, the general sat down at his desk. The *Havana Journal* lay open before him; its headline seemed to mock him. The photograph splashed across the front page showed three of his men with playing cards in their hands and their pants around their ankles. Other, smaller pictures showed the harvesters ablaze. His fists began to clench and unclench. He hit the intercom button. "Get me Sedillo." The little box came back with the reply.

"My general, he is at the depot investigating, you sent him to —"

"I did not ask you where he was, I said get him!!"

"Yes, my general."

"And tell the sergeant to make ready a squad of ten."

An hour later the general's staff car pulled up in front of the *Havana Journal* building followed by a military truck.

Two soldiers leaped out of the truck and took up positions by the door as the general walked in

and smiled at the receptionist. "I would like to see the editor of this paper; also the publisher. Regrettably there has been no time to make an appointment. But if you would be so kind, tell him he has a visitor. I am sure they will see me."

A door opened in a glass-walled office toward the back, and the editor quickly strode out holding a piece of copy in his hand and crossed over to a reporter's desk. "This copy is shit, Francesco," he said. "Rewrite it." Suddenly he was aware of the silence around him. The typesetters were quiet. Everyone was staring toward the front office.

The editor paled visibly when he saw who was at the front desk. The general nodded to him, smiled, and raised his voice so all the office could hear: "My friends, a matter of some delicacy concerning national security has come to our attention. The publisher and editor of this paper will accompany me, and together we will discuss the best way to address this most pressing problem. I am sure you understand the need for confidentiality in this matter. So I must insist that you not speak of it to anyone. The penalties for noncompliance are quite severe. In the meantime, as of now, this building will be closed for some much-needed renovations. Gather your belongings. My men will see you to the door."

After the staff had vacated the building, the street in front of it was cleared. The publisher and editor were hustled out the door and into the back of a waiting truck. Soldiers entered the newspaper office armed with sledgehammers. The shades were drawn. The general passed by the back of the truck on his way to his staff car. He fought to keep his temper in check.

"Gentlemen, we will speak of this further at a place where we will not be disturbed. The latest edition of your newspaper has caused much ... concern. Also, there is an urgent need to find out who supplied you with a number of slanderous photographs. You will find, gentlemen, that freedom of the press has its limits. Yes, and as to the renovations to your headquarters? I can assure you my men are experts. When they have finished with it, you will hardly recognize it."

CHAPTER FORTY-SIX: THROUGH THE LOOKING GLASS

Maria felt fearful as she searched through the sea of faces at Havana's central train station. She had never seen so many people in her whole life. When at last she saw Miguel pushing his way through the crowd toward her, her heart opened with joy. At last ... at last, she could bathe in the warmth of her brother's love, stand next to someone she could trust completely, and feel safe. It was that feeling inside her she had been missing more than any other. Feeling that no one was watching her, that she was able to say whatever she felt needed to be said. The feeling she had felt with Wilfredo when they watched the kite soaring above them.

Since she'd had the encampment built, she had felt the old coldness seeping into her. She had not felt it since she was a child living in her special place. Before Kate showed her what home could feel like. None of the men dared to look directly at her, but she could feel their eyes on her, watching. Watching for her to make a mistake. And now, added to this coldness, she felt fear. Her papa had called her "my little one." How she longed to be a little one again.

Miguel reached her and squeezed all those thoughts from her mind as he lifted her in a bear hug and spun her around. His eyes met hers and she could see that his were filled with playfulness and warmth.

“It is good to see you, sister,” he said. “You look beautiful, as always” Miguel set her down, wrinkled his nose, and passed his hand back and forth in front of it. “But your smell ...”

“It is the smell of you, my brother,” she said. “The smell of bullshit. I hope this fancy hotel of yours has a great big bathtub.”

“Come. We have rooms at the Inglaterra. It was Papa’s favorite hotel.”

Maria stopped in her tracks. She could feel her face fall and the tears well up in her eyes. Miguel put a sheltering arm around her and spoke gently. “We have much to discuss, my sister. Come.”

Maria had never been to a big city and her eyes grew wide with amazement as the taxi made its way to the hotel. The size of Havana, and all its myriad sights and smells, astonished her. This side of her brother, the denizen of a grand metropolis, she didn’t know. So this was where he had gone to the grown-up school. The university. He seemed so at ease here. It seemed a place more suited to giants than to ordinary people. She had to concentrate to keep her mouth closed as she stepped into the hotel and looked up. The ceiling of the lobby seemed to reach to the sky and the plasterwork was a pageant of sweeping swirls and figures of animals.

“Our rooms are at the very top of the building, on the fourth floor. You can see the whole city from your window. Come and see.” Maria felt a pang of discouragement. She suddenly felt very tired and the thought of climbing to the top of this giant building did little to comfort her. She was making her way toward the grand staircase, wide enough for ten people, when Miguel beckoned to her. He was standing in a little box room off to one side beside a man in a purple uniform. He motioned for her to join him.

Suddenly she felt fear. He wanted to share a secret perhaps? Perhaps someone had recognized her? Who was this man in uniform? Reluctantly she entered the tiny box room and looked over at Miguel. The look in his eyes was playful again. Time seemed suspended somehow, and Maria's thoughts were racing. Even if she whispered, the man in uniform would hear her. She looked over at the man, but he was ignoring both her and Miguel. He pushed a button on a panel in front of him. Suddenly moving doors appeared in front of her and closed her in. A trap!

Instinctively, Maria crouched down. There was a jolt and the floor beneath her seemed to vibrate. She felt a strange sense of movement. She braced herself against the walls of the tiny room with panic in her eyes. She looked to Miguel. The world was not making sense. He was laughing and being playful. "It is an elevator, Maria. To take us to our rooms. Try to relax." Maria narrowed her eyes as she looked at Miguel. She felt angry and strangely foolish at the same time. Then there was another jolt and the movement stopped. The doors opened and the man in uniform called out, "Fourth floor."

They made their way down the hallway and Maria felt her feet sink into the deep red carpet. It was all so hushed and quiet. Miguel stopped in front of their rooms and handed her a key with a big brass tag attached. "Your room is this one: 422." He smiled at a secret only the two of them shared. "I know you like the even numbers. And look, we are neighbors. My room is this one, 421, right across from you. You can rest now for a few hours. We will talk over dinner. Meet me in the dining room at seven." Miguel winked at her. "I think you will find the food here better than rations at the camp." They kissed on both cheeks and took their leave of each other.

Once inside her room, Maria looked about her in wonder. Her surroundings reminded her of a book she had read as a child. About Alice going through a looking glass. She felt as Alice must have when she became very small. The ceiling, once again, was high above her. Even the windows were much taller than she was. They were framed with satin curtains tied back with gold brocade. As her eyes moved about the room, she noticed rich upholstered furniture sitting on each side of a low table with a glass top. On it was a huge vase filled with fresh flowers. She breathed in their perfume, only to become painfully aware of her own smell of stale sweat.

She wandered through an archway and found the bedroom. The bed was several sizes too big for someone of her size and seemed made for a giant. The bedroom led to a large bathroom, with gleaming white fixtures and faucets trimmed in gold. Maria retraced her steps to the bedroom and sat on the edge of the giant bed. She felt disoriented—lost and somehow very lonely. She realized it was not her that was small. It was looking at all these things that made her feel that way. Her thoughts went to the guilt and shame she had felt living at the hacienda while the workers were made to live in grass huts with dirt floors. But that was nothing compared to this! This room, these rooms! On the taxi ride over to the hotel, she had seen many beggars in the streets holding out their hats for coins. Some of them sat or were sprawled out on the cement pathways. They looked wounded somehow. It was as if they had been beaten. Yet no one seemed to care. People walked around them without even looking! She realized now that the disparity between the rich and poor would be harder to overcome than she had thought. The differences were everywhere and much greater than she could have imagined. She looked behind her at the giant bed. It would be impossible to sleep, feeling like this. She went to the bathroom and filled the tub with water that was as hot as she could stand. Miguel was right, she thought. I stink. The whole world stinks. If I hope to get rid of any of the stench, I would do well to start with myself.

CHAPTER FORTY-SEVEN: A RECKONING

Maria was dressing when she heard a knock on the door. Her head snapped up. It was not Miguel's knock. Too tentative. Her mind raced through possibilities but she could come up with nothing that made sense. Besides, she felt safe here. She quickly finished buttoning her blouse, crossed to the door, and opened it. A boy in uniform (the hotel people wore uniforms, she had learned) held out a garment bag. "Delivery for you, señora, from Señor Sandoval." She took the bag from the boy and gave him a quick nod of thanks. She was about to close the door, but still the boy stood there as if he had no intention of leaving. He looked at her expectantly. She grew impatient. "Yes?" The boy now looked at her with some sort of puppy-dog expression in his eyes. Exasperated and annoyed, she slammed the door. Men, especially the young ones, could be such idiots.

Her jaw dropped in surprise when she opened the bag and found a new dress and shoes that would make walking all but impossible. And with it? A smaller bag containing lipstick and ... what were these buttons? Earrings? After surprise came the anger. Miguel knew her better than this. Then she noticed a note in the smaller bag. She opened it to read: *We are being watched.* She was beginning to feel like Alice in *Through the*

Looking-Glass again and she did not care for the feeling one bit. And besides, the dress was shit brown. Miguel knew her favorite color was blue.

At six o clock Maria entered the dining room feeling like someone else. The dress was itching her skin, she had trouble keeping her balance, and she had to resist the terrific urge to scratch. She spotted Miguel and their eyes locked. There was a man with him. Taller than Miguel but much thinner. They rose as one as she approached the table. The man smiled politely.

"Señorita, it is indeed a pleasure to meet you at last. Your brother has spoken highly of you, but he neglected to tell me of your great beauty."

Maria felt herself blush but returned the polite smile and turned her eyes angrily to Miguel. He tilted his head ever so slightly to the left and her eyes followed his movement. Most of the diners were couples or small groups, but in a corner off to the side was a solitary man who made a sudden show of picking up a newspaper and busying himself with it. She looked back to Miguel and he gave a slight nod of his head.

"Maria, I would like you to meet Antonio Guiteres. He is the gentleman from the university I told you about earlier. Señor Guiteres will be collecting soil samples at the plantation ... to further his studies ..." Maria's eyes darted from Miguel to Guiteres in search of a clue to this puzzle. She did not understand what was going on and that was not a position she liked to be in. For now, though, there seemed little choice.

Her brother spoke again. "I have taken the liberty of ordering, Maria. I know how much you like camarones and it seems it is the specialty of the house. Shall we order some?"

They sat and Miguel took his time pouring wine into the fine crystal glasses. There was an awkward silence during which Maria's frustration began to grow.

Well, if this is to be the way it is, she thought, then at least there is food. She reached over and snatched a dinner roll from a basket, hunched over her plate, and hungrily tore the roll apart with both hands. She took a huge bite and was reaching for the wine to wash it down with when she caught Miguel glaring at her. She darted a look sideways at Guiteres, who seemed quite amused with her savagery.

Feeling suddenly guilty, she remembered the lone diner and glanced in his direction to see if he was looking at her, but he was buried in his newspaper. She set down the roll and straightened herself in her chair, smiling and frowning at the same time, her cheeks bulging with bread. It took a great deal of time and chewing, but finally she was able to swallow the last of it.

The rest of the dinner passed without incident; there was what seemed to Maria endless chatter about agriculture of all things, and she was again growing impatient. After coffee, Miguel produced cigars, offering one to Guiteres. They made a great ceremony of lighting up while Maria looked on, annoyed. Apparently this was another pleasure she was expected to do without.

At last, the lone diner rose from his table, paid his bill, and left. Maria saw no further need for patience. "Miguel, you shit, what is going on?" she asked.

Miguel kept his voice low. "Sister, go to your room. Make sure no one follows you. We will meet in my room in ten minutes. If you happen to be followed, you are to stay in your room and wait for me to contact you. Go now."

Fifteen minutes later Maria was getting answers to questions she hadn't dreamed of asking and found herself rapidly entering a world she hadn't known existed.

Antonio Guiteres was not at all like anyone she had ever known. He seemed to be a master of disguise. Between the restaurant and Miguel's room, his easy charm had disappeared and his laughing eyes had grown deadly serious. He spoke at length and with intelligence and urgency. His voice was soft and held Maria and Miguel in rapt silence.

"Maria, I would have liked to show you the university. There are many good people there who share your vision of a better world. Unfortunately, these are dangerous times, perhaps much more so than you imagine. Events are moving very quickly. First of all, Machado has announced his intention to serve a second term as president after promising to step down. The election will be a farce as he has outlawed all the opposition groups, preventing them from putting up any candidates. It is no secret the Americanos use him as their puppet. There were protests, of course ... first coming from the university. So at Machado's insistence the university council has formed disciplinary tribunals. I have been expelled and my position as head of the student union is untenable. They have also expelled Julio Mella and outlawed the Communist Party. And now there has been an attempt on Mella's life. We have managed to get him out of Cuba and he is on his way to Mexico."

Miguel was startled. "But Mella is a member of the Communist Party. You are not with them."

"Miguel, we are all in this together. I am a socialist and want a democratic solution, but I will work with the Communists, I will work with the radicals ... I will work with you against American imperialism. What is the saying: 'The enemy of my enemy is my friend'? In any case we need each other now more than ever because Machado has become more brazen in imposing his agenda. This raid of yours was a success of sorts, Maria. But what did you imagine its consequences would be? In the old way of things, perhaps it would have signaled a small victory. A vindication of sorts. But as I have said, these are dangerous times. The newspaper that published the article about your raid has been closed, its offices vandalized and destroyed. The publisher and editor have been arrested. And unfortunately ... I have to tell you ... they have since disappeared. We need information now more than ever on every step Machado takes. Your brother is in a unique position to help right now. He has agreed to accept the Americanos' offer to manage the business affairs of your old plantation. We will set up a shell company in his name. It will give us a secret base and an insight into—"

Maria exploded. "The Americanos offered you this, Miguel? You accepted? An offer to suck on their tit while they fucked you?"

Miguel held his hands up in fatigue and resignation. Maria rose to her feet in a fury. Guiteres grabbed her by the arms in a fierce grip and forced her sit back down.

As he spoke to her his voice turned to hot steel.

"Listen to me now and listen carefully. This is no schoolyard, yet you act like a child. You take a few baby steps and imagine yourself to be running with wolves. This stunt you pulled at the rail yard. Your quote to the papers: 'It is a demonstration of nonviolence.' 'No one was hurt!' What do you imagine Machado will do to those soldiers who have embarrassed him? What will happen to their families? You make a rag into a flag and have the insolence to brag about your accomplishments in print. What has happened to those courageous souls at the paper, ah? But of course you are safe from any reprisals. Or are you, Maria? Do you not think they are already looking into where the cloth from this flag of yours came from? What the significance of your emblem can tell them? What do you suppose will happen when they find out, ah?"

From across the room Miguel's words cut harshly into the fierce whispers of Maria and Guiteres. "Enough! If you want my help in this, Antonio, you will start by showing respect to my sister!"

Maria felt her head pounding and tried desperately to find the equanimity she needed so badly right now. To escape her feelings somehow. But there was nowhere to turn. And Guiteres was speaking the truth. She squeezed her eyes shut as hard as she could, but the hot tears found their way out in spite of her efforts. She felt as if she might collapse. Summoning all she had in her, she focused on her breathing and her racing heart.

Guiteres turned away from her, rubbing his face with his hands in exasperation. An ugly and heavy silence descended on the room.

Maria was the first to gain control and speak. She had found the infusion of ice in her veins that she so badly needed. "He speaks the truth, Miguel. There was no disrespect intended. I have let my heart take control of my head and have endangered the lives of many innocent people. Strong emotion can only blind one to objective truth."

Guiteres examined the words she spoke and looked at her in utter surprise. "I ... don't ..."

"I do not attend a university, Señor Guiteres, but still, I learn."

Antonio Guiteres looked at Maria with new eyes. Older ones. His voice, soft again. "Yes. Certainly. But how do you come by this ... quotation?"

"I have an excellent teacher," she said. After a brief silence, she continued. "You have heard this expression 'go fly a kite.' There is more to it than you know."

Antonio and Maria studied each other for a moment, each of them finding new respect for the other. And infuriatingly for Maria, attraction. Perhaps purely physical. Her sense told her strongly it was time to leave.

"Gentlemen, I'm sure we have much more to discuss, but if you will forgive me, for now I need to ... rest. Miguel, my brother, I apologize. Of course I will support any course of action that will further our cause."

She turned to leave, but on a whim, turned back and plucked a cigar from the box on the table. She lit it slowly and deliberately, taking comfort in her steady hand. Her eyes took aim at both men through the smoke. They met her gaze briefly and then looked down, whether in contrition or embarrassment she could not tell. As she closed the door behind her the two men exchanged a small smile at her last words.

"I have got to get out of this fucking dress!"

CHAPTER FORTY-EIGHT: THE HUNT BEGINS

In over a month Tristan Sedillo had been unable to find any work. Anything at all. He had spent time in two of the villages close to the rail depot but had found nothing unusual to report. Just the same miserable campesinos living out their stupid lives. On Sunday they went to mass to thank a God that was nowhere to be seen in the nothingness of their world.

If only the general had given him some men ... he could have gotten information quickly enough. As he knew well himself, the threat of a beating could loosen a man's tongue. He should have been given a car and a squad of soldiers. But instead he was handed peasant clothing and an old mule. The general insisted he remain invisible. Just another poor campesino looking for work. He was to keep his ears and eyes open and perhaps win the others' trust. But what did Tristan Sedillo need with their trust? He was no longer like them and he would not grovel. And he surely would not go to mass. But the eyes and ears part ... This he could do. And what better place to find out a village secret than at a cantina? What better role for him to play than the town drunk? They would see him as harmless enough and eventually forget he was there. Then perhaps he would hear something. A secret meeting perhaps. Perhaps one of them would flash the sign of the blue diamond. But nothing had happened at all.

Time was running out for Tristan. Only one village remained. The one close to the old Sandoval place. He had hoped it would not be necessary to go there. He might still be recognized. He was badly frightened by the thought of Miguel finding him. Besides, there was probably nothing in this village. But he was terrified of returning to the general with nothing to report. There was no easy way out of this dilemma. He would have to think on this. He threw his sleeping blanket over the old mule and led him down the dirt road leading out of the village. The sky above was gray and threatening. Perhaps he'd get a soaking. He badly needed something to cheer him. Well, there was rum in his saddlebag. He would have a taste to help him decide what to do.

Soon enough, he came to the crossroads where the great highway was under construction. The carretera. It was said when the highway was finished it was to run the entire length of the island. Over seven hundred miles. But for Tristan it came down to taking a single step in one direction or another. Go to the last village and perhaps be found by Sandoval, or go back to the capitol and report to the general that he had found nothing. Neither direction was the right one. Then both directions were the right one. Tristan felt his guts twisting inside him and the cold fear start up again. He let the old mule graze and sat down to finish the rum. After a while he grew warm and his worries did not matter so much anymore. His guts relaxed and he felt better. It was good to take your time in making a decision such as this. He looked out at the peasants toiling away at constructing the great road. His thoughts began to darken again in spite of the rum.

It was the white suit. The white suit had been a mistake, he thought. The general only laughed at the sight of him in it. What had he been thinking? The general knew him for what he was ... a nothing ... a nobody. He should have saved the three hundred dollars. He could have easily found work, perhaps on the highway construction. The government paid good money to its workers, better than at the plantation. And he was still young and strong. The other workers would have looked up to him. He could have become a foreman. A leader of men. A leader instead of ... an informer. He realized that telling the general about the rebels had been a mistake. Every night he was having the same dream ... a dream of facing his own death ... only to wake up just before it happened. Working for the general was a mistake ... So many mistakes and now he had to make another choice. Whatever choice he made, he thought to himself, it would probably be a mistake. A mistake by a nobody. He wished he could be invisible like the general said ... invisible...

Wait!

Perhaps there was a way after all. The general had given him field glasses ... they rested in his saddlebag, unused. After all they weren't of much use to a drunk in a cantina, but what if... what if he were not seen in the village at all, but just looked in from the outskirts. Sandoval would never know he was there —if Sandoval was even there himself. Tristan swallowed the last of the rum and threw the bottle into a drainage ditch. He was feeling much better now. He had a plan. He just needed to fill in details.

How could he find out anything if he could not get close to the people? Well, if there was anything going on, any plans being made; they would be meeting at night, wouldn't they? There were plenty of shadows to hide in. Stay close to the walls of buildings ... he might just overhear something. He would just keep hidden whenever possible, that was all. He would keep his head down, not talk to anyone. Become like he had thought of himself before ... A true nobody. No one would notice him. But still ...What if, after all his subterfuge, he found nothing? The last piece of the plan fell into place and Tristan chuckled to himself. The answer was simple. If he found nothing, he would simply keep on going, far from the capitol. He would disappear. The general was a busy man. A nobody like Tristan would soon be forgotten.

Tristan felt much better now. All those bad thoughts were just that. Bad thoughts. And thinking of mistakes? That was a mistake too. There were no mistakes. There was only him. Tristan Sedillo.

He walked over to the old mule, took up the rope, and began leading him down the great road toward the village. A flock of grackles screamed out at Tristan as they scattered from the branches of a nearby tree and swooped into a darkening sky. Low overhead, the thunder rolled.

CHAPTER FORTY-NINE: A BIGGER PICTURE

The morning air was filled with the sound of hammers and saws. Sounds echoing in a cloudless blue sky. If things had gone another way, they could have been cheerful sounds. The hacienda was being rebuilt. But for Maria, it would never again be her home.

She reminded herself she was only here to meet with Miguel and Antonio. What she wanted most was to be back at the encampment. She wanted to strike against the Americanos again, and soon. Standing in this place that no longer belonged to her only fueled her impatience. At last the security watch that had been posted gave the all clear and she made her way inside to one of the finished rooms. It smelled of dampened sawdust.

Miguel and Antonio did not notice her entry. They were studying a pile of papers spread out on a table in front of them. She watched for a time. Occasionally Antonio would move from one set of papers to another.

"Can I play too?" she asked coyly. Both men looked up and smiled.

Antonio spoke first. "Maria, come in, sit." She crossed over to the table and sat down with her eyes on Miguel. Her brother seemed changed somehow. Older. When he spoke, his tone was not so much that of a loving brother to a sister but more like the voice her papa had used when he spoke about the business of the plantation.

"Maria," Miguel said. "Now that we are in this together, we need to move forward in a different way. The three units that were part of our original plan will now be combined into one. But they will continue to operate independently. Antonio will oversee general operations. This will involve many separate groups, including yours. I will be in charge of gathering intelligence. Antonio?"

Antonio took a moment to study Maria and she felt like he was looking right through her. Still she held his gaze and did not blink. Finally he seemed to come to some resolution and spoke. "Maria, I would very much like you to continue to work on this with us. I know of your passion. I know of your ability to rise above it and to see the bigger picture. I know too that you believe in our cause and have agreed to work with us."

He paused for a moment. Maria eyed him warily. His look was very intense.

"What you do not know is the size of the organization you are involved in. If you continue with us, you will see that much more than the Americanos and imperialism are at issue. What is at stake is nothing less than revolution. You will need to decide if you want to go that far. But I will tell you some things you need to know now in order to make a decision. Things that Miguel can verify. Then you can decide. Agreed?"

Maria shifted her gaze to Miguel, who was beginning to feel that the air was becoming very heavy in the room. He tried briefly to lighten the mood. "As long as Antonio doesn't tell you about his great-uncle. I'm not sure anyone could verify ..." The small attempt at a joke died. The air in the room grew heavy again. Miguel looked from Antonio to his sister and nodded. "Listen well, my sister. This business is beyond what you think. It may not be for you. But Antonio speaks the truth."

At this point Antonio took over. "Maria," he began, "I share with you the desire to improve the lives of our people. Not just by taking on the Americanos, but by total revolution. We are committed to the overthrow of Machado's government and believe it will come about sooner rather than later. Our forces now number in the thousands. Made up of workers, intellectuals, and politicians. They grow every day. As I have said before, Machado promised the country he would resign at the end of his term, but instead has banned all elections and become a dictator. Revolution is the only way forward and something I have committed my life to along with many others ... and we have been preparing. Revolution is not just attacking the government with guns and bullets. That has to happen, yes, but what then? What happens when a revolution is successful? We have to have a detailed plan. We have to have policies ready to put into place. We need to have the right people."

Maria's mind was working furiously. This was much bigger than she had thought possible. Could such a thing as a total revolution actually be about to happen? She worked at slowing down her heart. She pointed at the table. "So, these papers? They are about this ... plan, about these ... policies?"

"Yes. The papers list people's names, governing bodies that must be created, what person is best qualified to lead what ministry. What portfolio the ministry should be given."

Maria looked at the papers again, her eyes widening.

"We are creating a provisional government, Maria. And we would like you to play a part in it."

Maria was uncertain now. What did this mean? She rose to her feet. "But what of my unit and the operations we have undertaken? Of Manuel's unit? We have plans to ..."

Antonio shrugged. "It depends on your decision, Maria. We want you to join, but you need to know the risk. You can choose to work independently. We will in no way hinder you, but we will not be able to help you. It may be that you will be able to continue your own operations without actual bloodshed. But if you're caught, you could easily find yourself in prison."

Antonio rose and came around the table, closer to her. His voice was now lower but his tone was more urgent. "If your choice is to work with us, Maria, you may see some of your dreams come true. There will be tremendous sacrifice. And there will be bloodshed. No one is looking forward to it, but sadly it is inevitable. And to be blunt, you must be prepared to give up your life for the cause of the revolution. Are you sure you are willing to go that far? Your brother seems to think you are. But perhaps it would be better and safer to play a smaller role."

Miguel tried to catch his sister's attention, but it was as if he were not even in the room. Maria and Antonio had locked eyes, face-to-face. Miguel knew the look in his sister's eye well. She had been challenged. Before she could speak, he called out suddenly, "Maria!" Reluctantly, almost fiercely, she pulled her gaze from Antonio and glared toward Miguel. "Soldier is in the barn. It has been a while since you've seen him. It might feel good to take him for a ride. You need to think ... and I need to speak with Antonio . . . in private."

There was a brief silence, after which Miguel dropped the sternness in his voice and sounded like her brother again. Maria ... please."

Maria held Miguel's eyes for a level moment then shifted her gaze to Antonio. Both men looked at her expectantly. She turned on her heel and left the room.

CHAPTER FIFTY: HEARTS AND MINDS

Minutes later, Maria had already mounted Soldier. She bolted from the barn at a gallop, intending to return to the encampment. The speed and the wind suited her thoughts. Antonio infuriated her. No, that was not right. She was attracted to him, a little in awe of him. That is what makes me so angry, she thought. She brought Soldier back down to a walk, and her thoughts slowed with him as she turned the stallion toward the sea and what used to be her special place. She had a decision to make and this time she had a choice. So much of her life had been determined by things that were out of her control. It was time to change that. But what were her choices? Her people were working at the hacienda right now because there were no machines. Was this not a good thing? But Antonio had been right about her foolishness at in thinking this could be done without violence. Her mind kept going back to the papers on the table.

She reached the sea and dismounted, walking Soldier along the shore. How could she torture herself on such a beautiful day as this? The gulls wheeled overhead in a bright blue sky as if they were calling to her. She stopped to look up at them. She cleared her mind and concentrated on her breathing. She leaned her head onto Soldier's neck and felt the living strength of him.

The horse gave her comfort. Perhaps he even understood what

she was feeling. It was good to have someone understand. It helped in a way that ... Suddenly Maria stood away from the horse and looked up at him. It was as if the horse had somehow passed on an idea to her. "Come with me now. Let us go and see Wilfredo."

She found the old man tending to his little garden at the back of his house. As always, he seemed to know she was there before she said anything. As she rounded the corner that led to the little house she could see he had his back to her and was busy digging. But still he knew; though he continued his digging, she knew that he felt her arrival.

"What brings you here today, child? I thought you had no more time for lessons."

Maria was annoyed that he still called her child. If anyone else had tried to address her in such a fashion, she would have given them a kick in the proper place to remind them. As it was, she felt a touch ashamed of herself, letting herself be annoyed by such a small thing. She tried to cover her embarrassment.

"It seems you have eyes in the back of your head, old man."

Wilfredo rose to his feet, but it took him a while to straighten up. Even then he did not look at her, but at his garden and then to the sky. "The beans are doing well. They will make a good crop this year. Yet the grapes have no sweetness in them. I suppose that is the way of things. Everything has its own time."

He turned and studied Maria for a moment. "I will fetch the kite."

"Wilfredo, the kite is not necessary. It is a distraction. I have questions that—"

"Questions are good. Let me ask one of you. Do you think flying the kite is for your benefit alone?"

Maria understood. She smiled in apology. "I will be quiet

now."

Wilfredo returned her smile and went into his house to get the kite.

Only later, when she had practiced her breathing, when they were in the field and both had studied the path of the kite for a time, did Maria speak. "I often feel like this kite, Wilfredo. Always I am at the mercy of the wind. And often the wind is more cruel than merciful."

Wilfredo remained silent.

"I think of things, Wilfredo. I want to help my people. I have tried to do this in a small way, without hurting anyone. I am angry because I know in the end my work will amount to nothing. It will take something much bigger to bring about change. Bigger and much more violent. But, Wilfredo, I cannot kill. I will not kill. Yet still the desire for change burns within me."

"These things you think about ... do you trust them to be true? Do you think of them with your head, or do you feel them in your heart?"

"They are true. They have made my heart beat for as long as I can remember. But I also think of them every day in my head."

"You speak of helping your people in a small way. Do you not think this has value? It is not always possible to—"

"But it *is* possible! There is a revolution coming. I have been given a chance to be a part of it! It is the bigger thing I spoke about. It will succeed."

Wilfredo's eyebrows went up. He was silent for a moment. "I see ... but still you are troubled?"

"There will be violence. There will be killing. If I choose to join the revolution, I must make a commitment to it. I must be a part of it."

"I can see the difficulty such a choice would present to you. It puts one side of you against the other. But let me ask you something else. Do you not see any other way?"

"It has been made very clear to me," Maria said. "There is only one way."

"This clarity you speak of sounds like it came from someone else. I'm sure that someone believes there is only one way. But do you believe this to be true? Again I ask you: Do you think it with your head? Do you feel it in your heart?"

"I am afraid of it in my heart. In my head I think . . ."

Maria's eyes suddenly widened in surprise, as if some truth had been revealed to her. She let go of the kite string and Wilfredo had to make a grab for it. When her thoughts returned to earth, her face was lit up with happiness. She rushed over and gave Wilfredo a big hug and a sudden kiss on the cheek.

"I love you, old man. I don't know why I do not listen to you more. Perhaps it is because you say so little."

Maria smiled up at him. "I must go now. I ... Wilfredo, you are blushing!"

Wilfredo did his best to assume a stern face. "I do not blush. I am an old man."

Maria laughed to see him so flustered. "Old man ...? Do you think that in your head, Wilfredo, or do you feel it in your heart?"

As he watched her gallop off, he gave a slight wave of his hand and felt a great peace in his heart.

CHAPTER FIFTY-ONE: SUNDAY COFFEE

Early on a Sunday morning the general's staff car pulled up outside the corner café bordering the capitol square in downtown Havana. His guards checked the perimeter. Traffic was light, and as for street life, only the usual. A scattering of peasants in filthy clothing moved about the freshly renovated square like lost turtles. A few pulled old wooden carts, some slumped on benches. Others shuffled about with their heads down. They looked strangely out of place among all the newly sculpted concrete and marble. A distant church bell called stragglers into mass.

The all clear was given with silent nods, then the rear door was opened and the general stepped out into the blinding sunlight. He chose an outside table to take advantage of the slight breeze. He ordered an espresso and a small portion of helado for his sweet tooth. The morning newspaper was brought to him and he felt satisfied. There was an article on the president's optimism about the country's future. Another item on an American actress due to visit. A bit of troublesome news on the economy but that had become universal of late. Not a scrap of anti-government garbage, though. It showed what could be accomplished when a little pressure was brought to bear in the right places. He felt a shadow fall over him and looked up. Jimenez, the head of his special force, la Porra, stood at military attention before him, his arm crooked in stiff salute.

"Your punctuality is much appreciated, Jimenez. Please join me. Let us share some coffee together. I wish this meeting to be informal. You must try the ice cream. It is delicious."

"Thank you, comandante. I consider time spent with you to be an honor."

A nervous-looking waiter appeared and more coffee was ordered. There was the hasty sound of scraping chairs and the few remaining patrons in the café rose to leave.

A silence grew between the two men and nothing further was said until the coffee was set in front of them and the waiter had disappeared.

"Look around you, Jimenez," the general said. "Tell me what you see."

Jimenez dutifully scanned the square. Perhaps there was a threat in the vicinity? He could not see one and the general's mood was jovial. Expansive even. He was at a loss.

"Is there something in particular, comandante? What should I look for?"

"Progress, Jimenez," the general replied. "Progress. Feast your eyes on the new capitol building. The central square. There are beautiful sculptures in the park. We are making great strides, do you not think so?"

"Sí, my comandante. It is true. There have been many accomplishments."

"Yes, of course it is true. And not just in the capital itself. There is the carretera. Over seven hundred miles of new highway. And an airport! It is said we are creating the Switzerland of the Americas."

Jimenez looked about him with dutiful reverence. "Sí, it is very wonderful."

"Yet every day we are forced to look upon the ignorance of our citizens. All this fresh white concrete and marble is wasted on them. They are blind and stupid as to what is growing before them. Still, one must realize they are also necessary. They provide us with—what is the expression? Yes. They are properly termed a 'human resource.'"

Jimenez remained silent, wondering where all this was leading.

"What is troublesome, however," the general continued, "is that there are those who would see all this progress come to an end. They have different ideas on resource management. The communistas. The socialists. This new group, what do they call themselves?"

Jimenez was relieved to be on familiar ground now. "They call themselves the ABC, commandante. The abecedario. Their leader is unknown, but Antonio Guiteres' name has surfaced as a possibility. As to the group itself, we are not sure of their agenda as yet or the significance of the letters in the name. We are investigating."

The general waved his hand dismissively. "The significance of the letters is of no importance to me. The leaders of these various groups—it is they who must be dealt with. You see our citizens out there? They are dull and plodding. Easily led. I do not mind when they go to mass. The priests are impotent and have the proper amount of fear in them. Let them prattle on. But the leaders of those who oppose us must be silenced. We will begin with Julio Mella."

"Mella, the Communist? But, comandante, he is not even in the country. There was an attempt to silence him while he was in Havana, but he managed to escape to Mexico. We believe he is no longer a threat. Of course we are tracking down those who might have helped him."

The general regarded Jimenez for a moment. "No longer a threat, you say?"

There was a brief but uneasy silence. Two or three grackles flew down, alighted on the table, and began pecking at crumbs. The general studied the birds for a moment, seeming almost amused. Then suddenly, with a bang he pounded on the table, causing the birds to take flight. Moments later, they perched on a nearby branch and began cawing raucously at the two men as if scolding them.

"Where in Mexico?" the general demanded.

"Comandante?"

"Where in Mexico is Julio Mella?"

"We believe him to be in Mexico City, comandante."

The general looked up to the grackles and made kissing noises at them. The birds still scolded the men from the safety of their branch.

"These birds can be such a nuisance, don't you agree, Jimenez?"

"Comandante?"

"They brazenly come to our table, jabbering away, and take what is not theirs. The minute you try to stop them, they fly off; but as you can see, Jimenez, never too far away. And just listen to them scold us. No matter how agreeable you try to be with them, their insolence knows no bounds. And here is something else. You know as I know, the minute we are not looking, they will be back."

Jimenez began nodding. He now understood why the meeting had been called.

"Go to Mexico City. Find Mella. Make sure he does not come back."

“Sí, comandante.”

“Then we will see about this other one. What was his name?”

“Guiteres, comandante. Antonio Guiteres.”

CHAPTER FIFTY-TWO: A SEAT AT THE TABLE

It was that magical time of day when sounds become less connected to and grow closer to nature. The softening light hushes them somehow; they begin to drop away one by one and the gentle, patient murmurings of the night begin. The song of crickets serenaded Maria as she walked Soldier to the barn. She led him to his stall and removed his saddle, bit, and blanket. She saw to it he had a fresh bed of straw and plenty of hay. She brushed him until he shone and spoke lovingly to him. In the soft golden light of the lantern, she prepared a warm bran mash for his supper. She smiled as she heard him nicker softly. After she had seen to his needs, she turned down the lantern and, steeling herself for what was to come, made her way to the hacienda. Horses were so much easier to deal with than men.

Miguel looked relieved to see her. "We were beginning to worry."

The papers were gone from the big table. In their place lay dirty dishes, an empty wine bottle, and an overfilled ashtray. Miguel was clearing them away. "Are you hungry? We have tortillas, corn, and some wine ... I am not used to this cooking business, but still ..."

Maria shook her head, her gaze traveling across the room to where Antonio was busying himself at a smaller table, cleaning and assembling a pistol. He did not look up.

"Antonio, these words are for you. Miguel, my brother, do me the courtesy of letting me say what I have come to say."

Antonio looked up at Maria and their eyes locked.

"Antonio, I have given thought to what you have said. You want a decision. You will have it. And with it comes a proposition.

"You say if I do not join with you, I cannot be a part of this revolution. You say if I remain independent, you cannot help me. This may be true. But perhaps I can help you anyway." She paused, then continued: "My decision is to remain independent. I will not answer to you. But I will work with you. We share some ideas and differ on others. I am prepared to give up my life, but I will not take anyone else's. That is my commitment. And if I work with you, there will be a price." Again she paused.

Antonio waited for her to go on, but instead Maria fell silent and looked to him, expectantly. When Antonio spoke, his voice was steely. "So now you think you can dictate to me —"Maria shook her head. "One dictator at a time is enough, don't you think? No, I believe I said that I had a proposition, not an edict."

Antonio reflected on this. He looked to Miguel, but Miguel would not meet his eyes. It seemed to him that there was more to this woman than he'd thought. He was on the defensive and didn't care much for the feeling. Still, he had to admit, it was mixed with a grudging admiration. He glared at her. "Go on ... I am listening ..."

"What if you did not have to take power?" she asked. "What if power was simply handed to you?"

Antonio sighed with exasperation. "Maria, I have no time for games. If you have something to say, Say it!"

"I have an idea I will share with you. But first the price must be discussed. If you believe this idea will work, if it is put into effect, you agree to let me have a seat at the table. To share what is written on the papers. To include me in this bigger picture of yours."

Antonio nodded. "If your idea is that good, I would be a fool not to give you a seat at the table. I am not in this to feed my ego, Maria, no matter what you may think."

A moment of truth was shared between them. They had come to an understanding. And finally, an easing of tension.

Maria spoke in even tones. "In order for you to be given power, Machado's hold on power must be taken away, no? And your plan is to fight him. And perhaps you have the people on your side. But he has the army on his, so the struggle will be a long and bloody one. Agreed?"

Antonio nodded almost imperceptibly.

"What if this struggle could be shortened considerably?" Maria asked. "If we could gain the upper hand quickly? I believe it is possible. Answer this question for me. How does Machado hold on to his power when there are others much more powerful than he is?"

"You mean the Americanos? But what—"

"The Americanos use Machado as their guard dog. He protects their interests. He keeps them feeling safe and secure. So what would happen if the Americanos did not feel so safe or secure?"

"Then they would unleash the guard dog," Antonio said. "There would be more killing. Maria, I do not see—"

Maria interrupted him. "But what if there were no enemy for the guard dog to attack? What if the enemy was seen to be Machado himself? A guard dog with no teeth? A guard dog that chased his own tail? The Americanos would dispose of him like a used tissue. That is, if there was a suitable alternative. A group such as ours that perhaps had in place a provisional government."

Antonio listened intently. And Miguel was now drawn in like a moth to a flame.

"Sister, what you say makes sense. But you talk with questions. How could what you suggest be done with Machado?"

"By making him look ridiculous. By having the people laugh at him. Listen to me. We draw a cartoon of him. Like the political ones you see in newspapers. We put it on leaflets. We fly an airplane over the Americano plantations and drop these leaflets. Thousands of them. For the people to see. For the Americanos to see. No one is killed. No property is damaged. No enemy is found. I do not say it wins the war. But it will win us the first battle. And the dog starts chasing its tail."

There was a silence. Antonio looked over at Miguel, then back at Maria. "Such a plan could work. I am not saying it wouldn't. But even if we could get the details of such a plan in place, it would cost a very large amount of money. Miguel?"

"I can provide some money but . . . no. Certainly not that kind of money."

Maria smiled. "I think I see a way the Americanos could pay for it."

Both men looked at her in stunned surprise.

"This Americano William Merrick, he is coming here soon, Miguel?"

Miguel was hesitant. "He comes to Cuba next week, but not here. He goes to Santiago."

"Even better, and much less likely to arouse suspicions. My unit will meet him there. We will take Mr. Merrick on a vacation to the hills. Tourism is so much better when you are among the people, no? I'm certain the Americanos will be glad to pay for his safe return."

Antonio couldn't help himself and broke into laughter. "Yes, Maria, I'm sure they will."

He rose, crossed over to the big table, and pulled out one of the chairs. He gestured to Maria. "Would this chair suit you? I'll get those papers you wanted to see. We have work to do."

CHAPTER FIFTY-THREE: THE BROTHERS

Group two, Manuel's unit, had done its job well. Through hard work and a judicious donation of small gifts, they had gained the loyalty of everyone in the village. Any government soldiers passing through were viewed with fear and mistrust. Soon it would be time to move on to the next village. But Manuel was in no hurry. He had found a good woman, one who did not have so much fire inside her, and life was good.

Just as the passage of only a few days can change winter into spring, a few days can radically change a man's thinking. The seven others in Manuel's group, as well as Manuel himself, had always referred to themselves as rebels. Now they were known among the villagers simply as the brothers. There was mystery to their doings at first. The men did not stay or live in the village. They camped outside. But every morning they would come in. They spent the days helping the villagers, whether by picking fruit or thatching a roof. In the beginning there was talk of an upcoming revolution, but the needs of a village seldom permit much time for discussion or politics. So the brothers were kept busy laying water pipe or fixing the school bell.

Miguel had seen to it that they were supplied with uniforms and guns as they became available. These were kept at their camp, where there were to be daily drills and simulated maneuvers. Manuel saw to it that this practice was carried out—at first. But then, somehow, the drills became every other day and then only once in a while. It was not that the brothers were lazy, but somehow it felt more useful to be mending fishing nets or fixing a broken axle on a wood cart. The requests that came Miguel's way now were not for ammunition or mess kits but for woodworking tools and a new pulley for the well.

In the early morning light, when the roosters were busy with their duties, the women would be down at the river washing clothes. They would look up to see the brothers coming into the village, not stiffly marching in formation but laughing and jostling each other as they went along. There was a feeling of camaraderie among them. They always sat together at mass. Manuel saw to it that they all stuck together. It was just that now they were finding it harder to remember what they were sticking together for. And just lately Manuel had been spending one or two nights every week away from camp. There was a woman who gave him comfort and peace . . . it was hard to resist.

And so, with the brothers' help, life had become easier in the village. Everyone seemed to sense it. It was becoming a special time. The weather was not too hot or too cold. The breezes were gentle and cool. There would be a fine crop of fresh corn soon. Because the burden was lighter, there were fewer squabbles. More laughter was heard. Many prayers of thanks were offered, yet it did not seem enough somehow. The villagers needed to celebrate their good fortune together somehow. And so it was that they decided to stage a festival.

The planning of it kept them busier than ever. In the center of the village square a huge pole was erected and paper streamers strung from the top of it to nearby rooftops. Strings of little electric lights, until then used only at Christmas, were dusted off and made ready for the celebration. A huge field tent used for shelter during the harvest was brought out and put up in the square. Colorful piñatas were constructed from paper and flour paste and stuffed with candies. The women worked together to bake special treats: churros, empanadas, and little cakes. The brothers helped bring in a wonderful fruit crop: mangoes, bananas, limes, papaya, and melon. Meat from coconuts was put through a press and a sweet cream was made from it to use in puddings. The children ran about excitedly through all of this preparing, playing a game. They would each try to get a finger in the icing bowl. The winner was the one who could get a taste without being hit with a spoon.

Soon all was in readiness. The men wrapped colorful sashes around their waists. The women wore their best dresses and put flowers in their hair. All the little ones were scrubbed up and dressed in white. It was time to go to the square. All good festivals should start with a procession and this one was no exception. Leading the procession was Eduardo the juggler. Behind him came two townsfolk holding a banner that read *The Festival of Good Times*. Then came the wood cart piled high with fruit and a big steel kettle that held punch. Following that, Fernando and his dancing horse. He blew steadily on a bugle but the sound was terrible, for Fernando had never learned how to play it properly. The rest of the townsfolk followed him,[BH1] walking four abreast, talking and laughing. The children and dogs ran alongside them.

Once they had arrived at the square, the women began to put out the food and the men unloaded the cart with the big kettle. Soon enough all was arranged. The festival began as most celebrations do, demurely at first, then growing bolder.

One of the brothers brought out a guitar and began to play. Another brought out his harmonica and joined in. An old man in the gathering crowd saw them and went to get his violin. The top was taken off the big kettle and punch was ladled out. The music was not playing long before the singing started. And once the volume of the singing grew loud enough, the dancing began. A few of the children laughed in excitement as they darted about the dancers, playing tag. Some children rode on their fathers' shoulders. A whole group of children gathered in a corner to hear Wilfredo read to them about a giant and a beanstalk. Everywhere there was music and laughter. As daylight faded into darkness the electric lights came on and the color and splendor of it all was something to behold. The celebrations went long into the night.

By and by, the melodies of the guitars grew gentle and softer. A little boy climbed onto his mother's lap and yawned. An old man nodded off and began to snore softly, all the while still holding on to his glass.

And on a hilltop above the village, Tristan Sedillo put down his field glasses and wept.

CHAPTER FIFTY-FOUR: FRIENDS

Maria and Miguel ate a breakfast of eggs and sausage in the hacienda's new kitchen. Maria thought it looked nothing like the old kitchen. Perhaps it was just as well. The memories of this place were many, but somehow they all ended the same way. She found it hard to understand how Miguel could live here. Just being in the kitchen brought back old pictures in her mind. The old cook stove where she had made her first disastrous efforts to learn how to cook. Well, perhaps "cook" was not the right word. The thought made her smile. Miguel had seen to breakfast. He would not even let her help, saying just having her in the kitchen made him fear for his life.

She watched him fix their breakfast with curiosity. The wood stove had now been replaced by an electric range with cooking rings that became red-hot when a switch was turned. The icebox was also a thing of the past. They called it a refrigerator now and it made too much noise for Maria's liking. Still it was one of the newest inventions. The Americanos had certainly spared no expense. After they had finished their meal Miguel took a last sip of coffee and rose from the table.

"I am going to the village. I have train tickets to Santiago for Manuel and the group. They will make sure the locals there will look with favor on your upcoming little enterprise."

Just then, Antonio came into the kitchen, sleepy-eyed. "Am I late for breakfast?"

Miguel shrugged him off. "Too bad for you. I am going to the village."

"You are no good in the kitchen anyway, Miguel. I mean you no offense, but now we have a woman to cook for us. Maria, cook me some eggs. My stomach feels as though my throat has been cut."

Miguel looked over at his sister and saw the thunder clouds gathering on her brow. Antonio had his back turned and did not notice. Miguel's smile turned into a grin of mischief.

"If you eat what Maria cooks for you, a cut throat will seem like a minor injury. Adios!" And with that, he was out the door. Antonio did not look at Maria but shuffled over to the table, rubbing the sleep from his eyes.

Maria crossed to the counter and frowned down at the eggs. "How many eggs do you want?"

"Ah?"

"How many eggs do you want ... one or two?"

"Three. I will have three. I am starving. Just hurry up, will you?"

"Antonio . . . ?"

"What is it now? How hard can it be to . . ." He turned to face her, feeling somewhat exasperated.

Maria's aim was excellent. The first egg burst squarely on Antonio's forehead and began to run down his face. As he lifted his hands to wipe it out of his eyes, he felt a second egg burst on his chest. As he turned in panic and began to run out of the kitchen the third egg exploded on the back of his head.

"Perhaps it is better you asked for three. They say that breakfast is the most important meal of the day!"

They did not speak to each other again until late that afternoon. Even then a restless tension ran like a hot wire between them. But there were things that had to be discussed. They sat across from each other at the big table, going over the papers concerning the provisional government and its policies.

It was Maria who broke the silence. "You are certain about all these people? That they are the right ones?"

"Maria, these are not my decisions alone. Ramon Grau. He is the one who will lead us. Some of these others, including myself, are from the student directorate. I know them to be good people. They have my complete trust. There are others I oppose, such as Batista. He is more right-wing, but we need him, as he has the support of the military."

Maria's eyes opened wider at this. "You would allow this right-wing person Batista into the government?" she asked incredulously.

"It is not ideal, Maria. But we will work with the consent of the people, unlike Machado, who just takes what he wants. So there must be left-wing and right-wing: it will take both to fly."

"So this Grau, he will listen to you about Batista?"

'Batista is a military man. He has no head for politics or policy. Ramon Grau knows this. And he will support our ideas, Maria. Listen to me; I know of your passion for getting women the vote. Just as I know of my passion for the eight-hour workday and Miguel's passion for student rights. Together we can bring them into reality. And think of all we have worked on together during the past few days. A minimum wage, independence from the Americanos, and the redistribution of land. It will all be possible. It must be made possible. We are so close!"

Antonio fought to control his voice and his agitation. He rose from the table, crossed to the window, and looked out. Maria sensed the rising emotion in him. She wanted to reach out.

"My brother and myself, I know where our passion comes

from. It has lived with us a long time. But yours ... where does yours come from Antonio?"

Antonio felt something ease in his belly as he listened to her words, and he gave a brief laugh. "You might say it lived before me. My grandfather fought in the Mexican revolution; my great-uncle John Walsh fought with the Fenians for Irish independence from England. The tales he told of Ireland, ah . . . ? So it may be that I inherited this passion that I was born to be a revolutionary.

Maria felt a deep chord strike within her. "Ireland?"

Antonio looked over at her. "Yes, why? What is it?"

Maria thought of the song. Kate's song. She tried to sing a few words, but the music evoked a state of impossibly loneliness and the words to the song would not come out. Instead she studied Antonio for a moment, then looked away.

"It is nothing. Only that Mama came from ... Ireland. She spoke about what she called the troubles. Little bits of the story. That's all she would tell."

"I could tell you all of it. But, excuse me for saying so, Maria, and I must be delicate here. Miguel looks a little like his mother. If you squint a little, he could even pass for an Irishman. But you ..."

Maria's heart had been so filled with memories of Kate. And now it quickly sank and she felt forlorn, like a piece of driftwood on a shore. Her voice turned cold. "Kate was not my real mother. I do not remember my real mother. She was killed in the . . . in the ..." She wiped furiously at her eyes. "I was there. Where your grandfather was. Fighting. In Mexico. The revolution. An old man saved me, took me away from the killing ... I don't even remember much of it now, I ...."

She was having trouble going on. She sensed Antonio moving closer to her. She didn't want him to. She didn't need his pity.

She didn't want to cry anymore. She wouldn't cry anymore. She regarded Antonio frankly.

"So now I am here. Kate was the only mother I ever knew. And now she is gone. And I am still here. Do you know what the workers used to call me? Do you know?"

She glared fiercely at Antonio but he did not react as she expected. There was no pity on his face. He met her eyes directly and with steadiness. She faltered for a minute. "The girl who came from the sea. That is what they called me. And so perhaps that is what I am. And all that I am. The girl who came from the sea."

"Maria, you are much more than that." He reached for her. To hold her. To comfort her. But it turned into more. It turned into want. It turned into need, for both of them. Desire coming more from desperation than from anything else. They tore at each other's clothing and fell to the floor as one. Their coupling was sudden, fierce, and brief.

Afterward there was nothing to say. They avoided eye contact. There had been no wrong or right about it. But both knew it would not happen again. The tension between them was gone, leaving only traces of sadness. They dressed in silence. Antonio crossed over to the table and sat with his back to her, busying himself with the papers. Maria looked through the window, seeing nothing. After some time had passed, she spoke over her shoulder toward Antonio's back.

"Will we remain friends?"

Antonio did not turn to face her. She turned back toward the window. After a moment he

answered, his voice soft. "Yes, Maria, we will remain friends. I would like that very much."

Miguel arrived a little later. He was not in a good humor. "What is this?" he demanded. "Not a single smell of cooking coming from the kitchen? I have been the one who has worked all day. I suppose I must do all the cooking too? You do not know what kind of day it has been." He looked reproachfully from one of them to the other.

"You know," he went on, "one of you could have made something. Or the other one. Or what about both? The two of you cannot seem to get together on anything." He strode angrily into the kitchen. What made him even angrier was he could have sworn he heard them laughing behind him.

CHAPTER FIFTY-FIVE: THERE IS ALWAYS A CHOICE

Tristan Sedillo opened one eye. The other he couldn't get open, for some reason. And there was pain. He lay still so the pain would not be so great. Consciousness came slowly and he had to fight to clear the fog. When, finally, he was fully aware, his first thought was that he might be in danger. It dawned on him that someone might see him in this state. He mustn't be seen!

Fear gives a man energy and Tristan sat up quickly. A thousand firecrackers exploded at once inside his head and he desperately wanted to lie down again. But he had to make sure he was safe. He looked around him with his one good eye. He was safe. He was at his camp on the hill. An empty rum bottle lay a foot or so away. He touched his head tenderly, the way a mother might touch a hurt child. He found caked blood. Then the memory found him. He had done this to himself. He had smashed himself in the face with the bottle again and again. He had been watching the village. There was a party. A festival. He felt sad because he couldn't be part of it. No one would invite him. Not him. No one would ever invite him to anything ever again. He couldn't be a normal person. He couldn't be around laughing children. And he had done this to himself. And then he had grown angry. He had made it so he could never go back. Never. And then he hit himself with the bottle. Because he was stupid, stupid, STUPID.

Well, it's done, he thought. He looked about him for the burro. The animal was tied to a nearby banyan tree. At least he had shown some sense in doing that. "I take care of you, don't I, Cha," he told the burro, then winced to hear the sound of his own voice. It sounded like a rusty hinge. He patted the burro and remembered a happier time. The day he had been talking to the burro and thought to name him Cha-Cha. Because he was so slow. His little joke. But no one was laughing and he was talking to a burro because there was no one else to talk to. No one to share his joke with. "I am a lonely, stupid little man, Cha."

As he began to lead the burro down the hill, he thought he would report to the general. About the brothers. The ones who came into the village every day and disappeared every night. He recognized one of them as Manuel from the Sandoval place. Some of them wore parts of military uniforms. That should be of interest to the general. The rest was a mystery to him. Where they came from. Why there were eight of them. Why they were always together. Nothing else seemed at all suspicious. The activity in the village was dull and normal. The women: washing clothing and pounding out tortillas, the men fishing and working in the fields, the children playing their games and flying kites.

Perhaps this information would not satisfy the general. A few pieces of military clothing? What of that? What then? If the general decided he was of no use, he might be imprisoned or worse. The general would not want him talking about what he had been doing. He would surely be killed unless ... What if he reverted to his escape plan? Just keep going as far from Havana as he could get. The general was a busy man. And the general had already called him pitiful and that other word ... insignificant. It meant of no importance. Perhaps if he got far enough away, he could find a village where he could hide. He would grow a beard. Then, after a time, he would be safe. Forgotten. Just a wandering campesino looking for work. And he could fit inside the village. He would go to mass. He would be kind and make friends. He would work hard. He could start again. Maybe even have a family. "And then, Cha, we would no longer be lonely," he told the burro. "Who says you can't go back ah? You see, Cha-Cha? There is always a choice."

Having come to his decision, he turned and led the burro in the other direction as he made his way down the hill. Away from the way he had come. Away from his past. Away from the general. He would stay off the path. It would be slow going but that wouldn't matter. He was good with his machete and could clear a path for himself. And it was important to keep out of sight. His mouth was dry. He would have to find water soon. The pain in his head would not stop, but the thought of a new life burned brightly in him and made it easier to bear. He would use the sun to find his way.

Tristan hadn't gone far in the dense undergrowth when he stumbled upon a small clearing. Five huts in a circle. He immediately squatted down to avoid being seen, then turned to the burro, looked up at him, and put a finger to his lips. He led the animal away from the circle and tied him a few yards away. He returned to his hiding spot and waited. Not a sound. Just a few birds. The place seemed to be deserted. After observing a long time, Tristan cautiously made his way toward the nearest hut and peeked in. Two sleeping mats and nothing else. Looking all around him for the slightest sound or movement, he edged along the circle to the next hut and looked in. He saw old blankets. But there was something underneath them. When he pulled back the blankets his mouth fell open in surprise. Guns! Rifles, pistols, grenades! They were all laid out neatly. Under another blanket he found boxes of ammunition. Under yet another a few military uniforms and ... money! He covered it all back up and left everything just the way he had found it ... except for the money. That, Tristan took. Then, with his heart pounding, he edged along to the other huts. They were all empty except for sleeping mats. He left the circle, untied the burro, and then, moving as silently as possible, put as much distance as he could between himself and the encampment.

It wasn't until later that Tristan put it all together. Eight men coming and going from the village. Every day. From where? Now he knew. Eight sleeping mats. This put things in a new light. The general would be very happy to get this information. For the second straight time Tristan would have weeded out and identified rebels for the general. Once, perhaps, was lucky, but twice?

"He will have to take notice of me now, won't he, Cha? He will no longer be able to say I am ... this word ... insignificant. Perhaps he will even let me lead the charge. Give me a jeep and some men ... no offense to you, Cha, but I could not lead such charge on a burro. You know, Cha, I should not have been so hard on myself. Tristan Sedillo always finds a way. Always. Look at the facts. I have critical information, a generous amount of pesos in my pocket, and there is a cantina just up the road from here where we can celebrate with some rum.

"Our troubles are behind us now, Cha," he said in conclusion. "Our troubles are over."

CHAPTER FIFTY-SIX: FROM A KING TO A PAWN

William Merrick dined at the hotel on stone-crab bisque. It was excellent. He was feeling quite satisfied with himself. The business in Santiago de Cuba was complete, gift-wrapped with success. The harvesters for the eastern operation had arrived without incident and had been put to work immediately. Management had beefed up security as instructed. He had to admit he found the sight of guards armed with machine guns to be a bit intimidating, but at least they guaranteed that there would be no trouble from the locals.

Maybe the incident to the west of Havana was an isolated occurrence after all. But the damned flag, this blue diamond business, the whole thing stank of some kind of pinko plot. That fucking Machado had better get things under control ... Merrick's thoughts shifted. Now, now, Billy boy, remember your blood pressure. After all, it's a beautiful afternoon; a little leisure time is in order. Tonight, the dinner with Bacardi on his yacht. Now, there was a stand-up guy for you. He'd taken his whole booze business international in the past two years, so, of course, the yacht was one big fat tax write-off. But what the hell, more power to him. Anyway, he decided it was time to cool off with a swim.

A couple approached him as he was signing his bill. A youngish man with a camera and a young woman. A very attractive young woman.

"Señor Merrick? William Merrick?" the woman asked.

"That's right."

"My name is Marissa Sanchez. I am secretary to the mayor. And this is Felipe Ortega. Could we take a moment of your time?"

"Not really convenient, sweetheart. I have—"

"But, Señor Merrick, we will make it worth your while. It will only take a moment. Please."

Merrick took his time looking her up and down. Low-cut blouse. He liked what he saw. "Okay, okay. You are a doll, aren't you, sweetheart? I'm gonna give you five minutes. Just so I can admire the scenery. Okay, fire away."

The young woman gave him an appreciative look. "Thank you so much, Señor Merrick."

"Call me Bill, honey."

"The mayor ... he asks to have his photograph taken with you. In our city, an election comes soon and he thinks it would be good publicity for him to be seen shaking hands with such an important business person as you. The office is only one block away ..."

"Sorry, doll, can't help you. I'm busy, and besides, United Fruit can't be seen handing out endorsements to political candidates, so if that's all—"

"Please, señor, the mayor, he ... says I must bring you or I am not to come back. My job, señor ..."

"A real asshole, your boss, huh? Goddamn men in this country ... treat women like shit. You say he's gonna make it worth my while? And just how's he propose to do that?"

He saw the girl look down and away from him. Almost as if

she was ashamed. She seemed to have some difficulty answering. "He says I am to make it worth your while, señor. If you ... like what you see."

Merrick looked over at the cameraman, who looked away and tilted his head up toward the ceiling as if he hadn't heard a word. So that was the way it was going to be.

"Well, now that's a horse of a different color ... Okay. Ten minutes. Let's get this over with." Merrick reached over and tilted the girl's chin up. She looked very frightened. "Listen, doll, don't worry, I'm American. I like to do things with a little class. I'll treat you right. We'll give the mayor his photo; you'll keep your job, and then you and me ...? We'll go for a swim, have a few drinks. I'll even take you to a party tonight. Get you loosened up a little ... then? Believe me, you're gonna want it."

The girl smiled a tight smile. She seemed relieved somehow. Maybe she was overcoming her shyness and warming to the idea of being with him.

"We will show you the way, Señor Merrick."

"Now, now. We're gonna be such close friends. You really need to call me Bill," Merrick said

as he followed them out of the hotel and a little way down the avenida. They made a turn and then started down a narrow side street. Something about the street struck Merrick as not quite right.

Then, as if out of nowhere, the camera jumped in close to his face, the flashbulb exploding. He was blind. He felt a gag go into his mouth, felt his hands being tied, heard the girl's voice, a raspy whisper in his ear.

"You and me, Bill? We'll go for a swim, have a few drinks. We just have to get you loosened up first."

There was a sharp hospital smell ... Ether? Then, nothing.

William Merrick was on vacation.

Maria's unit had performed flawlessly in getting Merrick to the encampment. Number seven complimented her on her acting.

"I hope each of you will do as well in your roles when I am gone," he said. "Now, gather around me, the next part of our plan will be revealed to you. Tomorrow I go to Havana. The wire to United Fruit will be sent from there so it will be impossible to trace. Number two, you will be in charge of the encampment while I am gone. The strictest discipline must be observed by everyone and you must see to this. We have reason to believe unit two has been compromised by this very thing. Lack of discipline. As a result, it is not clear if the village below us is friendly to us or hostile. Numbers three and four and five, you will be guarding the Americano in shifts. No harm shall be done to him. Is that clear? He is to be treated with respect. We are soldiers. He is a civilian. He is to be kept as comfortable as possible. Number six, you will position yourself on point as lookout. Work out the shifts to coordinate with the others. Number seven, you have secured warehouse space in the village?"

"Sí, comandante. Very private."

"And the equipment?"

"Darkroom and developer all in place, comandante. I have a source for the paper and printing machine. They can be purchased and brought here as soon as we receive funding."

"Very good, now we will have a little recreation before supper. Number four, did you set up a space for bochas?

"Sí, comandante."

"Good. The Americanos will want proof we really have their gringo. Seven, I want you to photograph him enjoying a game with us. Then I want you to show me how this darkroom of yours works. I will go and talk to Merrick."

Maria walked across the clearing to where Merrick was sitting tied to a pole. She knelt down and removed the hood they had placed over his head. "Well, look who's here! It's Señor Merrick. Did you sleep well, Bill?"

Merrick looked about wild-eyed and panic-stricken. He struggled to move but the ropes held him firmly in place and the gag kept him silent. It took him a moment, but slowly he calmed down and stared incredulously at the woman in front of him. The low-cut blouse and skirt were gone and she was completely clad in military garb.

"Listen to me carefully, Bill," she said. "You are on a little vacation with us. You are in no danger. You will not be harmed in any way as long as you do exactly as you are told. You are our guest here and part of a little business transaction we are doing with your company. We will even take all the restraints away if you promise to be good. But this is the important part, Bill. You will be watched very closely day and night. If you try to escape, we will kill you, do you understand?"

Merrick, wide-eyed, nodded.

"Do you promise to be good?"

Merrick nodded again.

Maria took the gag out of his mouth and began untying him.

Merrick looked at her with new eyes. Strange, she was not being rough with him. This little doll was more like a nurse than a soldier. But he could see others. Some were watching. And they definitely did look like soldiers.

"Jesus, you people ... this place. What *is* this place? Christ, you had me fooled! I can't believe ... you can't believe you'll get away with this. Kidnapping? You'll all be shot. You must know that."

The girl said nothing but began untying his legs while he rubbed his wrists. God, she was almost gentle about it.

Merrick dropped his voice. "Look, a nice girl like you shouldn't be caught up in this kind of thing. I bet they've forced you into it, huh? Listen, you get me out and I'll see to it you go free. I'll tell them what you did, see? Hell, sweetie, I'll even ..." His hand had found her breast. In an instant she grabbed a handful of his crotch in a vise-like grip and squeezed; hard.

"Oh Christ, please, Oh Jesus, no ... let me ... ahhhhh . . ."

Maria held on. "Just to be clear, Bill, no one is forcing anyone to do anything. That is clear, is it not?"

"Yeah, yeah, oh shit, yes, I mean I'm sorry I . . . Ah, please ... *please!*"

Maria took her hand away and rose to her full height. "We are taking a little afternoon recreation, Bill. We would like it if you would join us. But there is no hurry. I can see you are in some discomfort right now."

Merrick's curiosity eventually got the better of him and he made his way over to where the group members were taking turns playing at what looked like a game of horseshoes. And as strange as he felt, within fifteen minutes he was playing right along with them. Under different circumstances, this could have been a lot of fun. And the strangest part of it all was that they were all laughing and joking. They even clapped him on the back when he scored extra points. In the middle of a throw, though, they had taken his picture and his uneasiness returned. He liked the game. Hell, who didn't love a good game? He often thought of life that way. Like a good game of chess. But now it seemed like he was no longer a king. And pawns, he realized, were dispensable.

CHAPTER FIFTY-SEVEN: THE SAD CLOWN

The capitol building struck fear into the heart of Tristan Sedillo. It seemed to him only God could live in such a place as this. His courage failed a little more as he ascended each of the fifty-six steps up to the entrance. He remembered the first time he had climbed these steps. In his white suit. Thinking he belonged here. Thinking himself such a big man.

I don't belong here, he thought. I am a little bug who could be squashed any second. I should turn around. Perhaps no one has seen me yet. The first plan is better. Get yourself far from here. Far from ...

Tristan looked up as he entered the dome-topped edifice as if he were seeking God's help. His breath caught in his chest. The ceiling was impossibly high and ended in ... ended in an eye. An eye that was watching him. He began to tremble. It was too late. He could not go back. The statue in the entrance hall had seen him too. The statue of the woman with a spear and shield ... solid gold and ten times his height. There could be no escape.

Tristan could not look down. He was certain there would be no floor. Dizziness swirled in his head and made the marble columns lean crookedly. He felt his heart pounding and his breath inhaling and exhaling very fast.

A security guard approached him. "What is your business here?" the man demanded. His voice was somehow the anchor Tristan needed to ground himself to the present. He answered somberly, as if he were passing down his own death sentence: "I am to report to the general."

"Speak up. Speak up. You are mumbling."

Death would be better, thought Tristan. Just to be done with everything. He gathered the little courage he had left in him and tried to speak forcefully. "My name is Tristan Sedillo. I am to report to the general. It is important I speak to him immediately."

The guard began to chuckle. "You have been in the sun too long, Machacho. Look at you. Such a sad clown. You are filthy and stink of rum. You ... report to the general? That's funny."

Another guard crossed over to where they were standing. "What's going on?" he demanded.

"This one says his name is Tristan Sedillo. He says he wants to report to the general."

Both guards were laughing openly now. Their encounter with Tristan was proving to be great sport. The second guard gave Tristan a mock salute.

"My apologies, Your Excellency, the general has been called out of the city. But perhaps you can give us your report, ah?"

"The general says I must report only to him. When will he return?"

"Well who can say, Your Excellency? The general does not favor us with his timetable. But are you sure you won't report to us? We would love to hear what you have to say."

Tristan's feeling of dread had now been replaced by a sense of panic. They were making a joke out of him. If he failed in this

...

"You must understand. Please. Time is very important. The general must hear what I have to say very soon or he will be very angry. Not just with me but with you ..."

The two guards exchanged looks that said this man is crazy or drunk or both. Still, the matter would have to cross the general's desk on his return. It was probably nothing. Still, one must be cautious.

The second guard spoke to Tristan in mock reverence. "This information sounds to be of vital importance. We will take steps to keep Your Excellency safe until the general's return. Please, come with us and we will show you to your rooms."

Ten minutes later Tristan was thrown into a cell and the steel door was slammed shut.

Blackness. A stone floor. No sound except the echo of retreating laughter and the distant clanging of another closing door.

Tristan curled up on the floor and tried to turn off his thoughts. He squeezed his eyes shut as tightly as he could, as if this might prevent the thoughts from returning. But there was no escape. I am a dog, he thought. If I had a tail, I would wrap it around myself to keep warm. But dogs are not tortured with thoughts. For them there is no past, no future. I must try to be like a dog.

The rum was wearing off and he felt like his head was being pounded from the inside. Was it from the rum, or from the thoughts that would not go away? Who could say? I should at least check out my surroundings, he thought. This was a good idea. And to reward himself for his good idea he got up on his hands and knees and crawled about his cell. Good boy.

His exploring trip did not take him very long or very far. Four cement walls. At least it felt like cement. Three arm lengths wide and two long. A pot for a toilet.

Tristan sat on the cold stone floor and leaned his back against the wall. At least there was something under him and he could feel something against his back. He could feel his backside and his back. Perhaps the rest of him had gone away. Nothing seemed real. But no. The thoughts were coming again. He was no dog. There were tears finding their way down his face. Dogs didn't cry.

Then a new thought came. The village. The village he had watched through the field glasses. The bright yellow sun shining on the little houses with their thatched roofs. The gentle waving green of the palm trees. The blue of the river and the women washing clothes. Yelling to each other and laughing. The children playing hide-and-seek. Squealing in delight when they were found. How they raced around. The sound of cicadas. Such a sleepy siesta sound. And high, high up in the blue sky with the white clouds, a kite. Drifting first this way, then that way, high above the sleepy village. The wind playing with its new toy. So free, so free.

And one small tender mercy was granted to Tristan Sedillo when sleep found him and took him away.

CHAPTER FIFTY-EIGHT: THE FIRST SHOT

Number seven led Maria through the winding streets of the village. They kept their heads down and Maria was very wary, but the villagers paid them no mind. This seemed unusual, as strangers in a small village are usually the object of much scrutiny and whispered debate. Perhaps Manuel's unit was doing its work a little better this time. They edged their way along the narrow streets until they arrived at a decrepit old warehouse. It looked like it should have fallen down a long time ago. Perhaps someone was saying a novena for it. Number seven checked the streets in both directions before they entered.

"You should put your cigar out, comandante."

"Why?"

"Inside is the darkroom. The picture must be developed. It is a little delicate. Ready?"

Maria nipped off the glowing end of her cigar and stuck the butt in her pocket. "Ready."

Number seven creaked the door open just enough for them to squeeze through. Once inside, he closed the door behind them and they were in total blackness.

"Seven, you idiot, I cannot see anything. What are you doing?" Without knowing why, Maria had dropped her voice to a whisper. Perhaps because darkness was a place for secrets.

"I will show you, comandante. One moment." Maria could hear him moving away from her in the dark. Every one of her senses was alive, sensing for danger. She heard the click of a switch and suddenly an area off to her left was bathed in a red glow. It was unlike anything Maria had seen before. Perhaps like unintentionally looking at an unexpectedly bright sun. You could see a red color even if your eyes were shut tight. It was like that, only ... there were things inside the room she could make out. Pieces of paper hanging from an indoor clothesline. A bench with three sinks. Pieces of paper stacked beside them. A big black box hung upside down with what looked like a spout coming out the bottom and a tray underneath.

"This is our darkroom, comandante."

Maria noticed seven's voice had dropped to a whisper too. It was like a conspiracy. She kept her voice low. "How do you know of these things ... the taking of pictures, cameras, darkrooms?"

"They teach us this at the university, comandante. It is called photography. It was one of many courses of study that I take there. This part ... photography... Well, I am not so good."

"I want to learn this thing. You can show me? From the beginning?"

"Sí, comandante, I will show you what I know. But I am not so good ... I ..."

Maria's voice rose to take command. They had been whispering like children. "We are not here to talk about you. We are here to develop this picture. What is the first step? What do I do?"

"I will show you," said number seven.

He took the camera over to the bench, and though it was hard to tell exactly what he was doing, Maria saw him put the camera in a bag. Then he began moving his hands inside the bag.

Maria was fascinated. "What is it you are doing?"

"I am taking the film out of the camera, comandante."

Maria felt herself growing angry. "But how? I cannot see how you're doing this. I ask you to show me and you hide. You move your hands in the bag, like a magician, where I cannot see them."

"It is because light will ruin the film, comandante. It is called a changing bag. I am more practiced at this than you, so I can—"

She interrupted him. "I want to do it!"

"It is all right, comandante. This red light will not harm the film. I only show you the changing bag because sometimes you will have to change film outside in the day. It is like when you trained us to put together the rifle with the blindfold on. Please, comandante, it will be hard to show you what to do unless you have some patience ..."

Maria felt her face turn as red as the light in the room. Her voice dropped again to a whisper. She nodded to Seven.

"Yes. Of course. You are right. Go on ... please."

Seven showed her how to load and unload the camera. He explained the working of the camera. The viewfinder, like the sight on a rifle, told you where your bullet would go. The shutter. A click on the shutter button would act like a trigger, and cause the shutter to open and close more quickly than a bullet could move. And that meant the picture was there—on the film. One need only develop the film to obtain the picture.

Seven handed her the film, showed her how to unroll it and cut it. "Then, comandante, you can see here, in each of these frames, what the picture will be."

Maria peered closely at the frame Seven was holding up to the red light and her face clouded in disappointment. Her voice still a hushed whisper. "The picture is ruined. It is as if the faces have been stolen. There are dark places where the faces should be. Only their clothing has light."

"It is as it should be comandante. This is called a negative. Now take the negative and put it here, on this piece of glass."

Maria put the negative on the spout part of the big black box.

"This is called an enlarger, comandante. Put this paper underneath the glass. Good. Now we shine light through the glass like this ... Good. The picture is now on the piece of paper, only much bigger."

"But I see nothing."

Seven smiled. "Sí, comandante, but now you will see the magic. We will give the paper a bath. Put the paper into the developer in the first sink. Hold the paper only by its very edges."

Maria was now entranced. Very slowly and deliberately she did as Seven instructed. She was aware suddenly of the absolute quiet. The only sound was the gentle ripple of the liquid in the soft red light when she placed the paper into the sink and submerged it. The liquid felt warm and soothing on her fingers.

She whispered over her shoulder to seven. "Now what do I do?"

"Keep washing the paper, comandante."

Maria turned her attention back to the sink. Her eyes grew wide and her mouth opened. It was impossible, what was happening, but it was happening right before her eyes. An image was growing out of the nothingness on the paper. Faintly at first, then growing in clarity, until she could identify almost every detail. The Americano, Merrick, playing the game of bochas, holding the ball up, about to throw. The soldiers watching him. Maria took a sharp intake of breath.

"Dios mio, it is a miracle!"

"It is photography, comandante." Seven smiled and continued softly, "Now take the paper out of the first bath and put it in the next one." He indicated the second sink. "This bath is for keeping the image from developing too much. Give it a wash for a few seconds. Good. Now, on to the third sink. This is called the fixer. Excellent."

When the developing process was completed, Seven showed Maria how to clip the photograph to the line to dry.

"Like hanging clothes on a clothesline, ah, comandante?"

Maria did not answer but studied the picture closely. She began to feel excitement build in her. "You have done well, Seven. Look, look at this. Come here and look at your picture. No, come closer. Look closely. See here? Where he holds the ball above his head and his smile?"

"Sí, the Americano is congratulating himself on making a lucky throw."

"It is not only that. See how our soldiers, in the back of the picture ... the shadow on them ... they look on him with suspicion and what else ... disappointment?"

"Sí, but—"

"Look at the shine of his fine suit and the shabbiness of those around him."

"Sí, comandante, but I don't see what—"

"The Americano is in the center of what you call the frame. He is holding the ball over his head. It is as if the ball is Cuba and he holds it over our heads! Look at the smile on his face. He's gloating!"

"Sí, now that you say it that way, I begin to see what you

mean."

"You say you are not good at this photography, Seven. But I think you are very good! This is something I want to do very much. I feel a fire in me for this."

"Sí, but, comandante, I feel, for me at least, that the camera got this shot of the Americano was just luck, not skill."

"What? What did you say?" she demanded.

"The picture. It was just a lucky shot."

"You call this picture… a shot?"

"Sí, comandante. In photography, they call each picture a shot."

Nothing further was said until they were outside the building, the picture stowed safely inside a small brown leather satchel. Maria took out her cigar butt and lit it. She began to chuckle as she exhaled smoke toward the sky. "This is delicious, Seven. This is sweeter than the sweetest fruit. You see, this is how I will fight this war. And win it. They may fire all the bullets they like in every direction." She paused. "But I will fire shots." She gave the satchel a loving pat. "And I will choose my shots wisely."

The next day, at a little after one o clock in the afternoon, a holy sister of God passed in front of the Havana offices of the United Fruit Company. The nun paused and looked around her. No eyes met hers. From beneath her habit she withdrew a small brown leather satchel and deposited it into the big brass mailbox. The satchel contained a ransom note and a photograph. Sister Maria, her prayers for a safe delivery answered, slipped back into the shadows. The first "shot" in the war had been fired.

CHAPTER FIFTY-NINE: FREEDOM'S PRICE

It is sometimes said that a watched pot never boils. But just when Jacob Dalton thought the air in the room couldn't get any heavier, the teletype in the corner sprang to life, and keys began angrily hitting paper. Finally, the response he'd been waiting for. His associate, Sam, walked over to the machine and scanned the message as line by line it chattered into view. It seemed to take forever. Dalton, seated at the end of the long boardroom table, drummed his fingers.

"Well, Sam?"

"They've Okayed it, JD. Board of directors, all on-side."

"The whole laundry list?"

"Yeah, looks like it. The fifty thousand. The whole ball of wax."

"Bill Merrick is one lucky son of a bitch. Jesus. They saw that picture. We all saw it. Playing ball with them, for chrissakes. Big fat smile on his mug. And they still Okayed it?"

The teletype fell silent. Sam tore off the message and handed it to Dalton. "See for yourself."

"Well, well, well. They may have Okayed it, but they're not happy. Listen to this: 'pending safe release, William Merrick's employment with the company is hereby terminated.' Ha! Sam, you are now looking at the new director of Cuban operations for United Fruit."

"Congratulations, JD."

Maria's instructions were carried out to the letter. Less than thirty-six hours later, a small crop duster took off from Santiago de Cuba airport and flew west, low over the Sierra Maestra range. The pilot waited until he saw the flare fired up into the sky then pushed the package out of the plane. The parachute opened and the package drifted slowly down. It landed in the mountains, who could say exactly where? Except perhaps Seven, from Maria's unit. He was there to meet it. In the package was everything they had asked for. Fifty thousand well-used American dollars in small denominations. And some "very stylish" women's clothing in an extra-large size. Now it was time to fulfill their side of the bargain.

When he got back to the encampment, Seven gave the money over to Four. Four, in turn, would begin the process of feeding the dollars into their newly created propaganda machine. Some would go for the leaflets. Some to pay for the equipment. And some for the pilot, who would be handsomely compensated for remaining anonymous. He was the very same pilot who had dropped the package from the plane. A pilot who was beyond suspicion, since he operated a small but profitable crop-dusting enterprise under contract to none other than the United Fruit Company.

Seven entered the hut where William Merrick was playing poker with his guards.

"Señor Merrick, I have good news. Your company has complied with our wishes and you are to be released."

"Well, it's about goddamn time. No offense, boys, but onward and upward, as they say."

Seven gave a quick tilt of his head to the guards, who gathered up money from the table and left the hut.

Merrick chuckled. "It's just as well; I was losing my shirt to those clowns."

Seven threw a garment bag down on the table. "That is exactly what you are going to do, Señor Merrick. Lose your shirt. Take off your clothes and put these on."

Seven undid the garment bag. Merrick's mouth dropped open.

"It's a dress, for chrissakes!"

"Yes, but quite stylish, don't you think? And, as you can see, there are accessories as well."

Merrick was furious. "I'm sure as hell not putting on women's clothes!"

Seven took the pistol out of his holster and leveled it at Merrick. "You will do as you are told, señor. It is important to us that you are not recognized before you reach Santiago, and we cannot risk entering the city at this point. So here is what will happen. You will put on this clothing. A hood will be placed over your head, as before. You will be taken to a road west of the city. The hood will be removed and you will be free to walk. It should take you perhaps an hour to reach your destination, no more."

Merrick looked first at Seven, then at the clothing on the table, and finally at the pistol Seven was brandishing.

"Put on the clothes, Señor Merrick," Seven ordered. "Do not press your luck with us. We have been generous, so far."

Merrick stripped to his underwear and then, muttering profanities, looked down at the clothing in disgust. He picked up the dress.

Seven stopped him. "No, señor. First things first."

"A garter belt and ... stockings? You can't be serious."

"Let me answer you this way ..." Seven cocked the pistol.

"Okay. Okay. Jesus." Merrick picked up the garter belt. "How the fuck do I even put this on?"

Seven smiled. "How would I know such a thing? But you are a man of the world, señor, no? I am sure you have taken delight in removing such garments from women. So in this case ... you, ah, as it were . . . just do the opposite."

When Merrick had finished Seven pointed gun at him. "Now the rest."

Cursing, Merrick picked up the dress and stepped into it. "How do I do this fucking thing up? The buttons are all in the back!"

Seven smiled again. "I suppose you will have to practice."

Merrick fumbled with the buttons. When he finally succeeded in getting them done up, he turned and snarled at Seven: "Happy now? You fucking guys are going to pay for this."

Seven threw Merrick a wig and a pair of shoes. "That is no way for a lady to talk. Now *move*!"

Seven had the hood put over Merrick's head and led him to a jeep. He, along with Five, then drove him around in circles until they were sure he had lost his bearings. Next they drove him to the road that was his destination, hauled him out of the jeep, and removed the hood. Tears of humiliation streaked down his cheeks. Seven almost felt sorry for him. Almost.

"Look on the bright side, señor," he said. "You have your liberty, and a story to tell your grandchildren. And what's more, our comandante is certain you have now learned how to treat a woman with the proper respect."

Five and Seven exchanged good-humored looks and Seven shifted the jeep into gear. "Adios, señor. Or should I say 'señorita'?"

The two soldiers laughed, gunned the engine, and sped away,

leaving Merrick in a cloud of dust on a road somewhere on the outskirts of Santiago.

CHAPTER SIXTY: TESTIMONY

The general was not in good humor. In fact, he had not been in good humor for some time. The kidnapping of the Americano, Merrick, was only the beginning of his woes. It had cost him the trust of the business community. They no longer had confidence in his ability to control things. And they had made it plain enough that if he could not control things, there would be someone put in his place who could.

And now ... and now this. He grabbed up the leaflet, rose from his desk, and tore it to shreds in barely controlled fury. "You see this, Jimenez?" he said. "You see? They have made a cartoon of me! A joke! Spread it all over the country ... for everyone to see! Cartoons of me, dropping like rain from airplanes!"

"We are working on it, comandante. We are looking. We will find them . . ."

The general exploded. "You are working on it; you are looking ... while you are working on it, my close personal friend Vazquez Bello is shot to death in his car coming out of his club."

"Comandante, we—"

The general's voice went cold. "No Jimenez, not we. *You*. You will understand that looking is not enough. You must know where to look. And for that to happen there must be sources of information. Intelligence. An ability in which you are sadly lacking."

"Comandante, we are tracing every line of inquiry available to us. Every credible lead, no matter how small ..."

"Credible? What do you mean, credible?"

"Well, comandante, we cannot be expected to listen to the drunken ramblings of every peasant who—"

"What peasant? Who are you talking about?"

Jimenez was becoming very uneasy. "A month ago. Perhaps a little more. Some drunken peasant comes barreling into the rotunda bloated with his own sense of importance and saying he was on official government business, that he had to deliver a report. It was comical, comandante. It was nothing."

The general's voice turned soft. Dangerously soft. "And did this peasant have a name?" he asked his aide, uttering each word carefully.

"I cannot remember. It is of no consequence. This peasant—"

The general cut him off. "And where, may I ask, is this peasant now?"

The tone of the general's voice was getting vicious. Jimenez knew it well. It was often a prelude to death. He tried to control his rising terror. "We threw him in a cell. I have not kept track of what followed. He may still be alive, comandante, but —"

"Bring him to me immediately. And on your way to the jail, I suggest that you say your prayers. One prayer for him to be alive. And another for yourself. If he is not alive, Jimenez, you are to take your pistol out of your holster, put it in your mouth, and pull the trigger. I promise you that suicide will be quicker and less painful than what I have planned for you. Quicker but certainly no less final. Now *go*!"

"Sí, comandante."

After Jimenez left, the general crossed to the window and

looked down at the streets of Havana. A sense of rage boiled in him, but he was a man of discipline. The constructive way to deal with this was not to fly off in a temper but to plan. A well-thought-out plan of revenge. No, revenge was not the word. He was a civilized man in a civilized society. Reprisals. That was the word. There would be reprisals for the state of affairs he now found himself in. He had seen to the elimination of Julio Mella. Gunned down in a shopping plaza in Mexico City. And now they had shot Bello in retaliation. An eye for an eye. But he would not play this game their way. They had killed one. He would kill ten. They would learn how dangerous it was to cross him. And for making him seem weak and impotent? With these leaflets? He would hang a dozen of these so-called revolutionaries from the telephone poles for the entire population of the city to see. They would learn that they had underestimated him. They would learn the hard way. He would be their teacher. And it would be a hard lesson.

Moments later Tristan Sedillo half walked and was half carried into the general's office. He was little more than a skeleton with a beard, with eyes that were wild and feverish. Collapsing in front of the general, he hugged his legs and began crying uncontrollably. "Mi general, Mi general."

The general turned his stony eyes on Jimenez, who stood rigid at attention, a frightened man. He addressed his words first to the two guards who had helped Tristan into the office. "You two can go. Jimenez, get this man some water."

After Tristan was given a chance to collect himself, he was placed in a chair and told to give his report. Although Tristan sat quietly, his eyes were crazed and far away.

Perhaps he is too far gone to be of any use, the general thought.

But then Tristan spoke. "An encampment outside the third village, mi general. Guns, grenades. Eight ... men in the village. Eight sleeping mats at the encampment ... at first I did not understand—"

Jimenez cut in. "Comandante, there were—"

"SILENCE! The man is giving his report."

"But, comandante, the train depot, the harvesters. The blue diamond flag? The guards reported there were eight of them!"

The general looked over at Jimenez and then seemed to take a moment to reflect. He turned back to Sedillo. "Interesting. Go on…"

Sedillo was half babbling but his voice was full of urgency as he rushed to finish giving his report.

"Yes, yes, I have thought about the village! The eight men, they play with the children, they help the men at work, they even help the women! I have seen them. And the soldiers … when soldiers come through the village asking questions, the men and women just shake their heads no … I have seen this … with the field glasses you gave me. They are all in this together. The eight men have made friends with all the people in the village … Eight men, but perhaps there are more. I have seen them signal to each other! I have seen how they do it! They fly—"

The general interrupted, but was clearly reining in his temper. He spoke as if to a child. "Go slowly, my good man. Have another drink of water. What you are saying may be important. Think before you speak. Tell me what you can. What is this business about signals? How do you know of this?"

Tristan fell silent. He could see that they thought he was mad. Sometimes he thought this himself, but now was not the time for madness. This moment in time was important. His freedom might depend on what he said next. He tried to slow his thinking down. I can do this, he thought. I will go slowly. Like the general says to do. The general has saved my life. He is a good man. He has given me water. He has given me a chance to save my life. Tristan felt tears coming but fought them back.

"Mi general," he said. "I think a long time in the jail. I think of the village and children because it was a happy place and in the jail it is necessary to think of a happy place. I think of how I see a child's kite in the sky over the village. But then I think of what you say about finding the blue diamond flag. And then I say to myself, maybe they are the same. The kite is like a diamond. The shape is the same. I think perhaps the eight men work so hard to help the people so the village will keep their secret. And with the kite they send signals to another group of men. Maybe an army of rebels. That is all I know. Maybe it's a crazy idea. Maybe I am wrong ... Please do not think me crazy, mi general. I try hard to do the job you gave me to do."

There was a silence. Tristan held his breath. The general seemed to study him, and after a moment gave a little smile.

"You have done well, Señor Sedillo. Or should I say Sergeant Sedillo? You have been a good soldier. So now I will make you an officer. I will see to it you are given a room at a good hotel. You are badly in need of a bath. Take two days to relax, then report to Captain Jimenez for duty. Oh, and one thing more ..."

The general crossed over to a set of shelves in the corner of his office and returned with a canteen. "This was presented to me by my commanding officer a long time ago," he said. "I think you should have it. It is filled with water. I remind you to keep it that way. Water. Nothing stronger. Do I make myself clear?"

"Sí, mi general."

"That will be all. Wait in the outer office. In a moment Captain Jimenez will see you to your hotel."

Tristan picked up the canteen, stood up, and moved slowly toward the door. An emaciated, shuffling skeleton. He turned back to the general before stepping out the door. With all the strength he could muster, he stood as straight and soldierly as he could and with a shaking hand gave the general a trembling military salute.

The general turned to Jimenez. "You can go."

"Sí, comandante. But the hotel? Where should I send him to?"

"Send him to Hell."

"Comandante?"

"Do you not hear? I said get rid of him."

CHAPTER SIXTY-ONE: WHAT A PICTURE IS WORTH

Following the success of her propaganda campaign, Antonio and Miguel both felt Maria should remain in Havana. Government forces had descended on Santiago de Cuba and were combing the area for revolutionaries. Not that it was less dangerous in Havana. Gatherings of more than four people had been outlawed, and every night now gunfire could be heard in the streets. But Antonio felt it was the right time for her to meet with some of the people who had only been names on paper up to this point.

So Miguel met her at the Hotel Inglaterra one afternoon and suggested they take a walk. The weather was not ideal. Overcast skies and a brisk wind cast a pall on what should have been a joyous reunion of brother and sister. These days it seemed like secrecy was their constant companion wherever they went. The streets of the capital were eerily quiet even in the middle of the day.

Maria forced herself to keep her voice low but light. "So, my brother, where are we going? Will you buy me an ice cream?"

Miguel smiled. "If you are a good girl, perhaps I will buy you one later. We are going to the university. It is just around the corner from here."

"But, Miguel, you told me it was closed."

"It is. But I thought you would like to see it anyway. And nearby there is a safe house. Some of the people I would like you to meet have gathered there."

They rounded a corner and crossed a square to stand in front of the grand building that housed the university. Maria looked at it in awe, and her heart was all but drowned in feeling of wonder. Not for the majestic building with its Greek columns. The feeling was aroused by the statue in front of it.

"Dios mio," she breathed. "I feel so small. It is like I am a child again."

Miguel looked over at his sister. "It impresses you, no?"

"It is the most beautiful thing I have ever seen."

Maria looked up, entranced, at an elegant bronze statue of a woman dressed in robes, her bare arms seeming to beckon in welcome to all who stood before her.

Miguel well knew what she was feeling. "It is called *Alma Mater*. The name is from the Latin language; it means 'generous mother.'"

"I so wish I could have studied here, Miguel, at the university . . . when it was open."

"A university is not just bricks and mortar, my sister; it is people. Come, I will show you."

He led her to a safe house two blocks away. And down into a basement filled with cigarette smoke, desks, people, and activity. The names Maria had seen written on paper came to life one by one as she was introduced to them. It was hard to take it all in. She felt at times like she was drowning. Many of them had kind words, but others seemed to look right through her without acknowledgment.

She was introduced to Jose Sanchez, a professor of mathematics. He chuckled to see her looking so overwhelmed and lost. "You mustn't let it fluster you, my dear," he said. "There are many of us working for the cause. And Miguel tells me you have done more than most. We are all grateful."

"Then you are another patriot who works without bullets?"

"Nothing so romantic as that, I'm afraid. Timetables. Transitional schedules. Miguel tells me you were very taken with the statue at the university ... *Alma Mater*?"

"Miguel tells me its name means 'generous mother.'"

"Well, 'nourishing mother,' really. An education can be a kind of nourishment, don't you think?"

Maria shrugged. "I do not know this word 'nourishment."

"Well, I think you will know it soon enough. Because there is someone here who has something for you. A reward for your brave work. Come."

Maria followed the professor over to a desk where a handsome young man was poring over photographs. Photographs that caught Maria's attention immediately.

"Maria Sandoval," the professor said, "may I introduce you to Walker Evans. Walker,[BH2] this is Maria Sandoval, the young woman you've been hearing so much about."

Evans stood up and extended his hand. It took Maria a moment to tear her eyes from the photographs. She shook Evans's hand firmly and gave him a small, nervous smile.

He beamed at her. "It is an honor, Miss Sandoval. Your reputation precedes you. They are calling you the mystery woman of daring exploits."

Maria felt off-balance. More words she did not understand. But this Walker Evans seemed genuine and there was true warmth in him.

"Mr. Evans, I am afraid I don't ... that is ... I'm surprised that you are ..."

"Yup. American. Guilty as charged. But one of the good guys nonetheless, I hope. I'm on your side, señorita. Well, at least trying to be anyway."

Maria indicated the pictures spread out on the desk. "You are a photographer?"

"Uh-huh. Down here doing some freelance work. Your brother tells me you're interested. In photography."

Maria answered quietly. "I think it is a miracle. It is a way of ... speaking."

Evans dropped his voice. "Miss Sandoval ... uh, Maria, Miguel has told me about your campaigns and about their ... methods. Of your belief in nonviolence. It's something we share. If you will forgive my boldness, I have something here to give you. Well, to the cause actually."

On the desk there was a small black leather case. Evans picked it up and handed it to her. "This is for you. For what you've done. For what it is hoped you will do."

Maria's eyes were narrow and questioning. "I d-don't understand," she stuttered,

"It's a camera. A Rolleiflex, to be precise. A very good camera. The latest model. I'll show you how it works. And perhaps you can 'speak' with it.

Maria opened the case and took out the camera. She marveled at how modern and new it looked. She turned toward Evans and her eyes began to fill. She blinked hard to clear them. "It is a wonderful gift. I do not know of anything I can say to thank you."

Evans grinned. "You could try 'thank you.' Now c'mon with me. I'll give you your first lesson."

Maria proved an excellent student and within an hour had

mastered the intricacies of the Rolleiflex, loaded and unloaded film from it, and taken some sample pictures.

Evans seemed satisfied with her progress. He looked at his watch. "Well, gotta go. Magic hour. But you think you got the hang of it now?"

Maria held up the camera. "Thank you for this, Walker Evans. I will use it to speak and I will have a lot to say."

"Well, y'know, Maria, there was this guy in the States, a few years back. Advertising guy. He had a saying: 'A picture is worth a thousand words.'"

Maria laughed with delight. "That is a saying worth remembering. Thank you again, Walker Evans."

Walker started to leave but suddenly turned back as if an idea had just occurred to him. "Listen, I'm meeting up with Hemingway at El Floridita. You know the writer? Would you like to join us there for drinks?"

Maria shook her head.

"Why are you shaking your head? Is it that you don't know Hemingway, or that you won't join us for drinks?"

"Both. I don't care so much for alcohol. And I don't know this writer or have much use for him."

Evans looked surprised. "You have no use for writers?"

"Perhaps I will again sometime. But right now ... I remember the thing you told me. This American saying of yours. A picture is worth a thousand words."

Walker Evans shook his head and laughed. He was still laughing as he climbed the stairs and out of sight.

As she was leaving with Miguel, Maria held on tightly to her new love, the camera. She looked over and saw Professor Sanchez give her a little wave. He silently mouthed a word to her. At first she did not understand the word his lips had formed.

Then it came to her. She smiled to herself, for she had now learned this new word and the wonderful meaning it held.

Nourishment.

CHAPTER SIXTY-TWO: CLICK

First light had not yet arrived when Maria again put on the nun's habit and left the hotel. She was going to shoot a roll of film in downtown Havana, and she knew that she would be in constant danger. Yet wearing the nun's habit in public, she had noticed, gave her a distinct advantage over other women: many of the townsfolk would smile or nod at her as she passed, but both policeman and soldier alike avoided her eye and looked away quickly when they saw her approach. Well, what of that? Not one of them attended mass, she was sure, but did they think that ignoring the presence of a nun somehow gave them immunity from the wrath of God? In any case, the habit offered her some protection. Seeing a nun with a camera, however, would be cause for concern.

Walker had told her about the importance of light in photography. He had talked of the magic time that happened at dawn and at twilight. He had shown her how to set the aperture to obtain just the right amount of exposure. Yes, she thought. Exposure was very important indeed. This new knowledge made her look at the streets with new eyes. Keep to the shadows and look for the light, she remembered. Choose the shots carefully. Her first shot this morning was of a concrete wall.

The pride of Havana, all this new concrete. Blindingly white in the noonday sun, almost pure. But this morning, in the gray light of dawn, it looked sinister. Some graffiti scrawled across a section of the wall caught her eye. *Down with Imperialists!* she read. *The War Will Never End.* And the exclamation marks were there too. The wall was pockmarked with bullet holes and streaked with blood. Maria checked to make sure she was not being watched. She eased the camera out from underneath her habit, chose her shot.

CLICK.

Next, on to the Malecon. A group of peasants had already gathered outside the gates to the government market. Food was scarce, so they had to get there early. Some of the shoppers were men who had their hands in their pockets. Some were women who looked at the sister with hard eyes as she passed. Eyes that seemed to speak of betrayal. Suspicious. Bodies leaned this way and that, trying to gain some degree of comfort during the endless wait. Some sat in the dust. One child hid his face in his mother's dress. Another was clicking two pebbles together, the closest thing to a toy that was available. Two guards stood behind the gates with their backs turned to the peasants. Their uniforms were new and black.

CLICK.

The sound of the waves could be heard beating against the seawall as Maria made her way down the street. A siren in the distance. A lone automobile passed her and disappeared around a corner. Farther along, in the shelter of a doorway, she saw a mother with some children. The door behind them was massive and shut tight, secured with a heavy padlock and bolted. There were three children. Two lay stretched out on the sidewalk, little sleeping skeletons. The third was the smallest and slept in its mother's arms. The mother sat on the sidewalk and held her child protectively. It appeared as if she hadn't slept in days. All were dressed in rags. The mother's eyes were hollowed out and she stared out toward the sea with defeated eyes.

CLICK.

One block over, Maria heard raised voices and walked toward them. As she rounded a corner she saw a policeman shouting at a man and his family. She approached with her head down, listening. The policeman yelled to the man that no more than four people were permitted to congregate together. It was the law. The man said there were six in his family; his wife and four children. The officer said they must get off the street. The man said they had nowhere to go. The officer blew his whistle and three other policemen came running up to them, their shiny caps pulled low so their faces were not visible. The woman pleaded with the officer to let them stay, When the man angrily protested, the officer raised his baton and hit him hard. He fell to the ground bleeding and the woman screamed, gathering her children around her. The other policemen began kicking the man. Other people watched from across the street, afraid to go near.

CLICK. CLICK. CLICK.

One of the officers raised his head and looked in her direction. Had she been seen? Maria quickly hid the camera, bowed her head, and began walking in the opposite direction. Her heart was pounding and she felt her pulse beating in her ears. She waited for the dreaded whistle to blow. It was agonizing to have to walk so slowly. A second. Two seconds. She quickened her pace. There was a side street just ahead. If she could make it ... she heard voices. She heard a siren.

"Clear the way. Clear the way."

"Get out of the street, I tell you."

Maria turned down the side street and leaned against a wall for support. She tried hard to control her breathing but felt dizzy. A couple of seconds later an ambulance drove past. It was not for her. It was for the man who'd been hit by the policeman. She was safe. She felt waves of relief and guilt at the same time. I cannot waste time with my feelings, she thought. I have a job to do. I must keep these pictures safe.

She forced herself to walk slowly down the cobblestones of the side street. She kept her head down. She had to remain calm and get to the university. To safety. To a darkroom ... Keep moving, head down.

Maria nearly tripped over the body. It brought her to a sudden halt. A man lay in the middle of the street in a pool of blood. He looked to have been shot several times. He was lying face-down with his arm outstretched as if reaching for something. Maria's eyes traveled past the reaching arm and saw a canteen lying on the street. Then ... the man's arm moved slightly. He was still alive, and was reaching for his canteen.

Maria retrieved the canteen and knelt beside the man. She didn't want to touch him, but she wanted to give him some water. As she gently turned him over and placed his head in her lap, she was careful not to hurt him. When she looked down, what greeted her eyes was the face of Tristan Sedillo.

Her breath caught in her throat and her eyes turned to stone. He looked up at her and his eyes opened wide in recognition and fear. His mouth began to work but no sound emerged. Maria was transfixed by the sight of the man who had taken everything from her. He gave a weak cough and blood leaked from his mouth. She continued to look down on him and slowly, deliberately, lifted his head to give him a sip of water. It mixed with blood as he swallowed. His eyes softened in gratitude or ... supplication?

Maria looked down and saw that her habit was stained with blood. Her habit. She was dressed as a nun. For a second she had forgotten.

She looked once more into Tristan's eyes and reached out her hand. She made the sign of the cross on his forehead. His mouth worked a little more without sound, his eyes filled with tears, and then the spark went out of them and Tristan was no more.

Maria knelt with his head in her lap for a long time. Then she gently laid him down on the cobblestones and turned him over just as she had found him. She placed the canteen just out of his reaching hand and took out her camera.

CLICK.

CHAPTER SIXTY-THREE: REPRISAL

On the journey back to the hacienda, the train had rocked Maria to sleep. She'd had a dream. About riding with Kate. In the strange way of dreams, they were both the same age. Like sisters. Her mama looking so young, bright and beautiful. Her green eyes flashing and her long red hair shining. They were both laughing at Miguel. Miguel, so much younger than her in the dream, just a boy, standing in the yard squinting up at them in the bright sun as they sat their horses. He held a little toy cannon. Papa Vicente ruffling his hair, telling him history stories of America.

But this was no ordinary dream. She was standing in the bright new kitchen, where the old kitchen used to be. She did not recognize this place. All she knew was that she was standing in what once was and could never be again. In the next room she could hear Antonio and Miguel arguing. Her heart felt sore. Weary. She had to leave this place. She walked out to the stables and found comfort and solace in the darkness. in the sound of Soldier nickering gently beside her. She picked up the brushes and began to tend to his coat. Slowly. Gently. The rhythmic movement of her hands brushing across his hide soothed her. She murmured softly to him. "We will find peace one day, muy buen. Perhaps we will build . . ."

Noises. From out in the yard. Miguel yelling for her to come. She dropped the brushes and ran. Outside, the soldiers from Antonio's unit were grabbing their weapons, clambering into jeeps. She felt Miguel's hand suddenly grip her shoulder roughly, turning her around to face him. "Maria, the village ... soldiers have struck the village! Antonio and I are both taking our units in, but I thought you'd want to—"

Maria spun around and ran back to Soldier.

There was only one thought in her mind. Only one name in her heart. Only one prayer in her soul.

Wilfredo!

She rode as she had never ridden before. Soldier must have sensed her desperation, her need, because he practically flew out of the yard like the wind, before the jeeps had even started to life. Lunging, plunging, racing across the field. His legs long and his feet sure. They crested the hill and galloped down toward the village. She could see now. Some houses were smoking. Some on fire. Some of them already ashes. She could hear the staccato of automatic gunfire. This, in a village where the only available weapons were pitchforks and machetes. She reined Soldier to a halt so abruptly that he reared up. They were at the back of Wilfredo's tiny house. The roof was smoking. Please, God. She leaped from the stallion's back and was running as soon as she felt the ground beneath her. She rounded a corner calling out his name. She saw the little white iron table and the two chairs where they used to sit and share mugs of tea. She called his name louder, more urgently. She turned to go inside, looked up, and stopped dead.

Wilfredo's corpse was hanging from the doorframe of his house, swinging to and fro. Wrapped around his neck was ... a kite.

A moan grew inside her. No. No. No. She had to look away. No. She bent over to be sick, but nothing would come out. Gentle, sweet, sweet man. Her breath came to her only in racking sobs. She tried to hold herself tightly and rock. But first she needed to ... she needed to ...

Somehow she got herself to the little white wrought-iron chair. Somehow she carried it over and set it under him. Somehow she stood on it, found her knife. As gently as she could, she lifted him up, and cut the rope from which his body was suspended.

Everything inside her mind and heart came crashing down with him. Her pride. Her ignorance. Her anger. Of what use was this anger now? Blood and more blood. She had done this. She was responsible. She and her kite flag. This sweet man who had taught her so much. She had killed him as surely as if she had done the deed herself ... How would she ever be able to live with that knowledge? She was a murderer, no different from the rest of them. How would she ever live in a world like this? It didn't matter anyway, for she had lost the will to live. She would not paint any more white crosses. There was nothing left to remember. She heard gunfire in her dreams now. All she had wanted was for it to stop. So perhaps death was not so bad after all, she thought. She would have done well to give herself over to the church. Become a lamb of God. But now it was too late. Far too late. She was a whore. A whore to violence and bloodshed. And she had welcomed them into her, unholy vessel that she was. So let death come now. But she would meet it with clear eyes. She would not give death the satisfaction of knowing it had defeated her. She could hear more gunfire, now, closer. A shadow moved over her. Her breathing was rapid and her mind was tired, but her senses were alive. So, she thought, welcome, death, come to me.

There was no way forward anyway. She waited, with her head down, but death did not come. When she looked up into the shadow, expecting to see the face of a soldier, she found

the eyes of a boy. No more than four or five years old. The smoke from the burning village rising around him. His finger stuck in his mouth, as if he were pondering some great mystery. But his eyes were empty. He looked down at her but did not see. His eyes were lost, like ... like her eyes had been lost ... so very long ago.

She took the boy into her arms and ran.

There was the sound of breaking glass behind her. More gunfire. She made it to Soldier and raced to get herself and the boy mounted. She turned the stallion's head and they galloped off through the smoke. A bullet sang past her ear. She huddled over the boy and bent as low in the saddle as she could. Somewhere to her left there was an explosion. Then another burst of gunfire. The pounding of Soldier's hooves leading them away. Suddenly she felt the horse shudder under her as a bullet grazed his right side. But he didn't falter. He didn't slow down. His hooves continued their smooth and even pounding.

He ran until the sounds of gunfire were left behind. He ran until they no longer saw the smoke. He ran until they were safe. And when she finally whispered into his neck, "Easy now, mi buena," Soldier dropped to the ground. He had done his duty.

CHAPTER SIXTY-FOUR: A NEW DAY

Maria's life now centered on the boy. That is, her life would center on him if there were a way forward, and that was far from certain. Men from Miguel's unit had made inquiries among the survivors in the village. Both the boy's parents had been slain and no one knew of any other relations. Antonio had been wounded in the fight, and one of the first sights the boy had seen after entering the hacienda was Miguel dressing the wound and more blood. Maria put her hand over the boy's eyes and turned him away from the sight.

This can't go on, she thought. It must all end. And end now. She came to a decision. As quickly and certainly as a reflex. She and the boy would sail away from here. Perhaps to America. She would make a new life for them in a new country.

She took the boy for a walk to the sea. As they made their way along the streets, her thoughts were only about the boy and how she might reach him. Help him. He was too young to shoulder the loss of his mother and father, and his way of dealing with it was to withdraw into himself. Maria's job was to find a way to bring him back. She was unaccustomed to such a role, but she was sure that she could learn. She knew this in her heart. When they reached the water's edge, she knelt down and spoke to him.

"What is your name, little one?" she asked.

The boy refused to meet her eyes and only stared vacantly at the water as it washed over his bare feet. Finally he spoke. Maria silently said a prayer of thanks to God.

"Pepito ... My name is Pepito."

"It is a good name. A very good name. So, Pepito, do you like stories? Do you know about pirates? About buried treasure?

Pepito looked up at her and for the first time he met her eyes. He seemed to be studying her. She could only smile at him and hope. Hope that it was not too late to save the child in him. "Are you my mama now?" he asked.

"I could be. If you want me to be. I would like to be. Perhaps we could try it for a while. And then you can decide. Until then, you can call me Maria."

The boy looked out on the sea and seemed to go far away from her again. Finally, he answered. "Papa told me stories about pirates. But Mama doesn't ... she didn't like him to. She says a rake is of more use than a sword."

"And she is right, Pepito. And anyway, there are no pirates here. But listen. I have a secret to tell you." Maria put a finger to her lips and dropped her voice to a whisper. "I know where there is some buried treasure!"

Her words seemed to bring Pepito back to life again. His eyes lost their faraway gaze and again met hers. His mouth had dropped open suddenly in wonder and curiosity. "Really?"

"Come, Pepito, and I will show you."

Maria took the boy to her special place. It had been stripped of all its contents long ago, but one thing still remained. "Will you help me dig?" she asked. "Here in the sand?"

Pepito nodded eagerly and they both went to work. Maria made sure he was the one to uncover the little chest with the pearl in it. She nodded for him to open it and his eyes went wide when he saw what was inside.

"You see? It is a pearl. Now come with me. Bring the pearl with you."

She took his hand and together they went to the shore. Maria took the pearl from Pepito. "Now watch what I do, Pepito."

Maria took the pearl and threw it out as far as she could into the sea. A little plop and it was gone without even a ripple.

The boy looked confused. "Mari ... Mama ... you've thrown away the treasure."

"It was not a treasure, Pepito. *You* are the treasure. You see, it is very important in this life to know what to hold on to and what to let go of. It is the final lesson my teacher taught to me. His name was Wilfredo. I wish you could have met him. He was a very wise man. He told me this day would come."

"What day, Mama?" the boy asked.

Maria ruffled his hair. Everything was going to be all right. She knew that now. "Be patient, Pepito. And a day like this will come for you too."

Maria's thoughts went to Wilfredo. The final time she had flown the kite with him, he had told her to let go of the string. She had not wanted to and refused at first, but he had become silent until at last she did as she was instructed. Only then did he speak.

"See it fly away? When you let go of the kite, it flies higher and gains its freedom. By holding on you keep it tethered. You want the feeling of freedom the kite gives you. To get it you have to let go of whatever is tethering you. The feeling is still there inside you. It was never in the kite. All along, it was in your heart.

"Listen to me now," he continued. "You want freedom for your people. You believe it is something you can win for them. You want justice for your people. You believe it is something you can achieve for them. So you hold on to hatred. You hold on to vengeance. It's like a game of cards you play with fate. You think if you choose the right card at the right time, you will win the game.

"Listen," he told her now.

"Only by letting go do you gain freedom.

"Only by letting go of hatred and vengeance do you achieve justice.

"And last and most importantly, the people you think you are liberating are not your people. They are just people.

"Stop taking things, Maria. Stop holding on to things. Learn to let go."

"I know you are not ready for what I am telling you. But I know that despite your lack of understanding, you have listened to my words. A day will come when you will be ready. And you will know this day when it comes," he concluded. "You will see it as a new day."

Maria brushed away her tears as she stood by the sea. She knew now that the day Wilfredo had spoken of had at last arrived. And that she was ready for it. She felt it deep in her heart as Pepito took her hand and they both looked out at the horizon.

It was indeed a new day. Full of promise and possibility.

-EPILOGUE-

One sunny morning in early July Special Envoy Sumner Welles was summoned to the office of the president of the United States.

"Sumner, good to see you," the president said. "How's the family?"

"All's well, Mr. President."

"Good, good. Sumner. I've called you here today because we've got a situation that's got to be addressed, and quickly."

"Sir?"

"Have you seen the latest issue of *Life Magazine*?"

"No, sir. I've been rather—"

The president cut him off. "Well, there's a copy there on the table. Turn to page forty-two."

Welles picked up the copy and looked over the cover. "Oh, yes. The 'crime in Cuba' spread. Walker Evans—"

"Not him. His photos don't concern me. It's this other one, the one who he's working with." The president searched through some papers on his desk until he found what he was looking for. "Sandoval. Maria. She took the photo that's on page forty-two. And quite frankly, it's giving me heartburn."

Welles leafed through the pages and found the photo spread. "Sir, I don't see the significance of this. People in bread lines. There's nothing unusual about that. Hell, we're in a depression ourselves—"

The president interrupted impatiently, "Page forty-two, dammit! What do you see?"

Welles found the photo, studied it for a moment, and then cleared his throat. "It appears to be the photo of a man lying in the street. He's reaching for a canteen."

The president's patience was wearing thinner by the second. "Not he . . . *It*, Sumner. It is a corpse not a 'he.' A very bloody corpse too. A bloody corpse in the streets of downtown Havana!"

"Well, sir, things are in a bit of a tumult down there as I'm sure you are aware. They usually are."

"Well, I can't have it. I won't have it. *Life Magazine*, for God sakes. I want you to get down there and tell this tin pot Machado to pack his bags. They are close to full-scale insurrection down there anyway. Intelligence tells me there is a student directorate or some damn thing that's already formed a provisional government in waiting. I want you to make sure they get a crack at it."

"That's true sir, but perhaps if we just let things take their course ... we could avoid the appearance of interference in Cuban affairs."

The president waved this away. "We have the absolute right to interfere, as you put it, under the Platt Amendment. Safety of the country. Do I have to spell it out? I don't want any more pictures of corpses in *Life Magazine.* We're already getting a black eye down there with the gangsters moving in, using it as their little clubhouse. They're laughing at us."

"Yes, sir."

"Get down there right away. And you get Machado on a plane and fly him out of the country. You can tell him he'll get no support from us in any way, shape, or form from now on. And if the little so-and-so doesn't want to go, you can reassure him that we won't as much as piss on him if his pants catch fire. Tell him we might even light the match! That ought to do it," the president concluded.

"Yes, sir." Welles turned to go.

"Oh, and Sumner ..."

"Sir?"

"Not those exact words. Use diplomacy. You're a diplomat. Sugar it up. And give my regards to your wife, Martha."

On August 13, in New York City, Walker Evans met Maria for lunch. They were wolfing down hot dogs at a little stand in the East Village when he asked, "So, Maria, did you see the *Times* this morning?"

"No, I was busy getting Pepito dressed and ready for his first day of school. We are not all persons of leisure like you." She smiled.

"Well, here, let me read it to you. Front page. 'Machado Flees in Plane; Machado in Flight to Secret Refuge.'"

"Good for him," she said. "I have found my refuge. Let him find his. All I can say is that I hope it is in hell."

"You and I might have had something to do with this, you know; The *Life Magazine* thing?"

"Dios mio, Walker. You are so vain. I am sure the world is capable of making its own decisions without your participation. Still, I am very thankful to you for all you have done for me: lending a hand at the embassy, the papers, helping to get Pepito and me settled ..."

"How's the apartment?" he asked.

"It is not a life I am used to. But I do love the university. Another thing I have to thank you for. And for all your help with

Pepito."

"He's a good boy. What's happening with Miguel?"

Maria shrugged. "My brother is a dyed-in-the-wool idealist. He has moved to Havana. He and Antonio will continue to work in government, he tells me. He has promised to further my goal of giving women the right to vote. He will show me how good life can be, he says. He is coming to New York for Christmas. I'm hoping I'll get to show him this thing you call snow."

"Any regrets about leaving Cuba, Maria?"

"For me? No. I regret how things worked out in this life for the mother I cannot remember. I regret how things worked out in this life for the mother I cannot forget."

Maria finished her hot dog and brushed the crumbs from her shirtfront. "I must go and pick Pepito up from school." She gave Walker a kiss on both cheeks. "And, Walker, for Pepito and me? I want to be the mother that made things in this life work out better."

On impulse, Walker raised his camera and took her photo.

Maria looked surprised. "What was that for?"

Walker grinned. "I could tell you, but it would take a thousand words."

She gave him a smile, turned, and walked off into the afternoon sun.

ACKNOWLEDGEMENT

I would like to thank all the people who made this come true. My Mary who continues to be my inspiration and my always. My sister Barbara and her wonderful partner Ann who helped make it shine. My daughter Emily who helped with her insight. Thanks to the folks at Kindle Direct Publishing. Thanks also to Audrey and our wonderful hosts in Ensenada Carel, Eric and Luz.

ABOUT THE AUTHOR

George Houston

George is an actor/writer/musician and a proud papa of four. He currently lives in Northern Ontario. This book is a joyful part of his bucket list.

Made in the USA
Monee, IL
26 September 2020

42571290R00184